The Ladies Farm

The Ladies Farm

A
Novel

Viqui Litman

Doubleday Direct Large Print Edition

CROWN PUBLISHERS / NEW YORK

Published by Crown Publishers, 201 East 50th Street, New York, New York 10022. Member of the Crown Publishing Group.

Random House, Inc. New York, Toronto, London, Sydney, Auckland
www.randomhouse.com

CROWN is a trademark and the Crown colophon is a registered trademark of Random House, Inc.

Printed in the United States of America

ISBN 0-7394-0551-9

**This Large Print Book carries the
Seal of Approval of N.A.V.H.**

In Loving Memory of
Martha Harris Litman and Fred Litman

Acknowledgments

Special thanks are due to the Every Other Tuesday Night Writers Group: Steve Copling, Deborah Crombie, Dale Denton, Jim Evans, John Hardie, Diane Sullivan, Rickey Thornton, and member emeritus Aaron Goldblatt—who slogged through this manuscript many times with patience and insight; our guiding light, Warren Norwood; the sustaining members near and far of the Ladies Lunch—Karen Brachman, Rebecca Isgur, Judi Preston, Sylvia Weiner, and Edie Yentis; my editor, the delightful and highly skilled Ann Patty; and my agent, the late Jane Cushman, whose judgment, guidance, and obstinancy made this book a reality.

The Ladies Farm

Chapter 1

Oh, joy! thought Della Brewer when Barbara Morrison pulled her red Thunderbird up to the curb in front of the Ladies Farm. *My lover's widow come to disturb my life in the country.*

Della held her seat on the squeaky glider and concentrated on the *Times* editorial. She had a deal with Dave Eleston, who was kind of a Methodist ringer, singing in a Fort Worth church choir for their televised early service even though he lived in Sydonia and had never been a Methodist. Della prepared the ads for Dave's Quick Stop, which ran weekly in the *Sydonia Tribune*.

In exchange for this service, Dave brought the *New York Times* and the *Washington Post* back from Fort Worth every Sunday morning.

Della thought Dave drove the hour from Sydonia to Fort Worth and back again every Sunday just for the chance to catch a glimpse of Rita, his ex-wife, who operated the hair salon at the Ladies Farm and lived in the room over the solarium. Since divorcing Dave, she had remarried her first husband and only recently re-divorced him. Dave drew encouragement from this and spent as many hours as he could Sunday mornings after church sitting on the Ladies Farm porch, hoping Rita would spend a few minutes with him. But Sunday, as Rita reminded everyone, was the only morning she could sleep late without someone showing up with a hair crisis.

So after Dave had come and gone, Della lounged on the front porch with a carafe of coffee and several pounds of newspapers. Meanwhile, Rita slept, and the others—Pauline and Kat—having awakened early and breakfasted wisely, were out doing something useful. Which meant that Della would have to greet Barbara when she reached the porch.

She didn't care, really. Richard had been dead over a year and, even when he'd been alive, Della had stopped hating Barbara. He stayed with Barbara because he wanted to, Della reminded herself. He wanted to be married to her more than he wanted to be with you.

Okay, maybe she hated Barbara a little.

But who wouldn't? A rich, fat bitch, waddling up the walk in some sort of bronze silk pajamas, the sun glittering off her gold chains. She hadn't even caught on that it wasn't chic anymore to gold-plate the trim on your car. Let alone that really rich people drove a Lexus or BMW, not a Thunderbird, and that those cars were silver or white, not bright red. How could you not hate her?

Barbara looked up at Della on the porch and smiled. "Della, you look gorgeous. How do you do it?"

Della just hated her more. Why shouldn't Barbara be kind? She had everything: the money, the house, the jewelry. She was Richard's widow. Della was only his secret love.

Della smiled and leaned even further into the glider cushions. "Must be the clean country living," she said as she did a quick inventory. Barbara was right about one thing: Della knew she looked much better than Barbara. I'm way thinner, she thought. My skin's smoother. My eyes were always better. And I have the good sense not to make myself up like a circus performer. "Certainly not anything I do on purpose."

Barbara waved her hand to dismiss the comment as false modesty, causing her bracelets to clank. She mounted the two steps and settled with a small groan into the cushioned rattan chair that, with the glider, formed one of the three conversation groupings on the porch.

Tiny eyes, Della thought. Glittering brown buttons surrounded by flesh. In younger days, Barbara's porcelain skin had been set off by a head of shimmering chestnut hair, but even that subtlety had been abandoned for a mass of flaming orange, creating a vivid halo even on the shaded porch. Della rested the paper in her lap, but she did not speak again and a few seconds passed while Barbara settled in.

She's staying, thought Della as she smoothed her denim skirt. She's burrowing.

"So," Barbara resumed the conversation. "What's new with you?"

Della could not remember Barbara visiting the Ladies Farm. She must have visited Pauline and Hugh long ago, Della mused, when Hugh was still alive. But after Hugh died and Richard, in the role of concerned friend, asked Della and Kat to see if they could help Pauline turn the struggling bed and breakfast around, Barbara had not visited Sydonia. Of course, that was when Della and Richard became more than the coupled-up, PTA and Cub-Scouting friends they had been when their children were young; maybe Richard had discouraged his wife in some way from intruding upon this good deed that he and Della were performing together.

"Nothing's new," Della said evenly, warming with her memories. "That's why I live out here. So life can go on undisturbed, day after day." She smiled. Richard used to tell her that her smile lit up her eyes. Even now, especially now, she knew they were her best feature.

Annoyance flickered across Barbara's face, then she returned the smile. "Life here agrees with you," she said. "How's Pauline? And Kat?"

"Out and out. But fine, of course."

Barbara sighed, closed her eyes, and leaned her head back until she faced the porch ceiling. Della sneaked one more look at the horoscope. Richard had been a Gemini and she invariably checked his as well as those of her two children, a Leo and an Aquarius. She glanced last at her own, but Barbara started to speak before Della could ascertain whether or not she was having a good day.

She remembered finishing a meal at a Chinese restaurant with Richard once, and picking up a fortune cookie. Richard had stayed her hand and gently opened her fingers to take the cookie. "Here," he had said, picking up the remaining cookie from the plate. "This is your true fortune."

His cool, smooth hand on hers, his eyes almost moist behind his glasses, the studious expression: All those were as real to Della as Barbara sprawling on the porch. Della saw the blasted pieces of the fortune cookie crumbling onto the tablecloth, she saw his forehead furrowing in concentration as she read aloud, she heard him laugh, and felt the warmth of her own blush as neighboring diners turned to stare.

But the fortune eluded her. Surely she had tucked the slip of paper into the tin box that held her most precious Richard Moments. Surely, in the packing and moving, her single apartment, her townhouse, and finally here to the modest bedroom and sprawling, windowed office of the Ladies Farm, surely in all that moving and cleaning out and discarding she had preserved her fortune. She just didn't know where.

"You have a room for me?" Barbara jolted Della from her reverie. "You can check me in, can't you? I want a room at the Ladies Farm."

Chapter 2

"Well, how long is she staying?" Kat demanded.

Pauline, pouring coffee, glanced quickly at Kat, then back to Della before she finished filling the third mug and set the carafe down on the oak tabletop. They were huddled in the kitchen, where Kat and Pauline had spread out the buttons they had collected in a morning of yard-sale shopping.

"How should I know?" Della said, sliding the red mug toward herself. The business end of the kitchen, with stainless steel appliances and track lighting, lay behind her. She and Kat, who settled next to her, faced the uncurtained windows overlooking the side yard. There was a view of the carport, filled with their utilitarian vehicles—an aging Accord, a dented Suburban, a hail-pocked pickup (they used the insurance money to erect the carport)—and a sliver of the lawn that led down to the river.

"Maybe because you checked her in. You did check her in, didn't you?" Kat, even on Sunday morning, sounded like a businesswoman. Without looking at her, Della knew that her crisp camp shirt stayed neatly tucked into her sharply creased jeans and that the hand that clasped her coffee mug was perfectly manicured, with artificial nails trimmed to the proper dress-for-success length.

Della sighed. "Yes, Kat, I checked her in. I ran her credit card through the reader, I got her signature on the guest card, I even pulled the room number in the availability tracker."

"So how long is she staying?"

"She took the room for a month."

"A month!" Pauline's whisper annoyed Della even more than Kat's cross-examination.

"A month," Della repeated. She leaned back in the chair. She'd picked the one that rocked, and it jolted her lower back as it settled onto the left back leg. "Dammit," she muttered, then motioned at the chair in explanation. "She's in Governor Ann."

Originally they had envisioned naming the rooms, like the streets of Sydonia, after heroes of the Texas War of Independence. Then they'd decided on Texas women and named the largest room—a suite, really—after Ann Richards.

"For a month?" Della could see Kat adding up the revenue.

"Full treatment, too," Della continued. "Meals, makeovers, classes." After Hugh's death, when Della and Kat were recruited to revamp the bed and breakfast Pauline and Hugh had run as Sydon House, they concluded that there was no way the enterprise could ever make money. Specialize, they had advised Pauline, who was determined to hold on to the property. Offer classes, beauty treatments, all the things women love and pay for. You can rent to men, they had said. Just cater to women.

It had made perfect sense for Kat, who maintained a medical practice consultancy in Fort Worth, to live at the Ladies Farm. In exchange for her residence, Kat managed most of the business aspects of the rather specialized bed and breakfast.

Della's move to Sydonia had not approached Kat's well-considered and rational solution to managing the challenges of mid-life at the end of the century. I fled, Della reminded herself for the thousandth time. Richard died and I thought the loneliness would kill me and the only one I could tell was Pauline. And Pauline offered refuge.

"Is she in her room?" Pauline whispered now. Della ignored her own irritation and smiled indulgently.

"No, she's gone for a ride on our country roads," Della whispered back. "But she hopes we'll serve lunch upon her return."

"Cut it out!" Kat snapped. "We need the money and she's entitled to lunch."

"Appropriately lean and tasty," Della rejoined in her whisper. While guests often checked in on Sunday afternoon, the Ladies Farm almost never had guests for Sunday lunch, and the four proprietors had come to regard it as the meal they enjoyed with each other. Seeing Pauline's forlorn look, Della placed a hand on her friend's shoulder. "It's not so bad, babe. We've got lots of pasta salad. And gazpacho."

"I just don't know what she could do for a month," Pauline said, shaking her head.

"She asked about jewelry classes."

Kat snorted.

"She's good with her hands," Pauline recalled. "And she knows color. And style."

Della remembered the extraordinary needlework that had adorned the walls, the sofas, and even the chair seats in Richard's home.

"And she needs more jewelry," Kat said. She gave her head a vehement shake and Della, as always, watched with fascination as Kat's glossy hair rose away from her head and then settled perfectly into place. Until living with Kat, Della had thought that taffy color could come only from a bottle and that kind of hold only from a can that would destroy the ozone layer.

"I thought you'd be overjoyed," Della observed. "The Governor Ann paid up for a month. Shoot, we could hire her a full-time trainer for that."

"She doesn't want the aerobics?" Pauline ventured.

Kat set her mug down on the table.

"Pauline, we've stopped whispering!" Then, turning to Della, "She doesn't want aerobics, does she? Because our insurance premiums will go . . . they're already sky-high!"

Della knew why she herself resented Barbara and she thought, considering Pauline's role as her confessor, she understood Pauline's gentle terror. But why was Kat so edgy?

"Well, much as I'd love aerobics for the entertainment value, I really don't think she's here for the workout. I think she's here for the same reasons as the rest of us. She wants a little peace and quiet. She wants to paddle a canoe on the Nolan River and take a walk through the woods on the Highlands Trail and get a facial and a new hair style in her spare time. That's all."

"And the jewelry class?" Pauline asked.

"Oh, I suspect she wants whatever crafts we're offering. Buttonology or whatever. I don't see her in 'Journals as Spiritual Journeys.' Maybe 'Tarot Reading.' But you can work her into your regular schedule."

Pauline frowned at Della's dismissal of the crafts. In fact, the classes Pauline taught in the barn netted more than the makeovers and aerobics. "You're right," Della attempted appeasement. "She's probably great with her hands."

A sudden picture of those puffy, manicured fingers on Richard's body made Della draw a breath in alarm. Hand job? Surely not, thought Della, watching the others to see if they noticed anything. Damn! When did it stop?

"I know she's good with her hands," Pauline was saying, her own hands resting atop her mug as if she were trying to warm them over the coffee. "It's her mouth that frightens me."

Oh, great, thought Della. There's a picture.

Kat was sliding the buttons into groups. Her coffee stood untouched. She looked up. "Let's just concentrate on the program. Della's right; you can work her into your regular classes."

"And if she's too much for you, I'll make her a reporter for the *Silver Quest*," Della said, smiling. She loved being the even-voiced, level-headed one about whom Kat would never guess the truth.

Pauline relaxed a little, then looked up behind her. The shuffling along the oak floor could only be Rita, dragging her butt down for breakfast. She stuck her head into the kitchen. "Dave gone?"

"Hours ago," Della said. "Why does a night watching rented movies with your granddaughter make you look like a hooker who's just worked both sides of the street?"

"Della!" Pauline protested. "She just got up."

"We all just got up at some point," Kat said. "We don't all look like . . ." She paused.

"Like a hooker who's just worked both sides of the street," Rita finished for her. She shuffled over to the cabinets and pulled down one of Pauline's handmade mugs, then shuffled over to the table and rested there a moment, mug in hand, before she poured her first cup of coffee.

"It's just habit," she said. "There's no beer and no cigarettes and no men in my life, but when I get up in the morning, I still feel like I got to watch out for the wet spot." She squinted at Della as she walked around the table and pulled out a chair. "You know what I mean?"

Her lavender robe, a Christmas gift from the three of them designed to discourage her from appearing before the guests in her lace nighties, gaped as her shoulders slumped forward, exposing an alarming amount of cleavage. "Who's the guest?"

"How did you know?" asked Pauline.

"Gucci," Rita sighed, lifting the full cup to her face and inhaling dreamily. "Gucci in the hallway." She sipped. "I had a boyfriend once who used to bring me Gucci. Turned out his wife worked at the perfume counter at Nieman's."

"What happened to him?" Kat never had patience for Rita's stories.

Rita looked up, shrugged. "Oh, you know, that was Larry. Between our marriages."

"You mean," Pauline asked, "even when you were married to other people, you still were . . . seeing him?"

Sometimes Della didn't know how she had ever confided in Pauline. Even now, married and widowed, facing her guests' most intimate secrets daily, Pauline seemed far too innocent to bear the weight of her friends' confessions. But she had been a faithful confidante, with never even a disapproving silence.

Rita frowned a little, and her forehead furrowed. "I do believe that Dave and I were divorced by the time Larry came back around." Dave was Rita's husband between her two marriages to Larry. He often told Della that he persisted in his pursuit of Rita now because she had married Larry twice, a sure indication she would do the same with Dave.

"I think I was dating that boy from Dallas," Rita continued, "the one with the car lot." She looked to Della again. "You remember him?"

"The art lover who used to come get you in an Eldorado with longhorns mounted on the hood?"

Rita nodded solemnly. This past spring she had abandoned her Texas Big Hair for punk. She had dyed her yellow hair jet black, sheared it down to a spiky cap, and highlighted it with a changing rainbow of iridescents (this weekend's was teal) that blended oddly with her loopy earrings and mostly denim and rhinestone wardrobe. Della thought Rita's bizarre fashion sense succeeded only because, even surrounded by morning puffiness, the depth of Rita's blue eyes overwhelmed whatever ludicrous hair color or plastic bauble she sported.

Rita shook her head again, as if to clear

it, then fixed those eyes on Della. "So who is she? The guest?"

Della shrugged. "Just a friend of ours from Fort Worth."

"A widow," Pauline said. "Her husband died last year."

"Last February," Della amplified before she could think. "A year and three months."

"She have a name?"

"Barbara Morrison," said Kat. "Mrs. Richard Morrison."

"Is that someone I should know?" Rita, in her years in Fort Worth, had developed a clientele that included well-known names, some of whom still drove out to Sydonia on a regular basis for her ministrations.

"Richard had a medical supply business," Della said.

"Until he saw the impact of computers on practice management," Kat hurried to add. "He started repping software along with his cotton swabs and syringes and parlayed his nice little business into the biggest practice management program in the Midwest."

"And his wife—Barbara—worked with him in the office for a while," Pauline said. "They have one kid, in medical school in Dallas; Barbara lives in Fort Worth."

"I don't recall Barbara working in the business," Kat said.

"Early on," Della replied. "Probably before you knew them." She grinned. "Boy were we young then! I still remember her driving car pool with that van full of medical supplies. The kids just piled in the back. No seatbelt laws, I guess."

"Who got the business?" Rita asked. She had begun to glance around in a distracted way that signaled her interest in grazing.

"We're about to fix lunch," Della said quickly. They had baked yesterday for the purpose of filling the freezer with breakfast muffins, and Della dreaded another Kat-versus-Rita shoot-out over Rita's raiding.

Kat, however, was occupied with other matters. "They cashed out, sold it to a software house in Boston. So all they had to split was piles of cash."

"Nice life," Rita said. "What's her hair like?" She brushed a hand over the top of her own hair.

Della watched the black spikes spring back into place while Kat described Barbara's appearance. I never told Rita about Richard, she thought, watching Rita's eyes go wide at Kat's narrative. Week after week, year after year, she was cutting and combing and styling for Richard's pleasure, and she didn't even know he existed.

Della hadn't told anyone except Pauline, and that wasn't until Richard's death, when she couldn't control her grief. Pauline had listened and clucked and sighed and patted, pronouncing no judgment, shooing guests away as they sat at the table by the river and watched the turtles in the unexpected warmth of a February sun. Della supposed Pauline feared that the Ladies Farm wasn't big enough for Barbara and Della together, but Della would assure Pauline that there would be no scenes.

It's a good thing Rita doesn't know, Della thought. When she was done being pissed at me for not telling her, she'd be disappointed that there aren't any fireworks.

"What are you smiling at?" Rita asked her as they all rose to clear the table and get the late lunch ready.

"I'm imagining Barbara with your haircut," Della said, stepping aside to let Pauline scoop the piles of buttons into little Baggies.

"Well, I'm going to sharpen my scissors," Rita retorted. "And change my *shmate*."

"Yeah, yeah," Kat and Della grumbled in unison. One of Rita's favorite customers was the Jewish wife of a man who owned a sportswear factory. While their guests were either puzzled or tickled to hear Rita drawl Yiddish expressions, her housemates had grown so used to them that they barely noticed her language. What they did notice was that she was carrying off two frozen muffins and that, once again, she was avoiding kitchen duty.

"We have got to talk to her," Kat muttered, yanking soup bowls from the cabinet.

"Oh, why start trouble?" Pauline said. "She does her share."

"Just not on schedule," Della added. They worked without speaking for a while. Della imagined the others were reliving the part Richard and Barbara had played in their lives. Because their sons had been the same age, the six of them—Richard and Barbara, Pauline and Hugh, and Della and her then-husband Tony—had acted as one extended family from Cub Scouts through high school. Kat and, for a while, her husband Grant, had joined them later, right after Richard practically set Kat up in the consulting business.

He was in all our lives, Della reflected. Kat could barely spell practice management before Richard started referring clients to her. And Pauline had long ago confided that it had been Richard's and Barbara's money that had kept Sydon House going after the oil bust.

A serving spoon clattered to the floor. "Dammit," swore Kat, stooping down to retrieve it.

"We need some music," Pauline said.

"I'll do it." Kat was out of the kitchen before either Della or Pauline could suggest a CD.

"Do we trust her with this choice?" Della asked.

Pauline shrugged. Della braced herself for the onslaught, but instead of the screaming rock which Kat usually favored, Dolly Parton filled the kitchen.

Pauline inclined her head a little, then returned to shredding lettuce. "Maybe aliens," Della said, then giggled a little.

If it was revenge, it was an odd revenge. Neither Della nor Pauline minded country music. When Kat failed to reappear, Della decided her disappearance was the revenge.

"I guess she's pulled a Rita," Pauline murmured, but Della could tell that it was Barbara she was thinking about.

"Look," Della sought to reassure her friend, "if she were going to shoot me, she would have taken her shot on the porch. I don't think there'll be violence."

"You don't think there'll be bloodshed," Pauline corrected. She frowned down at the lettuce she was shredding. "Violence is another matter."

"As mad as she'd be, I'll settle for a little violence, especially the metaphysical variety, to the soul. Besides," Della loaded rolls into a bread basket, "she doesn't know unless you or I told her. And you or I didn't." She looked at Pauline, who shook her head in response.

"You or I or her husband," Pauline murmured.

Della jerked the last roll out of the sack, placed the roll in the basket, and crumpled the brown bag. "Dead men tell no tales. And I was the last one of us to see him alive. So we've got no worries."

Della knew her glibness neither shocked nor convinced Pauline, who continued to frown. How much lettuce do we need? Della wondered as she watched the huge bowl fill beneath Pauline's jerking fingers.

First, there had been the hysterical phone call from Barbara. As if Della were her closest friend and she had no one else to turn to. Then the whole maddening mess at the house, while she helped Barbara track her son Dickie down at the hospital where he was a resident and then, as Barbara sobbed wrenchingly, taking the phone and telling poor Dickie that his mother couldn't talk because his father had had a stroke on his way to meet her plane and had run the car into a ditch.

It had been hours before Dickie had appeared and she could escape to Sydonia to confess it all to Pauline. And what was there to do, then, but wail her regrets that she had let him leave early that morning because Barbara was expected back from Chicago? Della didn't want to relive it now. Stay buried! she ordered the resentment she had felt as she had comforted Barbara. Stay buried with the guilt that her final night with Richard had not been particularly meaningful, that she had been just a little short with him that morning because she knew he was anxious about picking up Barbara. And stay buried, Della demanded of the teeth-gnashing frustration that when she had returned to Fort Worth, she had had no role at the funeral other than that of sympathetic friend to Richard's grieving widow.

The present needs your attention now, Della scolded herself. Worry about what's gnawing at Pauline.

It was too much to ask, I should never have confided in her, Della thought, but she knew it was bogus. She could not imagine keeping it all to herself; she would have died of grief.

No one dies of grief, she lectured herself. That's the hell of it.

Della dumped the rolls into the warming drawer. "I'm checking on Kat," she announced, and headed out to the living room.

It was actually their lobby, with the desk at one end in front of a pegboard with room keys. Kat stood in front of the bookcase where they kept the CD player. She was holding the plastic case bearing the close-up of Dolly Parton and she was staring at it and, without making any sound at all, she was sobbing.

"Kat?" Della hurried across the room and put a hand around her shoulder. "Katherine? What's the matter?"

The hand holding the CD case rose and fell with the futility of the effort, and Kat let herself be led to the sofa where they sank down together. "He loved Dolly Parton," she whispered, her voice shaking with her sharp intake of breath. "It was his secret, he said. He loved her for those big tits of hers and he loved to listen to her." Kat wiped at her cheeks with the palm of her free hand and shook her head. "I was so stupid," she whispered. "I thought if we played it while we were in bed then he'd think of me whenever he heard Dolly Parton. But all he ever thought about were those big tits."

Della closed her eyes a second as she pulled Kat close to her. A mild, citrus scent rose from Kat's hair, and Della inhaled deeply as she felt Kat's shoulders shaking. You must not be angry at Kat, she lectured herself. You must not be ugly to Kat. And you must not tell Kat.

But Kat, of course, could not wait to tell Della. She choked out the whole predictable tale in a few minutes. How she met Richard at a Texas Medical Association meeting. How he convinced her to move her office from Dallas to Fort Worth because Fort Worth was ripe for practice management consultants. How she recommended his software and he recommended her services. "It was just business, and then it wasn't. I was so young then. It was before I got married."

"And it didn't start again?" Della fought the anxiety in her voice. "After you and Grant split up?"

"No." Kat shook her head, puzzling at what seemed to be a fresh question. "I don't know why, neither one of us seemed interested."

Della tried hard not to sound relieved. "It must have been hard to keep secret all this time."

"Oh, yes," Kat resumed.

This is how you comfort a friend, Della thought as Kat poured out the irony of Richard introducing her to Grant and then the disappointment that Richard wasn't even jealous when she and Grant got married. You don't even have to listen, Della realized, you just make these nonjudgmental observations every time she pauses and she picks right up. "You and Grant saw them a lot—Richard and Barbara—didn't you? I mean, without the kids. Not like the rest of us." You can watch the sunbeams on the oak floor and listen to the tinny rattle in the sound system as it vibrates along with Dolly.

"Oh, God! It was torture, seeing the way he let her baby him, practically spoon-feeding him dinner. 'Oooh, Richie, try this veal, here baby, just a wittle bite for Mama.' It made me sick. And he was so patient with her! Grant couldn't stand her, he only put up with it because he thought Richard helped my business."

"She called him Richie?" Della couldn't help herself; she knew there were lots of things she didn't know about Richard, things she would never know, but she hated the idea that some of them were things Kat knew. All those years when she had thought of him as just another Cub Scout dad, Kat already knew the sound of his voice in her ear, the taste of his skin. Della took a deep breath.

"The rest of the time she called him sweetie pie." The memory seemed to have vanquished Kat's tears, and Della felt her pulling away a little, straightening up. "Anyway, Grant never guessed, Barbara never guessed, and I guess Richard never told anyone. And I never did either, except my sister Joyce, because she lives in L.A. and whom could she tell?"

"Yeah." Della gave her a last squeeze. "Nothing beats an out-of-town confessor." As Kat started rubbing at her eyes, Della stood up and walked behind the counter, where they kept a box of tissues. "Here," she said as she returned, holding the box out to Kat. "I won't tell anyone either," she promised.

Kat took the tissue, and Della sat quietly for a few minutes while Kat sniffled and dabbed her leaky eyes. "I don't know why it hit me like this," Kat said. "I never cried like this when we split up."

"Well," Della advised, "you have to cry sooner or later. Maybe that's why you're crying now."

Kat shook her head. "Having her show

up . . . here . . . all these years, Grant and everything . . . I think it just made me sad, thinking that's the happiest I'll ever be with a man. A sneaky little affair with someone else's husband."

Della did her best to sound like Rita. "Sometimes sneaky little affairs are the best times of our lives. We just don't always know it right then."

Kat fixed her with a skeptical gaze. "That's my point. It's pathetic."

Chapter 3

It was all smaller than Barbara remembered. Driving back into Sydonia after tooling over the back roads, the courthouse she had recalled as a limestone castle loomed as just a moderately pleasing two-story landmark with turrets on two corners. The turrets were all that distinguished the courthouse from the county jail, which shared the town square.

"You're comparing it to Chicago," Richie would have said, but Barbara knew that even by Fort Worth standards, Sydonia was shabby. The boom in antiques on which Pauline and Hugh had banked was

only a jumble of dusty shops on two sides
of the square. Coupled with the usual
assemblage of title company, lunch
counter, hardware store, and law firm con-
sistent with a county seat, the retail estab-
lishments presented an image of 1950s
prosperity: commerce undisturbed by any
aesthetic ambition.

Cars backing from the angled parking
spaces around the square forced Barbara
to a crawl. She knew the red T-bird drew
stares, but she ignored them with a toss of
her head. Never mind, thought Barbara.
You don't need a thriving metropolis.

It was five blocks from the square to the
Ladies Farm, which sat at the end of a narrow residential lane. The house sat close to
the road, almost hulking. The two-story
addition of which Hugh had been so proud
jutted at right angles to the original frame
house and towered over the landscape like
a monolith erected by some brick-
worshiping clan. Barbara knew that Hugh
had been concentrating on the inside when
he built it, hoping that the river views from
the spacious rooms would enchant visitors
into returning. "Quaint only brings them in,"
he had told them when she and Richard

visited. "Comfort and convenience get them to come back."

She could picture him here, in stained work clothes, taking a break to show them the latest improvements while Pauline hovered anxiously behind, worried, Barbara supposed, that Hugh would somehow offend them with his starry-eyed dreams. Barbara thought Pauline never understood that it was Hugh's passion that won people over, his dreams that made him so charming.

Barbara blinked and shook her head a little. Now Hugh and Richard were both dead, and she was going to have to find a way to win over Pauline. Nothing would work without Pauline.

She could hear them all in the kitchen when she entered. "It's just me," she called out to forestall their having to stop what they were doing to check the front. "I'm just going up to change."

Even Della's commanding appearance had shrunk, Barbara thought as she labored up the stairs. Della had never been a beauty, but there had been some allure in the glow of her eyes and the perfection of her skin. Plus, even as she gained weight with age, Della somehow had maintained her shape, still nipping in at the waist, still overflowing top and bottom. But despite the dark hair and the green eyes (Did she wear contacts? She hadn't even put on glasses to read the computer when Barbara registered!), Della had faded.

Barbara pulled clothing from her suitcase, one garment after another, convinced that with all she had dragged to Sydonia with her, she had not brought the proper attire. She pulled on a pair of elastic-waist pants and buttoned her silk tunic. After all this planning, she still needed to prepare herself. It took twenty minutes to perfect her makeup. If Della had faded, Barbara knew, then she herself must be diminished in exact inverse proportion to her gain in weight. It doesn't matter, she told herself, trying to blot the curious eyes and knowing smirks from her imagination. They don't care if you're fat, and you don't care if they do care. Just go downstairs.

Which was how she found herself in the dining room, being examined by Rita, the hairdresser. "Honey, we've got to get that color out of there," Rita said, circling around to view the back of her head. "Strip off that color and get that hair conditioned. Then we can work with it."

Barbara stood still as Rita fingered her hair. "You won't leave it gray?" Barbara asked, trying, and failing, to keep the alarm out of her voice.

Rita motioned her to sit, and they all took their places—Pauline at the head, Barbara in the middle opposite Della and Rita, Kat next to Barbara at the long oak table—as she expounded the importance of re-texturing one's hair. "We'll just hack off all those split ends . . ."

"Hack off how much?" Barbara eyed Rita's prickly black cap and then looked to the others for support.

Kat patted her perfectly sculpted hair. "Oh, you should have seen the texture of mine before Rita took a razor to it."

"She shaved it?" Barbara's hand froze on its journey to the breadbasket.

"Oh, of course not! Rita does all our hair," Pauline chirped, shaking her head to emphasize the shimmer in her straight silver locks, clasped as always by a silver and turquoise barrette. "I've had dozens of texture treatments—she even dyed it auburn once—but she never cut anything except trimming the ends. Try one of those potato rolls," Pauline advised. "They're low in fat and they've got fresh dill and sun-dried tomato in them."

"I've given up worrying about low fat." Nonetheless, Barbara took one of the rolls. She peered at Pauline. "Did I know you with auburn hair?"

Pauline shrugged, but Barbara thought she didn't look that nonchalant. "I feel like you've always known me. But this was after the kids were in college, so you and I didn't see each other much."

"You did manage to stay out of Fort Worth," Barbara said. She turned to Rita. "And how long have you been here?"

"Well, I've lived in Sydonia all my life," Rita started. Every time Rita shook her head, her earrings, of which there were three in each ear, sparkled in the light from the bay window behind her. "In fact," she brightened, "it was me that told Pauline about this place, one time when I was doing her hair in Fort Worth. Isn't that right, Pauline?"

Pauline nodded, while Barbara tried to recall anything but that straight, waist-length hair, which started out ebony, then faded to brown and now to silver. Pauline had always seemed too pure for hair salons.

"So then, when I heard about Hugh," Rita continued, "I just came over and Pauline seemed so lost, and then Kat and Della started talking about having a salon and doing makeovers and all that . . ."

Barbara turned to Della. "You and Kat thought of this?"

"Pauline and Hugh thought of this." Della's chin lifted a little. "Kat and I helped refine it."

"It was Richard who called them," Pauline chirped. "I think he was so worried, after Hugh died."

"He was," Barbara replied. "He was so close to Hugh," she recalled. "And he loved . . ." she thought back. "I think he loved the whole idea of this place." Barbara smiled brightly, hoping they could forgive the tears glittering in her eyes. "Well, I guess it's Richard who brought us together, then."

She pulled at the roll, which was excellent, and put another piece in her mouth. She remembered Richard's shock when

Hugh died—the first death of a contemporary—and her relief that the project of saving the place for Pauline pulled him out of
his sorrow. She felt them waiting for her to
continue piecing the history together, but
Barbara didn't feel like moving forward.
She was groping around her memory, trying to recall if he had mentioned Kat and
Della. Kat made sense, of course. She and
Richard had consulted each other about
business for the past fifteen years. But
Barbara had never been sure what it was
that Della did, except, of course, disap-
prove of Barbara's becoming a stay-at-
home mom.

Don't keep them waiting too long, Barbara advised herself. "And now," she continued, "catch me up. Rita runs the salon.
And Pauline, you teach classes." She
waited for Pauline to nod. "Kat handles the
books and the business end." She turned
to Della. "And what is it you do, dear?"

"Why, I do all our public relations and
advertising," Della almost chirped. "Plus I
publish *Silver Quest*."

"Oh, yes," Barbara said. "That newsletter."

"Circulation's into six figures," Kat
snapped.

Barbara never stopped smiling at Della. "You must be quite proud."

"I hope you'll visit my office and let me show you how we put our little publication together."

Barbara ignored the sarcasm. "Oh, I want to learn everything about you girls and the way you live here." She saw Kat stiffen. I shouldn't have said *girls*, she thought. Kat's the type that probably hates being called a girl.

"It's kind of a tame vacation," Rita observed.

Barbara had started on her gazpacho and she paused before she raised the spoon to her mouth and swallowed. "I prefer a quiet retreat." The gazpacho was good, cold and spicy and thick with vegetables. Barbara took several more spoonfuls before reaching for her tea.

"Here, let me fill that for you," Della offered as Barbara drained the glass.

"Thanks," said Barbara, handing the glass across the table. "It's very good. Is it raspberry?"

"Currant and ginseng," Pauline replied.

"Pauline's special blend," said Della, handing the glass back. She hesitated a moment, but held eye contact. "You have beautiful hands," she ventured.

"You're sweet to say so." Barbara studied the left one a moment, holding it out and regarding it with a wistful smile. Her long nails were well manicured and she made time for a hot wax dip every few days. "My husband loved beautiful hands," she said. "Even when we were kids, just starting out in Chicago, he would hand me a few dollars. 'Here,' he would say, 'my wife can always afford a manicure.' He loved a beautiful set of nails."

"And your rings set them off so well," purred Kat.

Now Barbara fixed her brimming eyes upon Kat and could only nod. It's too soon, Barbara thought. It's too soon to have to go through all this.

"Is the one on your right hand the one that Richard had made for you?" Pauline asked gently.

Barbara turned slightly and nodded, holding up the hand with the square-cut amethyst.

"It was from Hugh's stone," Pauline explained. "I think he brought it back from South America." She frowned a little, trying to recall. "Anyway, one day Barbara and Richard were out here visiting and Richard saw the stone—it was a rock, really, Hugh used it as a doorstop—and offered to buy it on the spot. So he could cut it into a ring for Barbara."

"He didn't buy it," Barbara whispered, turning her hand to let the amethyst, surrounded by tiny pearls, catch the light.

"He didn't?" Pauline asked.

"When Richard told Hugh how I loved purple, Hugh wanted me to have it," Barbara was saying. She looked right at Pauline as she spoke, making sure Pauline understood her words. "It was a gesture of friendship."

Pauline did not change expression. She shook her head and finally reached over to put her upturned palm beneath Barbara's glittering fingers.

"Isn't that odd?" Pauline murmured. "All these years, I thought he sold that big amethyst. He was such a rock hound, and that was the only amethyst he'd ever found on his own."

"Well, he did the right thing, far as I can tell," Rita broke the reverie. "That amethyst's way too nice to be trapped inside some doorstop. It looks much better on Barbara's hand."

"Amen," Pauline said, smiling and giving Barbara's hand a squeeze before releasing her.

"You should have made Hugh get you one of those rings," Rita told Pauline. She held her own left hand up for Barbara to see. "Best I ever got was this little diamond chip and I had to marry that sucker twice to get it."

"It's a very pretty setting," Barbara said.

"Oh, this one's nothing compared to the original. That diamond was the eye on a horse's head. But stupid Larry, he wanted the damn thing back, so I said here, you take the horse, I'm keeping the diamond. I earned it."

Barbara, at a loss for words, looked around the table and was rescued by Kat, who assured Rita that she would have been well within her rights to keep the entire ring.

"You bet!" rejoined Rita. "And after all that, that SOB still wouldn't sign the settlement." She tilted her head a moment and spoke directly to Barbara. "I think it was Dave's fault. If he hadn't started coming 'round so fast, Larry wouldn't've cared. He just didn't want me back with Dave."

"And Dave is an old boyfriend?" Barbara ventured.

"Oh, Dave was my second husband. Kind of a breather between Larry," Rita said.

Barbara turned to Della and Kat. "Neither one of you ever remarried?" She knew, of course. But it was only polite to include them in the conversation. And it was obvious that Rita's recounting of her marital exploits only flustered Pauline, who had pressed her lips together and was staring down at her empty soup bowl.

Kat shook her head no and Della followed her lead.

"Well, it's hard to find a good man. I was lucky." Barbara sighed. "I'll never marry again. There won't be anyone like Richard."

"Oh, now, don't go saying that if you mean it," Rita advised. "Every time I swear off men, that's when they start hanging around. They have this kind of radar device; you know, that thing that points? And they just can't stop themselves from going after women who don't want men. If you really want to excite them, tell them you're a lesbian."

"Rita!" Pauline protested, laughing. "Barbara's just saying she misses her husband." Her voice softened. "All widows do."

"I miss Richard," Barbara concurred. "I miss him every day. I started missing him when I got home from Chicago that day," Barbara continued, looking at Della, "and he was in the hospital and I didn't know it yet, I just started calling everyone we knew, I was so anxious to see him. Of course," she turned to Rita, who had never heard the story, "he was already dead. I just didn't know."

Even Rita had no response to that. Barbara felt the emptiness of the long room, which the five of them had seemed to fill just a few minutes earlier. The vacant straight-back chairs that populated the unfilled end of the table struck her as ineffably sad, as if they waited in vain for the return of their rightful occupants. Barbara bit her lip.

"Well," Pauline said finally. "Who's ready for banana bread?"

Silently, they cleared the table and served dessert with dispatch, bringing the banana bread and hot coffee on trays and distributing dessert plates and silverware from the sideboard. In between trips to the kitchen, Kat hustled into the living room and simply switched off Dolly Parton. "Enough's enough," she told them as she returned. "Dollyfest is over."

"I didn't know she made so many albums," Barbara confessed, glad for a new subject. "I think you have some even Richard didn't have, and he was her biggest fan." She smiled at each of them in turn. "Everything is delicious," she said. "I feel at home already."

"Well, that's what the Ladies Farm is all about," Rita replied. "Especially if you're staying for a whole month!"

Keep smiling, Barbara told herself as she set her coffee cup onto its saucer. Keep smiling and stop delaying. "Oh, I'm staying for more than a month. I just said that when I checked in because I wanted to see how things were here. But this meal," she paused and made a sweeping gesture at the four of them, "I already know this is where I want to stay." The four women stared at her. "I want to live here."

They continued to stare.

It was worse than anything she had imagined. They don't want you, she thought, but she had known that. They hate you. She had supposed that too. It doesn't matter, she concluded. You're staying, and they have to take you in. You have to make them take you in.

"You ladies have the perfect life," Barbara struggled to fill the silence. "You share the work, you each pursue your own interests, you have a delightful time together. You lean on each other. If there aren't going to be any men, why shouldn't we live together?"

"But Barbara," Pauline said, "you have your house, your life in Fort Worth." She gestured with her hand to include everyone. "I know this all looks wonderful, but that's because it's new to you. It might not seem so enjoyable once you've been here a while."

"It'll seem downright tame," Rita opined.

"Well, perhaps. But tame, or at least quiet, is what I want now. I want some peace in my life."

Della had continued to stare, saying nothing. Finally, she spoke. "The peace here is an illusion. If you are troubled in Fort Worth, you'll be troubled here."

Barbara studied the troubled expression

in Della's green eyes, envious that, even now, they were round and unlined, almost innocent in their concern for Barbara's misguided notions. "There are troubles everywhere," Barbara conceded, trying not to lecture. "But I believe I can face them better at the Ladies Farm."

"Well, it's a pretty expensive therapy," Kat observed. "Especially if you keep your house in Fort Worth as well. Even if we work out some sort of annual rate—"

"Oh, I didn't mean as a guest," Barbara said, looking around the table and smiling at each one of them individually. "I meant as a partner: co-owner of the Ladies Farm."

"Oh, Barbara," Della said gently, pityingly, "Pauline's not taking in partners. Even the three of us," pointing to Rita and Kat, "you know, would love to buy in. But Pauline . . . this is her home. You see how it is."

Barbara met Della's kindness with her own. "Oh, but I already own my share of the Ladies Farm. Fifty percent."

"What?" That was Kat, who was addressing Barbara but looking hard at Pauline.

Pauline looked down at her hands. "I think what she means—"

"You told us you owned this outright. You and Hugh," Della said.

"And we did." Pauline looked up, eyes wide. "I just never expected Barbara to want, to exercise . . ."

"It's nothing, really," Barbara picked up. "You know, when we lent money to Pauline and Hugh, over the years, it bothered Hugh so much. He wanted to pay interest, but of course Richard wouldn't hear of it."

"So he traded you part of the Ladies Farm?" Kat's voice rose so high she almost squeaked out the question.

"No, no, no," Barbara shook her head. "You don't understand. Richard wanted to make sure," and now her voice trembled, "he always worried about me. 'What if something happens to me?' he would say. 'How will you live? How will you get along?' So when Hugh and Pauline insisted we had to take something back for all those loans, Richard and Hugh drew up an agreement, giving us half of Sydon House. That way, if either one of us were widowed, we would always have a place to go."

Kat, Della, and Rita turned to Pauline, who was nodding sadly and studying her hands.

"Well, but this isn't Sydon House," Rita said. "Though of course, we'd love to have you here. This is the Ladies Farm."

"The Ladies Farm is the legal successor to Sydon House," Pauline said, surprising everyone with her briskness. She looked evenly at Kat and Della. "Perhaps we need to meet to discuss all this, but basically, Barbara is correct. She owns half of the Ladies Farm." She turned to Barbara. "And of course, you can stay as long as you wish."

Chapter 4

Della had not seen Richard's grave since
the funeral. There had been no stone then,
of course; just that pit, and Barbara's wail-
ing, and the unseasonable heat that made
them all slick with sweat before they even
began the short walk from their cars to the
green awning.

There had been so many people, Della
recalled as she drove alongside the cemetery fence, that she could barely see the
coffin or hear the minister's words. In the
press of mourners, no one noticed that she
slipped away quickly, almost running back
to her car and speeding away from them,

away from Fort Worth and out onto the highway. To Sydonia, it turned out, where she had stayed and stayed as Pauline's special guest, until it became apparent to Della that she would stay permanently.

Fitting, Della thought as she turned into the gated drive. First I saved Pauline. Then she saved me. It had been Richard who called Della, right after Hugh's death, to see if she could help Kat talk some business sense into Pauline. They had met for lunch, she and Richard and Kat, to plot their strategy, and then Della had visited Pauline at Sydon House. Less than five years ago, Della thought, weaving along the gentle curves between the graves. Three years after the divorce from Tony.

And then one Sunday Richard visited Sydonia and he saw me there on the river, she recited silently. I was sitting in an inner tube, floating and talking to Pauline, and reaching for another beer from the six-pack that occupied its own tube.

"It was like high school," she could hear him say, and the words still thrilled her. "I saw you and I got a hard-on and I just wanted to coax you into the woods so we could make out." Della sighed as she pulled the emergency brake. He had moved a little more subtly than that, of course, meeting for lunch, then dinner, ostensibly all about the business plan for the Ladies Farm. But it hadn't taken long.

Because it was like high school, Della thought now. It was like the adolescence neither one of us had . . . maybe no one ever really has. Della got out of the car. We both worked so hard, all our young lives, she thought, and, suddenly, there I was in the river and there he was on the shore. Our kids were gone, our finances were stable, our time was our own, and neither one of us could see a reason not to have what we wanted.

Della had no trouble finding the right marker. She had known it would be one of those modern stones, flat and set in the ground, with nothing more than his name and the dates of his birth and death on a brass plate. But seeing it insulted her. She wanted a marble memorial to let onlookers know how much he had been loved. She wanted some description of how he had brightened the world, of how his eyes sparkled behind his glasses. Why hadn't they listed all the money he'd given to charity, all the committees he'd chaired, the causes he'd championed, the kids he had tutored, the teams he had coached? Wasn't there some way to make the stone convey the broad shoulders and the lop-sided grin?

Della flopped down in the grass and reached a hand out to touch the stone. "Oh, Richard!" she said. There was no place for her on that brass plaque, no acknowledgment that she had ever had a place in his life.

Della had supposed that the grave would stimulate memories and that she would be overwhelmed with warm feelings toward the man who had brought her so much joy at a time when joy had seemed impossible. Instead, she felt the distance between them and her nostalgia gave way to aggravation.

"Now look what you've done!" she scolded. "You had to be the great protec-tor. Your money wasn't enough? She had to have perpetual access to my only home?"

Somewhere beyond her sight someone was mowing, and the drone only empha-sized Richard's failure to respond. Della didn't know what she had expected. She had avoided the cemetery because a single encounter there with Barbara might give her away. Now, knowing exactly where Barbara was, she was safe from discovery. But maybe discovery hadn't been her only fear. Maybe it was silence.

He can't help that he died, she reasoned. But he could have prevented this mess. And he at least could have mentioned that dalliance with Kat!

"You thought you were being gallant!" Della accused.

But that meant, Della hoped, that Richard hadn't said anything to anyone else about his relationship with her. "Is our secret safe?" she asked. Then, in the next breath, "And what am I supposed to do with Barbara?"

Maybe he forgot all about it, Della thought. But how could you forget that you owned half a bed and breakfast? Or maybe he just figured that Barbara would never really move out there. Or maybe, Della thought, maybe that's why it was so urgent to save the place. All those hours you coaxed from me, she addressed the stone, figuring how Pauline could eke a living

from it: Were you just protecting your
investment?

Della remembered plunging in, taking
the lead. She and Kat had assembled all
the Sydon House records, performed a sta-
tistical analysis of guest profiles, compet-
ing bed and breakfasts, area attractions,
and even aesthetic comparisons. Then
they had written the business plan, she and
Kat, huddled in the office almost till dawn,
when they both had left for their jobs in Fort
Worth.

"I can't believe I did all that while I was
still working full time," Della addressed
Richard. "I don't think I could do that
again."

Now, though, a chunk of the mystery fell
into place. Kat and I, she thought. We both
worked nonstop because Richard had
asked us. It wasn't really for Pauline. And
then, no matter his intentions, we ended up
contriving a place where we both wanted to
live.

Still, none of this solves anything, she
thought. Surely, when Hugh died, Richard
must have remembered who owned what.
Of course, when Hugh died, he couldn't
possibly have asked Pauline to buy out his

interest. And Pauline would never have let him simply give it to her.

And, Della's mind raced now, he probably thought Barbara—no, make that he and Barbara, since he was planning to live forever—would never want to live at Sydon House. So he just let it ride, thinking they'd work it out down the road, when Pauline was stronger, when Sydon House was in better shape.

He was just doing what he thought was best for Pauline, Della told herself. Even after Kat announced she was moving down there, he never imagined Della would end up there.

And he was right. Once the Ladies Farm got started, Della had retreated back to her townhouse in Fort Worth. After all, she had to live alone to be available for him.

They had been careful, of course. Richard had given her money for a nondescript Buick that he parked at the Fort Worth Club building. He drove his own car to the building, went upstairs to the club, then took the Buick over to Della's and parked it inside her garage. For out-of-town trips, they flew to two separate cities, then caught second flights to their destination.

"How was San Francisco?" people would ask, and she would smile wistfully and say there was nothing more dramatic than the fog rolling in over the Golden Gate Bridge, all the while recalling the pristine sky over Vancouver Island.

She shifted around so that she was sitting cross-legged and leaned forward to stretch out her lower back. I'm too old to be sitting on the ground, she thought, but then, her back had been stiff for years.

Della had thought that being here with Richard might give her a clue about what to do, or maybe a clue about what he would have wanted her to do. But she remained uncertain. And angry.

Besides Kat and me, who else was there? Her rational side told Della that her anger was overblown. He married Barbara, she lectured herself, had a brief affair with Kat and then, years later, had a long affair with you. That doesn't mean there was ever anyone else. And it doesn't mean that anyone, even Barbara, meant more to him. But what if there were others? Della glowered at the stone.

Beloved husband and father. And, she told herself as she had told herself throughout the four and a half years of their relationship, you knew that from the beginning.

Maybe she could adjust to Barbara living at the Ladies Farm. She's not so bad, Della thought, remembering how Barbara had shooed them out of the kitchen while she stacked the dessert plates in the dishwasher. "I've given you girls a lot to talk about; go talk." That had ended in Kat berating Pauline until she cried, whereupon Rita announced that if Kat didn't stop her tirade and if they didn't welcome that nice woman in the kitchen, she was going to marry Dave and move her shop over next to his gas station.

Kat had finally apologized to Pauline and they had agreed to take a time-out and work on it at their regular Tuesday-morning meeting. Della doubted they could do anything to change the fact that Barbara was moving in with them. Instead, she had to decide if she could stay with Barbara.

"I never once asked you to do anything that would have harmed Barbara in any way. I never asked for a holiday with you, I never demanded your attention in the middle of the night or sulked because I had no escort when you were squiring Barbara to dinners and dances. She was your wife and I wasn't. But I don't want her for a roommate. I don't care how good you were to her; I don't have to be."

Carefully, she unfolded her legs and stretched them out in front of her, bracing herself with her palms flat on the grass. She tilted her head and studied the grave marker. What did you want from him? she asked herself.

She supposed it was permission to move out of the Ladies Farm. She'd rent a duplex in Fort Worth and edit the newsletter there. She'd have to find a job, of course. The newsletter itself would never support her, but she could probably freelance for the Convention Bureau or the Chamber of Commerce. Someone could use an expert events planner.

There would be no river and no canoe; there would be no oak floors or high ceilings. But some things wouldn't change much. Instead of the demands of guests, there would be the demands of clients. Instead of Flops, the bounding retriever–shepherd–setter and something they weren't quite sure what, there would be a demure and dignified cat.

"Who knows?" she asked aloud. "Maybe back in Fort Worth, I'll meet a man."

Richard had worried about her loneliness more than a meddling mother would. "Do not," he had said, holding her by both shoulders and stooping slightly so that they would be eye level, "do not leave yourself lonely over me."

Well if I did that, it wasn't because of you. It was because that's how I wanted it. And maybe I want to live alone again now, maybe I'm just not cut out to live with four other women and a bunch of narcissistic guests.

I've adjusted to the idea that you're not coming back, Della said silently. I don't need the Ladies Farm to distract me anymore.

She pushed herself sideways onto her hip, then rolled up onto her knees. Leaning forward, she touched the grave marker with her outstretched fingers. She had thought about bringing him flowers, but it seemed a foolish risk to leave something that, even days later, could raise questions.

Della stood. She had two pictures of Richard; one was of the two of them on a sailboat in the Gulf Coast, and the other was a close-up of him taken in a motel room they had shared in Toronto. The first picture resided in a safe-deposit box; the second was tucked between the pages of a paperback stored beneath her sweaters.

She used to take that picture out and look at it because she feared forgetting how Richard looked. Now, she looked at men his age and wondered if that's how he looked now, in some other place. Photographs did not help at all.

Turning, Della looked down the narrow drive that led to the older part of the cemetery. There were some irises she had cut at the Ladies Farm and she took those out of the car before she started down the hill.

She did the same things she always did: tugged a few weeds, laid down fresh flowers, traced the raised letters on the bronze marker. She and Tony, in what must have been the final joint effort of their marriage, had bought a stone bench under a stand of live oaks above the grave, and she seated herself there.

She didn't need photos here either, though she had hundreds. The angry adolescent with those aching moments of sweetness in his eyes, the boy tossing the football to his brother in the living room, guzzling milk from the carton in front of the opened refrigerator, shutting her out behind his closed bedroom door in favor of hours on the phone with friends she no longer knew; the dirty laundry on the floor, the stammered introductions to new girl-friends, the angry thrashing of musicians who used their guitars like weapons: All that was there in an instant and everything else was gone. "Oh Jamie!" she wept. "Oh Jamie!"

No resident of the Ladies Farm was allowed to go to Fort Worth without taking a shopping list with her. Even Kat, who still consulted three days a week, called home before starting back to Sydonia.

So Della stopped at the Kroger on her way out of town, picking up enough milk, eggs, and yogurt to tide them over till their next delivery. She passed up the California peaches—their own would be coming in soon—but she indulged in some South American pears. There was always a chance they could coax Pauline into making a pear tart.

That's the least she should do, Della thought as she lifted herself back into the car. Motor vehicles were one of the shared resources at the Ladies Farm and this one, a Suburban, had a large, cracking, leather bench seat that snagged her jeans as she settled in.

It was no joy to drive the thing through city traffic, but it did afford a certain right-of-way. Smaller vehicles simply yielded to her lane changes, enabling Della to return to her personal concerns. By the time she hit the farm-to-market road that wound back to Sydonia, she was mulling Kat's suggestion that the two of them simply buy out Barbara.

Della shook her head. "I doubt she's looking to sell."

The road crossed a gorge cut by the Nolan River; she crossed the river three or four times before reaching Sydonia and the green, wooded hills of this part of the drive reminded her how much she wanted to live here.

"Damn!"

If only it weren't Barbara. "If it were some stranger," Della told herself, "you'd adjust to it."

But it is Barbara. And you can't share a house with her. You can't sit across the breakfast table every day, or coax her to do articles for *Silver Quest* or show her how to use the registration software. It's too much to ask anyone.

This would be a lot easier, she thought, if Pauline had been up front in the beginning. But it was easy to see why she wasn't.

Barbara probably wouldn't let Della and Kat buy her out. But she might agree to Pauline buying her interest if she thought it meant a lot to her. "After all," Della posited, "wasn't Pauline's well-being one of Richard's most important concerns? Wouldn't Richard approve of ensuring Pauline's security in her home?"

"You don't have to sell out," Della imagined herself posing the situation to Barbara. "You could stay here. But really," Della paused, "really, Barbara, don't you think . . . wouldn't it give Richard pleasure to think . . . that you could give Pauline her peace of mind?"

Della sped by Castleburg Dairy on the right. Even with the windows closed, Della could smell it, but she smiled, even so.

"It's a long shot," she announced. "But we have a plan."

I'll talk to Pauline, thought Della. If she'll

let Kat and me fund this attempt and let us do the talking, Barbara might agree to it.

The Holsteins stood in groups by the road. Della imagined them discussing the weather, critiquing the quality of the pasture, comparing the progress of their calves. She wondered if they missed the ones who were no longer among them. The luckiest, she knew, were the ones whose daughters simply grew up and remained with the herd.

Some days she thought that after Jamie, there wasn't any loss she couldn't stand, any sorrow she couldn't bear. But most days, she felt that she had carried more than her share and it infuriated her when trouble imposed itself on her routine.

I feel like a Holstein, Della thought. I just want to chew my cud and watch the traffic roll by.

She crossed the Nolan one more time, then rumbled up the hill into Sydonia. She wanted to get home before Pauline started her Monday pottery class, but she took her time through the intersections around the courthouse. Even the high school kids had started drifting down to the square now that so many shops had been renovated, and no one looked before crossing the street.

Della waved to two blue-hairs who she knew were on their way to the pottery class, then turned onto their block.

The Ladies Farm had been built by Ora and Isaiah Sydon after they sold most of their farm to the Castleburgs and became residents of the town. By then they had found more prosperity in banking than in farming, and the house reflected a turn-of-the-century substantiality that people sought in banks. It sat alarmingly close to the street, and Della often imagined the four daughters flirting their youth away on the deep porch while young men maneuvered first carriages and then automobiles down the rutted dirt road.

By the time the road was paved, Ora and Isaiah had died and their useless sons-in-law had sold the bank. The house passed through a series of owners who began renting out rooms. When Hugh and Pauline saw it on one of their weekly excursions out of Fort Worth, most of the house was boarded up and the front two rooms were occupied by a family whose house-sitting prevented further vandalism while the owner, a widow who lived in a trailer near the Rio Grande, tried to sell the place.

It hadn't been called Sydon House when Ora and Isaiah were alive, but then, Sydonia had been called County Line until a group in the early fifties decided that advertising their location in a wet county was no longer becoming and succeeded in having the town renamed. Della pulled the Suburban into the drive and around to the back of the house.

She wanted to find Pauline, but she needed to get the groceries inside. No one around to help, of course. Nancy, their daily maid, would be attacking the upstairs rooms; Rita was in the salon, Kat in Dallas; and—she hoped—Pauline would stay in the barn, where Della could talk to her without Barbara.

She lifted two sacks into her arms, then judged a third to be safe to carry by an edge and grabbed the top of it; then, in a desire to finish the task, she grabbed the top of the fourth and last sack too. Mercifully the back door was hanging open and it yielded to a push of her hip.

"Hello?" Della called, but she expected no answer and was not disappointed. Almost doubled over by the awkward way she grasped her packages, she waddled across the kitchen to the cabinet next to the refrigerator, then let two of the packages slide onto the floor as she deposited the other two on the counter.

I'll just get the cold stuff into the fridge, she thought, then I can find Pauline. Della was closing the refrigerator door when she heard the heavy, determined step that preceded Nancy's arrival at the back staircase.

"Oh God! I'm glad you're here, they didn't know what to do, they all had to go with her—"

Della felt her stomach lurch. "Her who?"

"Pauline," Nancy said. "Pauline, she passed out or something in the barn and that lady, that guest?—"

"Barbara," Della supplied.

"—Barbara comes screaming up to the house, screaming so loud they heard her in the salon, and Rita goes running down there and she screams for me to call for help, so I call Dave, and he thinks to call the rescue squad, and meanwhile this lady Barbara's running around screaming and screaming and the lady under the dryer runs down to the barn where Rita is, and Dave shows up with the rescue squad finally, but no one can do nothing."

"Nothing? What do you mean nothing?"

"They tried. They gave her oxygen and everything." Nancy's pale eyes grew wide with the memory. "But finally, that one boy, the one who's working on his paramedic, he just pulls back and shakes his head and says she's dead. Just like that."

Chapter 5

There was more, of course. There's always more, thought Della. She hurried over to County Medical to find Barbara and Rita huddled with Dave in what looked like a room just for grievers. It was decorated in dove gray and mauve and, in addition to several sofas and upholstered chairs, there was a small table to accommodate people who had lists to make and plans to draw.

We aren't ready for plans, Della quickly surmised as both Rita and Barbara threw themselves on her. Rita gave a sharp hug and whispered, "Oh, baby. What are we ever going to do without Pauline?"

Barbara locked Della in a bear-like embrace, and sobbed huge, bosom-heaving sobs that left Della's neck and blouse soaking wet. "Here," Della said, gently disengaging Barbara's arms from around her torso, "let's sit over on this couch."

"Oh my God," Barbara kept whispering. "Oh my God, oh my God."

Della peered around Barbara, who was burrowing into her shoulder, and looked at Rita, who had settled herself on the sofa arm next to where Dave was seated. "What happened?"

Rita shook her head and motioned at Barbara, who was releasing clouds of Gucci scent with every quake. "She just came screaming up the hill: She's dead, she's dead! So I run down there and Pauline—oh, God, Della, I've had car wrecks and kids with broken bones and even my old Granny dying in her bed in my house with all of us right there, but I've never had anybody just up and die like that, with her eyes frozen open and this sort of vomit-like spit running out one side of her mouth—and she's just lying there, deader than doornails, and this one's screaming, and Nancy's called Dave, and he gets there and the rescue squad gets there, but nobody can do anything. Oh, God! Della, it was awful."

"Has anyone called Kat?"

"I tried her pager, but she's got the damned thing turned off, I'll bet. I tried the mobile, too."

"Try the pager again. If you try two or three times, she'll know it's urgent."

Dave cleared his throat and Della looked at him for the first time. "I'm thinking they had a son. Hugh Junior."

"Well, of course," Della said, trying to sound as if she hadn't forgotten Pauline's actual family. "And a daughter. Melissa and Hugh Junior. We'll just have to wait till we get back to the Ladies Farm so we can go through Pauline's address book. We'll call him just as soon as we can."

Rita busied herself with the telephone on the table next to the sofa and Della, who had been stroking Barbara's back, looked down at Barbara's flaming hair. "Barbara? Honey?"

She didn't look up but her shoulders stopped quaking.

"Barbara?" Della tried again. "Why don't you tell me what happened."

Barbara pulled back a little. Her face, red and swollen, had no makeup left on it.

"She was just l-l-l-lying there," Barbara shuddered. "Just curled up on her side and then she started sp-p-pit . . . vomiting." Barbara collapsed once more into Della's arms.

"She was on the floor already when you went to the barn?"

Della felt the sobbing stop long enough to permit a nod. Della shifted her gaze to Rita, who seemed to be dialing her fifth call. "Are you leaving her the number here?"

Rita nodded. "We can't leave yet. They called Dr. Pfluger, we need to talk with him. And we have to get hold of Hugh Junior, have him call the ER so they can call the funeral home." Suddenly she put down the phone. "I just can't believe this," she said, her face crumpling into tears before she could cover them with her hands.

"Oh, come here, honey," Dave said, half-standing to reach over to her. She went willingly, Della noticed, and was glad. She thought Rita should give Dave another chance. He was certainly an improvement over Larry. He was even a better father and grandfather than Larry, and those were Larry's kids.

Della returned to Barbara. "Barbara?" she tried once more. "Barbara, did Pauline say anything?"

"She was already dead," Rita answered. "Didn't you hear her?"

Poor Pauline, dying alone with her pottery! The image was so distressing that it took her a second to notice Barbara's wriggling. Again, she pushed back from Della's soaking bosom.

"Hugh," Barbara whispered. Her button eyes had a dull tone, totally flat.

"She called for Hugh?" Della asked.

"She just said it. *Hugh. Hugh.* Just like that. Then she started choking, and she rolled flat, and her head fell back, and she was spitting up, and I knew I had to get help," Barbara recounted.

"Her head fell back while she was spitting up?" Della repeated. She wanted to grab this woman by the shoulders and shake her. *You left her with her head back while she vomited? Have you lost your mind? She choked! She choked to death and all she needed was someone to tilt her forward!*

But she said nothing as Barbara nodded her confirmation.

Della breathed hard and unwound herself from Barbara. She stood up. "Rita's right," she announced. "We have got to call Hugh Junior. Why don't you all stay here, and I'll go back to the Ladies Farm and track down his number. That way, if Kat calls, someone'll be there."

Rita looked up from the comfort of Dave's embrace and nodded in a dreamy way that irritated Della. She didn't bother looking at Barbara, but hurried out to the Suburban. She didn't trust herself enough to think until she had gunned the engine and lurched out of the parking lot.

"Oh God! That bitch! That stupid, hysterical bitch killed Pauline." She reminded herself not to close her eyes while she was driving and she fought her impulse to head for the highway. You have to call Hugh Junior, she thought. You have got to make that call before you do anything else.

Pauline's cloth-covered address book lay atop her desk in the office behind the registration counter. The book's cover, a floral print in spring-toned pastels, had been hand-stamped by Pauline during one of her book-binding classes. There was a whole set of these things: journals, birthday books, purse-size reminder books, calendar covers.

Both home and office numbers for "Hugh, Jr." were written in Pauline's flowing hand. Typical of Pauline, all the entries were in peacock-blue ink and all had been inscribed carefully, with calligraphic flourish.

Della had dialed the number and it was ringing before she even realized what she was doing. What will I say? she panicked, but someone was already singing out the name of Hugh Jr.'s law firm and she found herself stammering out a request to speak to him regarding a family emergency.

"Hello?" The voice was so much like his father's that Della could not speak for a moment. Stupid! You were expecting the ten-year-old with the drippy nose who was always crying because the other kids picked on him?

"Hello?"

"H-h-hugh?" she finally stammered.

"Who is this?"

Della took a deep breath. "Hugh, honey, this is Della Brewer at the Ladies Farm."

"Is something the matter?"

"Hugh, I'm so sorry, there's been, your mother had an, ah, a heart attack and she died early this afternoon."

"Oh, Jesus." Now this was the voice of the ten-year-old. "What happened?"

Della related the story as quickly as she could, omitting the vomiting and emphasizing the lack of any previous symptoms.

"I just saw her last week. She was fine." His father's voice returned.

"I know," Della said. "She was so happy to see you and the kids. And Melissa called just last night."

"Oh, Jesus! Melissa! You haven't called her, have you?"

"No, you're the first one, really."

"I'll have to call her. And my uncles." Della felt she could see him starting to scribble lists, his face scrunched in earnest wrinkles, his pen flowing in that same even, though more masculine, hand that Pauline had instilled in him. Even in crisis, Della guessed, maybe especially in crisis, Pauline's children would tend to the details of order, harmony, and seasonal grace.

They agreed that he would contact the funeral home in Fort Worth to make arrangements to transport the body, and that she would fax him a list of friends that she and Kat would call from the Ladies Farm.

"This is Monday. The funeral will have to be Wednesday," Hugh Jr. said.

"Yes." She had not even thought about a funeral and she wanted to tell him no. Not for a few weeks, she would say. Give us a few weeks to get used to this.

You're losing it, Della told herself, and made herself sit back in the chair, an old mahogany banker's chair that Hugh had refinished and Pauline had recovered in a nubby mauve fabric that still smelled of her woodsy perfume and hand-milled soap.

"Hugh," she said.

"Yes?"

"Hugh, your mother, Pauline, she was . . . we're just lost, Hugh, your mother was so . . ."

"I'm so sorry," he was saying. "I know you and Mom were friends all those years. This must be so hard on you. And you were a friend to her," he encouraged. "If you and Kat hadn't gone out there after my dad died, she couldn't have kept the farm." He paused. "I guess you know that."

Della had seen enough deaths to know

that it was easier to console than to be con-
soled. "You're a good boy, Hugh. You
made your mother so proud."

"Yeah. Well."

They fell silent for a second and again
she pictured him, with his father's large
hands and his mother's sensitive mouth
and this terrible discomfort connecting him
to Della.

"Well," she said briskly. "You call Melissa. I'll fax my list and I'll tell the hospital
that they'll hear from the funeral home. And
you'll let me know about the funeral."

"Yes," he said. Another pause. "And of
course, you ladies—Kat and what's-her-
name? Rita? and you—you'll sit with the
family, won't you?"

"Of course," she said, wondering if he
knew about Barbara. There's time for that,
Della thought as they said their good-byes.
She hung up the phone and burrowed into
Pauline's chair. Make a list, Della thought.
People to call. Guests. Women enrolled in
Pauline's classes. Della closed her eyes
and pictured names and phone numbers in
peacock-blue ink on pastel paper. She pictured loaves of fresh-baked bread, cooling
in the kitchen. She pictured a work table

covered with unfired ceramics and a rafter hung with bunches of herbs drying in a cool breeze. I can't make a list, thought Della, feeling the tears begin to flow. She rubbed her cheek against the chair back. "Now look!" she sobbed to Richard. "Your stupid wife's gone and killed Pauline!"

"Well, God knows I would love to blame her for Pauline's death," Kat assured Della, "but you know as well as I do Pauline was vomiting because she had a heart attack and it wasn't vomiting that killed her."

"I know she had a heart attack," Della said. "But people survive heart attacks every day if they don't choke to death."

Kat took both Della's hands in her own. "Della, give it up. What difference does it make anyway?"

They were sitting in the canoe near the far bank of the river, where they had paddled to get away from Barbara. In all the excitement, they had forgotten they had guests checking in Monday afternoon and it had taken the two of them, with help from Barbara, Nancy, and Rita, almost every minute through Tuesday lunch to see to their guests' needs. Now, with Rita leading an excursion to the outlet mall and Barbara wandering through the empty house, the two of them were finally able to talk.

"Look," Kat said, "I've got a crafts lady coming over from the junior college who thinks she can take everything but the journal-writing class. You could teach that, couldn't you?"

Della blinked. She was still picturing Pauline on the concrete floor of the barn, head back, mouth open. "Journal writing?"

"Come on, you write *Silver Quest,* you write ads, you can write journals."

"When is it?"

"Tuesdays and Thursdays, ten to eleven-thirty, and a mini the first week in August."

"Twice?" The weekly classes drew from the local population, with several women driving out from Fort Worth once or twice a week. The minis attracted guests who wanted week-long programs. This week's had been counting on "Domestic Magic: A Houseful of Distinction from Everyday Discards." Thankfully, the four women from Houston were easily satisfied by a substitute curriculum of day trips, beauty treatments, and serious credit toward another week at the Ladies Farm.

"Come on, Della, we've got too much going on to waste time on this."

"This is what's going on," Della countered. "This is what made the Ladies Farm. We've got to maintain it; not just anyone can teach these things."

Kat looked smug. "My point exactly. Say yes."

"Yes." Della didn't know why she ever argued with Kat. It was a whole lot easier to concede immediately.

"We need to put together an offer for Hugh Junior and Melissa," Kat said now.

They drifted a little, but there wasn't much breeze or much current and Della, even in her sunglasses, squinted against the sun on the water. "What kind of offer?" She dipped a hand in the green water and dribbled it over her bare arm. When she looked back at Kat, Kat was staring at her.

"What do you mean, what kind of offer? Hugh Junior and Melissa now own half the Ladies Farm. They can sell this thing out from under us."

"They wouldn't do that. Besides, that's still only fifty percent. You need more than half to sell."

"You don't need more than half to ask a court to force a sale."

"Kat!" Della watched water dance off her fingers as she waved her hands in the air. "How did we go from mourning for Pauline into a court battle? These are Pauline's kids, not total strangers. We'll have the place appraised and buy out their interest."

She paused a second, looking at Kat's lacquered nails and crisp cotton shirt. "If they could sell to us, they could sell to Barbara." Della shook her head to clear the confusion. "You don't think she'd do that, do you? Bid on the Ladies Farm?" Only a few days ago, she had been planning to move away, but now, Della couldn't imagine anything more painful than Barbara buying the Ladies Farm out from under her.

"I don't know," Kat replied. "I'm counting on the kids accepting our bid. Then we'll own half."

"And then we can buy out Barbara."

Even in the rocking canoe, Kat's gaze was level. "Exactly."

Della felt a little tingle run through her, then wriggled a bit with conscience. "Of course," she said, "Pauline wanted her to stay."

"And look where that got her. Do you want her to stay?"

Della sighed and looked downriver. Cottonwoods overhung the bank as far as the little bend at Castleburg's, and they could hear the burble of water rushing over Little Sydonia Falls beyond that. There were turtles—at least eight of them—on the thicket of tree roots just before the bend, and Flops, the retriever, was eyeing them from the bank.

"We must have the only retriever in Texas that won't go in the water," she complained.

"Della," Kat issued a warning.

"I don't know," Della said. "Okay? I think she killed Pauline, and I really can't stand her. But she did get those Houston ladies to agree to the program. And she did offer to teach a needlepoint class."

"And for that, you're asking me to share my business and my home with my lover's widow?"

Oh, shit! Della started to laugh, then stopped herself. "I wish Pauline were here to talk to," she said wistfully. She imagined herself telling Pauline about Kat and Richard and, without any trouble at all, imagined Pauline telling her she already knew. Pauline always knew, Della thought.

"How about talking to me?" Kat demanded, and beneath the anger Della heard a longing that matched her own.

"I can't deal with this now," Della said, and found herself crying by the end of the sentence. "It's all too soon."

She took a deep breath. "Look," she said, "let's talk to Hugh Junior and Melissa and tell them we want to meet with them before they do anything. The end of the week, say. They'll probably be happy to sell out. The Ladies Farm isn't exactly a cash cow."

"This won't be any easier at the end of the week," Kat warned, but for once she didn't sound resolute.

"I know," Della said. "But I'll be more rational. Maybe by then I can figure out where I'll get the money to buy anyone out."

"All right," Kat said, and Della just stared. The easy abdication was far more frightening than Kat armed for siege. "Let's talk about dinner. Can we heat up one of those turkey pies?"

*   *   *

As it turned out, Rita kept the foursome at the outlet mall until closing, and their biggest worry Wednesday morning was maintaining their composure as they left Nancy in charge while the five of them—Kat, Della, Barbara, Rita, and Dave—left for the funeral in Fort Worth.

Hugh Jr. had asked Della if she wanted to speak at the funeral, and she had talked it over with Rita and Kat, but finally declined. "The minister's speaking. Hugh Junior and Melissa are both speaking. And her brother, Edward, is speaking. I hate long funerals."

"Amen," Rita said, and that had ended it.

Now, though, filing into the chapel and eyeing the closed casket, Della felt a little guilty. *In all ways,* she imagined herself saying in suitably measured tones, *Pauline was a friend.*

Della had a method for getting through funerals. First you read everything there was to read. Depending on the denomination, this could be a prayer card, a hymnal, a desk-top-published summary of the deceased's life, or just the manufacturer's name on the chair back. Then you thought back to the absolutely best time you ever had with the deceased. And you stayed there, reliving the thing in as much detail as necessary, until it was time to rise for the final hymn or prayer.

At that point you'd be overwhelmed with sorrow but the singing kept you from breaking down, and you could file out with your dignity intact. At the grave site, you just concentrated on whoever was collapsing closest to you, providing whatever comfort and support was needed. Before you knew it, you were back in the car.

As Della paged through the hymnal, she was surprised to hear that Pauline had once entertained dreams of performing great choral pieces. And when Hugh Jr. recounted how his parents had met at a workshop preceding a civil rights march, Della herself remembered how she had met Pauline at a PTA bake sale. Della had made brownies from a mix; Pauline had made six loaves of banana nut bread with whole wheat flour.

Barbara's sniffling interfered with Della's recall of Pauline's long hair. The hair had been her greatest vanity. It seemed to have turned silver overnight, but even then, Pauline continued to adorn it with jeweled barrettes.

A glance to her right showed Barbara dabbing at her eyes with a hankie. Beyond her, Della saw Rita rolling her eyes and patting Barbara's back. Kat, straight-backed and eyes fixed on the speaker, sat to Della's left and Della couldn't help thinking about Richard.

She imagined that seeing the three of them lined up this way would bring a smile to Richard. She could remember dozens of parties at Richard and Barbara's with Richard playing the genial host, welcoming Tony and Della with hugs and kisses, escorting her to the bar with his arm around her shoulder. He told her later that he had always envied Tony, had always been attracted to her.

Della watched Melissa step up to the lectern as Hugh Jr. returned to the row of seats in front of theirs. Barbara leaned forward and put a hand on Hugh Jr.'s shoulder. He jerked, then turned slowly and covered Barbara's hand with his own and nodded at his mother's old friend.

Meanwhile, Melissa had launched a somewhat sarcastic remembrance of the ingredients—all natural, no artificial additives—in Pauline's life. Barbara's sniffling had subsided and Della settled back, trying to picture Hugh and Pauline at the Morrisons' parties.

Suddenly, she recalled Pauline in a bathing suit at what must have been a Fourth of July party. Pauline at her rounded, curvy best, pulling herself up the pool ladder, water running from her peachy flesh, as Richard welcomed her into the folds of a dry towel.

Pauline froze in Della's mind, wrapped in the towel in Richard's arms. Oh, shit! Della thought.

Kat glared at her. Had she spoken?

Finally understanding that she was the only one still seated, Della rose and joined the singing.

You're wrong, she argued with the picture in her mind. Pauline wouldn't do that. Pauline died with her husband's name on her lips.

But the picture stayed with her. They finished singing and resumed their seats. The minister spoke and still the image remained, accompanied once more by Barbara's weeping.

Kat caught her eye for a second and frowned with a nod toward Barbara, but

Della didn't care about Kat's disapproval of Richard's wife.

She was so preoccupied with Richard and Pauline that she barely noticed when the minister wound down and they rose for the Twenty-Third Psalm.

Hugh Jr. had offered them a car, of course, but they had declined. Driving themselves to the cemetery saved them from having to come back to the funeral home after the burial.

"I like that Melissa," Rita said. "That's a girl with Pauline's heart."

Nobody reminded her that Pauline's heart had given out for no apparent reason at age fifty-seven.

"She's more like her father," Barbara said hoarsely, and Della leaned forward slightly to see around Kat to where Barbara slumped against the window. "Pauline was very kind, but Hugh . . . there was a heart. The way Melissa held on to those kids during the service? That was pure Hugh."

The others considered this in silence. Della didn't remember Hugh as especially affectionate, but you never know how someone is with his own family. It was high praise, though, from Barbara, who had

Richard for comparison. Richard was a born hugger.

At least Pauline and Hugh were not at the same cemetery as Jamie and Richard. Della didn't know whose idea this place was; maybe their church had a section here, or Pauline had made a hasty decision when Hugh died.

They stepped carefully onto the damp grass and walked to the edge of the awning. Hugh Jr. and Melissa and their families sat on folding chairs in front of the grave. Other mourners, many of whom Della knew, crowded beneath the awning.

Rita held on to Dave's arm, and Barbara seemed to be suspended between Kat and Della. Just once, thought Della, I'd like someone to hold me up at one of these things. "Here," she whispered to Barbara, "why don't you take this chair." She pulled an empty one from the back row and set it back a little so Barbara could sit. With a rustle from the layers of dark chiffon in which she had swathed herself, Barbara lowered her body into the chair.

She didn't know what Barbara could see, seated behind two rows of people on the sloping ground, but something set her off again, and she was sobbing by the time the minister took his place and described Pauline as waiting for them on some distant shore.

That didn't comfort Barbara at all. Her sobbing grew louder. Then, she made tiny mewing sounds, like a kitten, and people started turning around to look.

Della didn't care; let them look. They were lowering the casket into the grave, and Della was congratulating herself on her tolerance when Barbara began to moan. "Oh, Pauline," she moaned. "Oh, Pauline."

Kat looked at Della and Della looked around for Dave and Rita, but they had disappeared. Shrugging in acquiescence to Kat's demand, Della knelt next to Barbara. "Come on," she whispered to the hands covering Barbara's face. "Let's go get some air."

Barbara moved her hands to look at Della, but she didn't stop moaning. "Oh, Pauline! . . . Oh, Pauline! I killed her! I killed her!"

Della stood quickly, taking Barbara's elbow and yanking her to her feet. "Come on," she said, not at all gently. "She's in the ground, we're all done here."

Pushing and pulling, Della and Kat moved Barbara back to the car. Kat opened the car door while Della aligned Barbara with the front passenger seat and pushed gently on her shoulders. Barbara sat.

Kat, with a look that clearly stated *You can't possibly ask me to comfort my lover's widow,* fled toward Hugh Jr. and Melissa, to express her sympathy and to confirm they'd come out to Sydonia on Friday. Della hoped she rounded up Rita and Dave, too. She didn't want to hang around.

"Here," she said to Barbara. She reached into the back seat and pulled out a handful of fresh tissues. "Your handkerchief must be soaked."

Barbara took the tissues and blotted her face, then burst out crying again. "Oh, God! Pauline! Oh, Pauline!"

Della was still standing, facing Barbara, who sat on the car seat with her feet planted on the ground. "Barbara," she said softly, but Barbara was sobbing hard into the wadded tissue. "Barbara." Della squatted down to eye level.

She reached over and put a hand on Barbara's shoulder. The flesh felt warm through the silk and Della struggled to keep her hand there, imaging Richard's hand in the same place.

"Oh, Della!" Barbara sobbed harder, leaning forward until Della was all that prevented her from tumbling forward. "Oh, God, Della, I killed her!" Della, braced in her squat and pushing with all her might to keep this mound of quaking flesh from crashing onto her, barely comprehended at first. Shoving, finally, until Barbara sat back up, Della was panting when she replied.

"Oh, Barbara, don't be melodramatic. You ran out to get help. It wasn't your fault."

"No, no, no!" Barbara moaned, shaking her head back and forth. "It was my fault," she sobbed. "It was my fault."

Della felt ashamed at the jolt of pleasure, undiminished by recognition that her joy stemmed from her chance to be forgiving and magnanimous while Barbara writhed with guilt. She deserves to suffer, Della rejoiced, even as she patted Barbara's shoulder.

"She knew," Barbara wailed. "She knew when she saw the ring, and it killed her!"

"She knew?" Della could stand the pain no longer and forced herself to straighten up. Hot arrows shot the length of her spine.

"All these years," Barbara cried. "All these years, why couldn't I leave it alone? Why did I have to go there, have to talk about Hugh? It was like I couldn't stop myself, on and on about the amethyst!"

"Hugh?" Della dropped her arms to her sides.

"It was just one night. One night!" Barbara cried. "But it broke Richard's heart, and now it's killed Pauline!"

Chapter 6

We were just a bunch of middle-class Texans, Della thought. None of us was a prom queen or a CEO. We raised kids, went to church, lived in houses with two-car garages, and now it turns out we were all just humping like bunnies.

She blinked at Barbara, who had doubled over until her head was almost on her knees. Her silk floral back shook with grief. My God! thought Della. She cheated on Richard!

She looked around, trying to ground herself in the present. The crowd was dispersing to cars parked all along the service road that bordered the cemetery. Small groups dotted the flat ground in front of the wrought-iron gates.

She didn't see Kat, Rita, or Dave anywhere and guessed they were still with Hugh Jr. and Melissa. Della sighed. The door to the back seat hung open and she reached in again for more tissue. "Barbara?" she said.

Barbara looked up and reached for the tissue. "You won't tell the others, will you?" Barbara asked. "I know you don't like me, but—"

"Oh, for heaven sakes, Barbara, what makes you say that? Of course I won't tell them. Here," said Della, motioning at the tissue, "blow your nose. Do you have a compact?"

Barbara obeyed, then looked up with wonder. "Didn't you ever think about, when you were married, what another man would be like? Didn't you—"

"Who knows what I thought when I was married?" Della shifted from one foot to another. "Who cares now?" She nodded toward the clutch that Barbara had thrown onto the floorboard. "That yours?"

Barbara twisted around and then

reached, feeling with her hand until she retrieved the purse. There's no one around to appreciate this, Della thought, now that Pauline's dead. Me comforting Barbara over her unfaithfulness to Richard.

She felt her own eyes filling up and she turned away from Barbara. All she needed was another tear fest.

Nonetheless, her eyes stayed full and blurred the figure walking toward her. Until he said her name, she didn't recognize Tony at all.

"You okay?" he asked, then looked into the car. "Barbara?"

Barbara finished applying her lipstick and smooshed her lips together for a long second before she flashed a smile at Tony. "Well, hi there, stranger. How have you been?"

In a move that surprised Della with both its speed and grace, Barbara popped out of the seat and stepped forward to hug Tony.

Tony hated fat women, and Della noticed how gingerly he hugged back before Barbara pulled away. Weight had been an issue between them, and Della still bore great resentment to his criticism. At least I was never that obese, she thought now.

"Tony," Della said. "How are you?"

He shrugged. He was a little too narrow for someone so tall, and Della noticed that most of his own weight gain had settled in his gut. She had heard that he'd opened another two copy shops, and she wondered why he didn't buy himself a new suit.

"Heard from Robbie yesterday. One of Hugh Junior's friends called him."

Della nodded. "He called me, too. He said he'd be here in August."

Tony smiled a little. "He put Katie on the phone. That kid's some talker."

Della smiled back. This was what they talked about when they saw each other: their remaining son and their grandchild.

They stood for a second, Barbara beaming inanely and Della and Tony just looking at each other. "Sorry about Pauline," he said finally. "This must be real hard for y'all."

Della nodded.

"Guess what?" Barbara took up the slack. "I've moved out there, too!"

"Have you?" Tony asked, looking down

at where he had dug up a plug of grass with his boot toe.

"Barbara's sort of resident-for-life," Della explained, crossing her fingers behind her back.

Tony raised his eyebrows enough to show he appreciated the humor, then shook his head, "How are you doing out there?"

"Oh, I'm fine out there," Della said. "Out there's a great place."

Tony nodded again. "Be hard without Pauline."

"Yeah." She still thought he was a handsome man, but she wondered if his face would be so creased and his suit jacket so tight if they'd stayed together. She liked to think not. "How's the copy shop business?"

"Oh, great," he replied without enthusiasm. "Opened a second one in Weatherford, and one up in Denton. They've all got computers-by-the-hour in them."

"Sounds lucrative." Della couldn't figure out what Barbara was beaming about, unless it was just joy over the presence of an actual man. There were so few in any of their lives, it was always an excitement.

Tony had remarried after their divorce, a

woman with three kids who left him after a
year for a car salesman in New Mexico.
Della thought the whole thing was just forgotten; she never thought it had much to
do with her, but she supposed there was
something about the wife, Suzanne, that
made up for something she herself had
lacked. Suzanne hadn't been especially
thin or beautiful, but maybe she was easier
to get along with. That wouldn't have been
hard, after Jamie died.

"Barbara?" Tony asked. "How's Dickie?"
Maybe Della imagined the catch in his
voice.

"Doing great!" Barbara said.

"Still in Dallas?"

Della shifted from one foot to the other,
feeling the sun through her long sleeves.

"He may be moving to Houston," Barbara said. "He's got an offer from a big sur-
geon there, to work with him."

"Glad he's doing well. Richard'd be proud."

Barbara dimpled and launched into a
description of Dickie's accomplishments.
Della knew why Tony put his arm around
her then, and she was glad for it, to have
this support while they listened to Barbara
extol the son who had been Jamie's friend.

Dickie was a great kid, Della reminded herself as she always did, but it was never comfort enough against the cruelty that Dickie had grown up and Jamie was dead.

Thankfully, the rest of the gang showed up, and while Tony shook hands with Dave and Kat filled Della in on when Hugh Jr. and Melissa were coming, they somehow all loaded up into the car.

Della found herself waving to Tony from the back window. Nice guy in a bad suit, she thought.

Silver Quest was due at the printer's, and Della had barely started writing it. The ads, laid out by a part-timer who came in after school, were mostly in place, and the lead article, a state-by-state roundup of legislative activity, would not be tough. It was her column—the piece she usually wrote about women traveling alone; or how to dress to meet your daughter-in-law-to-be; or discussing safe sex, vaginal dryness, and impotence with a potential partner—that was causing problems. All she wanted to write about was Pauline.

"Well, write about her," Kat advised. "Our readers know who she is. Was."

"I can't," Della said.

"Can't?"

"Nothing's working." Della felt stupid.

"Nothing's working? You have writer's block over a newsletter?"

"Oh, of course not. The newsletter's not writing anyway, it's just reporting." Della paused. "I just can't get anything out."

"Well, write something," Kat repeated, turning back to the ledger she had opened on Pauline's desk. It was a shock every time Della walked in and saw Kat rummaging through Pauline's things.

"She was in love with her own handwriting," Kat murmured now, more in wonder than criticism. "That's why she wouldn't use the computer. Look at this!"

Della peered over Kat's shoulder, looking at the entries covering the page. *Tortillas, carton, $11.95. Bed sheets, white, $124.50. 100% rag writing paper, $23.95.* Her capital letters twice the size of the lower case, her descenders flowing down in gentle slants to the next line. And the ink like rows of flowers, first peacock blue, then green, then lilac.

"It's a work of art," Della said.

Kat sighed. "Yeah."

Della knew Kat was worried about getting all the financials into the computer in time for Hugh Jr. and Melissa, but Della knew she'd do it. Pauline's desk was in order, and so were her ledgers. If Kat wanted, Della thought, she could even hire someone to key in the data. But it was an act of faith with Kat. She had to key it in herself, the way she had every month that Pauline had lived and handed over those artful ledgers.

"I'll write it if you want," Barbara said.

"Jesus!" Kat jerked back. "I forgot you were here."

Barbara sat on—actually overflowed—the steno chair in front of the computer. With her back to the screen and one leg tucked up under her, she resembled a cherubic schoolgirl in her mother's earrings.

"They're already written," Della snapped. She hadn't noticed Barbara at all. "They need to be keyed in."

"I meant your article. About Pauline."

"Oh, Barbara," Della said. "That's so sweet of you."

"I can write," Barbara said. "And I want something to do."

"Maybe you could key the ledgers for

Kat." Della hated amateurs who thought they could write. Even newsletters. Every day brought manuscripts from hopefuls who had seen *Silver Quest* and just knew she would publish inspirational poetry, or spiritual testimony, or short stories, once she read theirs.

"I'm keying these myself," Kat said, rising from Pauline's chair with the ledger clutched to her breast. "Why don't you let her try," she challenged Della. "You just said you're stuck."

"Try," Della said. She wheeled around and started back for her own office, then changed her mind and headed for the back door. "I'll be on the river," she said.

The Nolan didn't offer solace. Della paddled around a little, but it was hot and she'd forgotten both hat and sunblock and spent most of her time envisioning brown tumors blossoming over her nose and cheekbones. What'd you expect, she grumbled to herself as she dragged the canoe back up onto the lawn. She shoved her toes back into her shoes and stomped over to a lawn chair beneath the live oak.

Flops, who'd spent most of Della's boating time patrolling the shore, followed her over and sat next to the chair. Della rested a hand on the back of her neck. "You holding up okay?" she asked, scratching as the dog pushed up against the pressure of her fingers. "Hmmmm?"

Let her write the thing, Della told herself. If she actually does, you'll be done with it. And if not, it will at least give you a starting point. It's a few hundred words. You can crank it out in no time once you get moving.

She leaned back in the chair and closed her eyes. The kitchen door opened and closed behind her, but she didn't move.

"You taking a siesta?" Rita asked.

Della heard ice clinking in a glass, but she didn't hear even a rustle from the ground as Rita moved over the grass. "You taking a vacation?" Della mumbled.

"Somewhat. Mrs. Pumphries rescheduled. I think Mrs. Myerhoff got her to change her day so they could come together."

"Your customers scared of people dying?"

"Either that or fat women who get hysterical over people dying."

"Well, that was probably pretty scary," Della conceded.

She listened to Rita nuzzling the black dog, pictured Rita's slick black cap of hair against the dog's neglected coat.

"You need a good comb-out," Rita was telling the animal in the tones she'd use to console a child. "You need a wash and a style." Then her voice grew serious. "You all are going to buy out those kids, aren't you?"

"I guess." Della roused herself, opened her eyes enough to squint toward the river. "If they'll sell. If Barbara doesn't outbid us."

"She wouldn't do that, would she?" Rita had settled onto the grass.

"You're going to get eaten by ants," Della warned. "Who knows what she'll do?"

"You think the kids know about Barbara owning half?"

"Hugh Junior mentioned it when Kat talked to him. Evidently, Pauline was so upset, she called him about it." Della closed her eyes again.

"Did he sound surprised?"

"Kat talked to him, I didn't. And it doesn't matter how he sounded. What matters is whether he'd sell to us before he sells to Barbara. And," she anticipated Rita's next question, "I have no idea whether he'll do that or not. Or if she'd even offer."

"Why's she here anyway?" Rita asked. "You really think she's just so impressed with the way we live she can't imagine living anywhere else?"

Della weighed the possibilities and imagined herself confiding in a breezy, chatty way that the three women Barbara might most want to kill were living here. The potential efficiencies were astronomical. Instead, she shrugged. "Who knows?"

Rita shifted gears. "Do you need any money?"

Della stared at Rita. "Are you offering to lend it?"

"Well, I've got some saved up!" Rita declared. "I'm not totally irresponsible."

Della stared, shook her head, then settled back in her chair and closed her eyes. "I don't know. I'm thinking, if this works the way we plan, the kids'll take back a mortgage and let us pay them out."

"And if Barbara sells out?"

"Maybe the same. Who knows?" Della concentrated on sounding noncommittal. "Have you thought about buying in?"

"It's a little soon," Rita said.

"It's a little soon for all of us."

"I just meant, you know, you and Kat

have known each other all along, and you all were the ones who developed the thing. I just do hair."

"Well, think about it," Della advised. "Kat and I have, and if you're interested, this would be your chance. Especially if Barbara sells."

Della looked down to watch Rita and Flops getting comfortable together, Rita leaning against one leg of the chair, Flops lying down with her head on Rita's thigh.

"You're both going to get bit," Della said again.

"You think Barbara'll sell?" Rita ignored the perils of ant attacks. "Or that Kat'll drive her out?"

"Kat's dug in. If the kids agree, and Kat and I buy Pauline's share, I'm betting Barbara doesn't last a month." Della considered. Unless, she continued silently, she wants to finish off Kat and me. "Without Pauline here, why would she want to stay? She's not close to any of us."

"I didn't get the feeling she was that close to Pauline," Rita observed.

Della concentrated on keeping her eyes closed and her mouth shut. But she did wish someone would explain why Barbara would want to move in with the widow of the man with whom she once had sex. Even once, long ago. After all, Della thought, I wouldn't move in with Barbara.

Della sighed, which Rita must have heard as a response, because she continued her inventory. "And Kat doesn't take to her at all. Barbara is a good cook, though."

Della didn't want to discuss Barbara's cooking, or her unrelenting cheerfulness about helping make up the rooms and running the laundry. "But she's not much good at CPR," Della countered.

"I kind of doubt anyone could have saved Pauline," Rita said. "You heard the doctor: It was a massive heart attack."

"Yeah." Della kept her eyes closed.

"So when are those kids coming . . . Melissa and Hugh Junior?"

"Friday. I thought you talked with them at the cemetery."

"Friday? No, Kat talked to them."

Della looked down at Rita's head. "So where were you when I had to wrestle Barbara over to the car?"

Rita tilted her head back to look up at Della. "I guess we were just in the crowd somewhere." She grinned. "Out of earshot, thank the Lord."

Della considered sharing Barbara's confession, but dismissed the chance. "I can't believe you didn't hear her moaning," Della muttered.

"Her what?"

"Moaning. Moaning. You know: *Oh, Pauline. I killed Pauline.*" Della regarded Rita more carefully. "I can't believe you didn't hear her, everybody there heard her. Where were you?"

Rita looked a little sheepish, and turned her attention to Flops. "Did you hear her, Flops?" she asked the dog, scratching her head. "Huh? Did you hear big, bad Barbara?"

Give it up, Della told herself. "We've got to stop talking about her," Della said, more to herself than to Rita. "She could be right behind us."

"Well, I didn't say anything bad, you and Kat are the ones complaining. Actually, I like her."

"You won't when you know her better. She's just one of those stupid, hysterical women who can't think of anyone except themselves. She couldn't even grieve for Pauline without making it about herself."

"Well," said Rita, "we all express grief in our own way." The grin on her face said it all.

"You were screwing, weren't you? At the cemetery?" Della couldn't believe she was asking, let alone that Rita was nodding that sheepish nod like a kid confessing to a particularly bad fart. "During the burial?"

"I guess," said Rita. "We weren't really watching what was going on there."

"On someone's grave?" Della couldn't prevent her rising intonation.

"Of course not! How tacky!"

Della couldn't believe the indignation, but Rita rushed right into the justifying details.

"I just felt faint, and you saw how flat and plain that cemetery was, no benches or anything, and there were no chairs left. So Dave walked me over to the maintenance shed. And we went around back where it was shady. And I was leaning up against that shed, but Dave thought I should sit. So he takes off his coat—that's his only suit, mind you—and puts it on the ground for me. So I sat down, and he sat down next to me and held me and, next thing I know, we're just going at it."

"Weren't you afraid someone would see you?"

"Nah. All the crew was at the grave. And there wasn't anything behind that shed except the fence and then the railroad tracks. And, you know something?" Rita cocked her head and looked up at Della.

"I don't think I know anything."

"It really did make me feel better. I mean, about Pauline and all. Like she was there, maybe, and was glad to see that life goes on."

"You felt she was there?"

"Well, not there exactly, but like, if she was, she'd be glad."

"Glad you were fucking at her funeral?"

"Oh, come off it. Are you telling me you never had sex anywhere but in your bed?"

"I'm telling you I never had sex in a cemetery during my friend's funeral." She gave a laugh. "And I certainly never tried to justify it by saying my friend would like it."

Rita didn't take offense, but she did press her point. "I didn't say like it, exactly. I mean, I think she'd be glad to know that someone cares about me." Her girlish smile was too much for Della.

"Cares about you? Cares about getting his, I would say. That choirboy!"

"Now, you leave off Dave, he was just trying to make me feel better. He is an ex-husband, and he does know me pretty well."

Della laughed. "I'm sorry," she said, but she kept laughing. "Oh, Rita!" She reached down toward her friend and put a hand on her shoulder. Just touching Rita started tears flowing, but she still didn't stop laughing. "You're right," she said beneath her streaming tears. "Pauline would be glad for you. And for just the reason you said: that someone cares for you."

Hugh Jr. and Melissa had hated Sydon House because it had forced them out of the Fort Worth suburbs and turned them into hicks. Even though Pauline had driven them to school in Fort Worth every day, they resented the distance that stretched between their friends and themselves.

"They treat us like servants," Della recalled Pauline mimicking Melissa in her complaints about running a bed and break-

fast. *"They expect us to clean up after them!"*

Pauline's decision to stay on at the Ladies Farm after Hugh's death had stunned them, Pauline once told her, but Della thought the kids had come to some understanding of it. Della was sure that Melissa and Hugh Jr. couldn't imagine their mother any other place, any more than she or Kat could.

Hugh Jr. brought his wife, Carrie, with him, and Melissa had her two boys, whose names Della forgot but who were captivated by Nancy's offer to take them down to the river. "I'll use the rowboat," she promised, then disappeared with them.

They started in the office, with Kat handing over Pauline's ledgers, as well as the printout of the financials for the Ladies Farm.

"We'll have to do an audit," Hugh Jr. said as he accepted the binder Kat had assembled.

"You should," Kat agreed. She glanced at Della. "Particularly because we'd like you to set a price on the place."

Hugh Jr. smiled. "Our thoughts exactly." He motioned to Melissa and Carrie, who sat on either side of him on the sagging sofa. Barbara occupied the typist's chair and Kat the straight-back one next to Pauline's desk. Rather than take Pauline's chair, Rita and Della had chosen to stand, leaning against the door jamb for support.

"What about you, Aunt Barbara?" Melissa asked.

Della held her breath.

The color rose in Barbara's face. "Me?" She seemed startled that they had noticed her. "Well, I want to stay on, of course. That is," she glanced quickly at Della, "if I'm still welcome."

Della saw Kat start to reply, but Melissa spoke—gushed—first. "Well, I know that's what mother wanted, Aunt Barbara. You belong here."

Hugh Jr. cleared his throat. "I guess what we were interested in, actually, is more the business aspect of this." He smiled gently at Barbara. "You understand. As executor, in an official capacity, I have a responsibility to the estate. So the real question is, were you interested in purchasing the remaining interest in this property? The real estate?"

"Purchase the remaining—" Her forehead furrowed and her lips pursed with the thought.

That little bastard! Della thought. He wants her to bid up the price! She caught Kat's warning glance and bit back her anger. We should have talked to Barbara first, she admonished herself.

Barbara finally figured it out and shook her head slowly, enabling Della to release a long, slow breath. Tears filled Barbara's eyes. "Your mother was such a wonderful woman. I'm sure she wanted these ladies to have the rest of the farm." She turned back to Della. "Just being allowed to live here brings me more happiness than I could ever have hoped for now."

Della smiled wanly. She means happiness from irritating Kat and me to death.

Hugh Jr. was talking about appraisals and letters of appointment, and Kat was making notes and nodding as if her future were not at stake.

"Well," Kat concluded briskly. "We'll get together after you've had time to look at the books. Let's take a look at your mother's things."

They all tromped upstairs, Kat hanging back to grab Della by the arm. "What the hell's the matter with you?" she whispered fiercely under the sound of feet clumping on the uncarpeted stairs.

Della shook her head. "I'm imagining you running her off."

"Get a grip," came the instruction. "Lose that loopy grin and stay with her and make sure she doesn't change her mind." Kat gave Della a little push up the stairs.

They crowded into Pauline's room, the only suite in the old part of the house, with a small sitting room and windows to the east, next to the bedroom that overlooked the street. These rooms in the older part of the house were small, and there was no bath in the bedroom. The ladies of the Ladies Farm shared two baths down the hall in the new part, where the walls were thin, the rooms were commodious, and every window looked out over the Nolan.

Della stood in the center of the room with the others, looking at the executive-stripe wall covering that Pauline had designed in the eighties and never replaced. Finally, Carrie approached the mahogany wardrobe as if to open it, then veered at the last minute to the small bookcase. "Look," she said, leaning over, "these are all books your mother covered in fabric."

"Journals," said Hugh Jr., following her. He turned to Kat. "We brought some cartons. . . ."

Kat nodded. "Let us go get them for you. We've been saving them, too." With that they dispersed: Kat, Rita, Barbara, and Della hurrying downstairs to get boxes from Hugh's van, while Hugh Jr., Carrie, and Melissa began sorting through Pauline's things.

"Leave them," Kat said on the stairs, after the third trip. She checked her watch. "We'll fix lunch for them in the kitchen after the guests have eaten."

From the river, they could hear an occasional raised voice, and Della supposed Nancy was helping Melissa's boys spot fish. "We need to make up rooms," Della said. "Since Nancy managed to snag river duty."

"I'll get the rooms," Barbara said, and the others jumped.

Kat looked hard at Della, and Della gulped. "There's no need for you to do all that by yourself," Della said. "We can do them together."

*   *   *

Della's offer did not surprise Barbara. No one at the Ladies Farm trusted her competence, and Barbara reminded herself once again to give them all more time. She followed Della to the second-floor utility room and helped her move the cart into the hallway. "I'll start the bath," Della said. Barbara nodded agreement and, letting the cart pass, pulled the vacuum cleaner from its corner, and followed.

The ladies had a system: One person hit the bathroom while the other did the beds and straightened the room. Nancy had explained it the day after Pauline died, when everything was still in an uproar and no one seemed to remember that there was a business to run. The straightener, Nancy had shown Barbara, always finished first and went on to the next room, where she started the bathroom and the other eventually came in and did the beds.

In the first room, occupied by a married couple on a trek out to California, Barbara and Della worked steadily and with little conversation, but Barbara's mind was shrieking questions. Everything had changed now. Now it was Della and Kat who controlled her future. Maybe she should just tell them, Barbara thought, stripping the sheets from the king-size mattress and bundling them into the sack that hung from the cart handle. But what would she say?

How could she explain that she had no interest in buying the Ladies Farm, that she just needed a place to live? Maybe she should just buy the place and let Kat and Della keep their money. They'd get it back eventually. But they'd hate me, Barbara fretted, dropping a pillow into a pillowcase and smoothing it down at the head of the bed. And I want to live with them.

Barbara switched on the vacuum cleaner, which roared over the sloshing sounds Della was making in the bathroom. The way Barbara remembered it, Della's lack of cleaning skills had been an ongoing joke, and it was odd to think of her swabbing toilets and scrubbing bath tile. Barbara herself got a lot of satisfaction from cleaning things. Clearing the carpet of lint and litter as she ran the vacuum cleaner over it gave her a sense of accomplishment. I guess, she thought, Della had a lot of career accomplishments. She didn't need to clean.

There were five guests: the married couple, two women in a double, and one woman in the single. The new crafts teacher had them out in the barn painting flower pots. The teacher had agreed to hold the pots for the married couple, who would pick them up on their return trip home to Baton Rouge.

After she finished vacuuming the third room, the single (which could actually sleep two since it had a double bed, but only a small dresser and a stall shower), Barbara stepped into the bathroom to see how Della was doing. "I'll get the commode," she said.

"Be my guest," replied Della, who was working at the shower stall. Nancy, who sometimes cleaned all six rooms herself, missed a lot, and the ladies made it a point of pride to correct her deficiencies on the days they did the cleaning.

Barbara squirted cleaner into the bowl and reached for the long-handled brush. "I'm sorry I made a spectacle of myself at the funeral."

"What?" Della looked up from where she was bent over the floor of the shower stall.

Her yellow-gloved hand held the soapy sponge in midair.

"I said, I'm sorry I made a spectacle at the funeral."

"Forget it," Della said, dipping her sponge in the running water and rinsing off the newly scrubbed stall.

"I don't know what came over me," Barbara said, still facing the commode. She swished the brush around the bowl and squinted into it to make sure it was getting clean. Then she turned to look at Della. "I've never talked about it, but suddenly, right then, I had to tell someone." Della's back was still to her, but the sponge had stopped moving. "I can't tell you how much I appreciate . . . how grateful I am . . ."

"Look," said Della, standing abruptly and turning the faucet knobs off with a jerk, "It's okay. I understand. And, I promise you I won't tell anyone." Barbara noticed that Della, as she finished speaking, put her hand to the small of her back and grimaced a little.

Barbara's eyes filled with tears, but she managed a thank you. "And," she took a breath, "thanks for letting me stay here."

Della looked away. "Well," she said, "there's no sense in making any big decisions until we see what the kids want to do with Pauline's share."

Barbara wavered a second, then forced herself to press on. "You know, Della, Richard left me . . . comfortable." She saw the skepticism in Della's eyes. "More than comfortable, I guess. And I don't want to start any fights here." She felt her lips start to tremble, but she kept going. "So if you need to borrow something . . . to take care of Hugh Junior and Melissa, I mean . . ."

She didn't know why Della looked so exasperated. "Kat and I can take care of Hugh Junior and Melissa." Della's eyes narrowed, and Barbara felt the same way she had years before when Della would squint at her and ask, "What do you do all day, anyway?"

"I meant that since I won't be bidding on the other half of the Ladies Farm, there's no reason why I can't make funds available to you. After all," she straightened her own back, "there would be no sense in just running the price up, as long as I can go on living here." Her resolve lasted only as long as the sentence, leaking out with each

word until she felt tears again. Still, she
stood facing Della in the bathroom across a
cart of cleaning supplies, both of them wet,
dirty, and clad in yellow rubber gloves.

Maybe Della felt sorry for her. "Oh, of
course you can stay here, Barbara. I just
meant that for Kat and me, this is business
and we should finance it that way. That's
all."

Barbara nodded, not trusting herself to
speak. They wheeled the cart out of the
bathroom and into the hallway. "I'll vacuum
this hall," Barbara said. "I guess we'll leave
Pauline's room alone today, let those kids
work in peace."

"Yeah," said Della, but she held on to
Barbara's gaze, and Barbara looked at her
quizzically. "Can I ask you one thing? You
don't have to tell me if you don't want."

"Sure," said Barbara. She braced herself, knowing Della wanted to know how
long she would stay.

"Did Richard really know?"

"Richard? Know?"

"About you and Hugh?"

"Oh!" Barbara was amazed that she herself had forgotten, though she noticed,
lately, that sometimes she went whole

days without thinking about it. "Yes," she replied.

"How did he find out?"

"I told him," Barbara said. "I couldn't live with it. I don't know how anyone does. But it was stupid, because I got the comfort of the confession, but I broke his heart. He pulled away from me then. He still loved me, but after that, everything was different."

It was funny that today she could talk calmly about this, but the Ladies Farm had brought tears.

"I'm sure he forgave you," Della said.

Barbara shook her head. "No," she said. "I don't think so."

They put the cart away in silence, and Barbara started back for the vacuum cleaner. They had to get cleaned up enough to help with lunch.

"He was a jerk," Della said suddenly as they closed the utility-room door.

Barbara didn't follow. "Richard," Della said. "Your husband. He was a jerk if he didn't forgive you that one thing."

Barbara shook her head. "Richard wasn't a jerk. You didn't know him the way I did."

Chapter 7

Pauline Freschatte was a real friend, Barbara typed on her laptop, then leaned back against the pillows. Alone in her room following lunch with Pauline's kids, Barbara realized she'd have to think all the way back to Chicago to remember times before Pauline in her life. Only Richard knew her longer. As adrift as the two of them had been, siblings scattered and parents estranged, she and Richard could not have imagined how to become a family without Pauline and Hugh to show them.

Barbara backspaced and retyped: *Pauline Freschatte was my friend.* And now that I need her most, she thought, breaking into tears, she's not here. Without looking, Barbara reached over to the bed-side for a tissue. After Richard's death, she had learned to accept these tear showers, wipe them away and go on. Still sniffling, she typed, *And once you were her friend, she accepted everything about you.*

Even that you slept with her husband, Barbara thought. Or maybe, she amended, Pauline didn't exactly accept that, she just kept her feelings to herself all these years and then had a heart attack over it. Don't think about that, Barbara ordered herself. Think about getting this written so Della and Kat will see how useful you are.

Barbara wished she could call Dickie, but there was no phone in the damn room, and she had already called him twice since Pauline's funeral. He had offered to come to Sydonia, but there was no point until he could see that she was settled here. Bar-bara checked her watch, then tapped out another two sentences. She still needed to find a phone with enough privacy from which to call both broker and banker. Maybe I could set up an E-mail address, through the web site, she thought, then wondered about the security.

Sliding off the bed, Barbara made her way to the window. From here she could follow the river as it wound into town. The courthouse tower and the First Methodist spire poked up out of the live oaks. Hugh and Pauline chose well, she thought, admiring the way the hill rose on the other side of the Nolan. For the millionth time she acknowledged how well Pauline and Hugh had complemented one another and wondered that she herself had ever been attracted to anyone so reticent. Not reticent enough, of course, but still, compared to Richard, Hugh's reserve had been fascinating.

As Barbara watched, Nancy beached the rubber raft, and Melissa's boys, Taylor and Brian, jumped ashore and raced toward whoever must be calling them from the side of the house. Brian, unable to keep pace with his older brother, gamely chugged along behind. For a second, Barbara recalled the three boys of the past—Dickie and Jamie fighting for the lead while Hugh trudged after them—and she ached for those sunburned legs and the sweaty, boy-smell that had filled so many family summers.

It must be hard for Della, Barbara thought, turning from the window: losing Pauline and seeing these kids—she reached for her laptop—and having me here.

Hugh Jr. had told Della that their goal for the visit was to collect their mother's belongings and leave the Ladies Farm behind them as quickly as possible.

"Don't y'all want any of the furniture?" Rita questioned as they helped carry boxes out to the car. "Not even that old armoire?" She sidestepped Brian, who sat on the curb and poked at tar bubbles with a stick.

"It's more trouble than it's worth for me to ship it to California," Melissa said. She glanced quickly at her younger son. "Don't touch that tar with your fingers," she warned, then continued to Rita, "And Hugh and Carrie have gone so contemporary..." Her voice trailed off and her hands waved in the air as she waited for Hugh Jr. to open the Volvo tailgate.

"Dave says he'll be happy to haul it for you," Rita offered to Hugh Jr. and Carrie.

"Pauline picked those pieces to furnish this house," Carrie insisted, setting her small carton on the ground. "They belong here, with you." She, too, glanced down at Brian. "Come on, Brinny," she invited the boy as she extended her hand. "Let's go give Flops one more hug." She smiled nervously at the assembled group, then fled with the child.

Della was relieved about the furniture. She could have parted with the bedroom things, but she didn't feel ready to face the office without Pauline's desk. "Are you sure this is all you want?" she asked one more time.

"We've got her journals, some of her books, and the jewelry," said Hugh Jr. "And we piled the things we think should go to Goodwill on the bed." He motioned to Melissa, who handed him her carton. "You're welcome to go through them. I know mother would want you to have whatever you liked."

Della nodded, since he seemed to be speaking to her rather than to Rita. She supposed he thought of her as the voice of authority for the Ladies Farm; she had been a fixture of his childhood as well as his parents' constellation: Robbie and Jamie's mom, Pauline's friend.

She shook her head to clear it because Hugh Jr. had continued. "...the appraiser next week, Dad's estate, handle mostly over the phone."

He was still talking to her as he arranged more cartons in the back of the station wagon. Then, after he withdrew from the back and slammed the tailgate, he said to her, "I'm not like my father, you know. I can handle business."

Della met his gaze while she debated whether to reassure him of her faith in his abilities or to rush to his father's defense. "Your dad handled business," she said finally. "He just had a bad break or two. And I'm sure you're quite competent." She tried to smile, but her voice had begun to quiver. "I know because your mother...your mother always was so proud..." Her face had grown hot and ridiculous tears filled her eyes, but she wanted to continue "...so proud of both of you."

From behind, Melissa put her arms

around her. "It's okay, Aunt Dell," Melissa whispered.

Della nodded. Of course it was okay. Hugh Jr. already looked sorry for upsetting her.

When he started to apologize, she told him not to worry about it. "It's just . . . the way you spoke about your father. I never thought . . . none of us ever thought of him as no good in business."

"Yeah." He shrugged, looked down the street to where it dead-ended at the Castleburg fence. "I just meant, you know, you could trust me to handle this. I was afraid you still think of me as a kid." He walked over to her, smiling a little, with a light in his eyes that was pure Pauline. "And my father's kid at that!"

Della chuckled. "You will always be a kid in my heart, Hugh. You and Melissa and Robbie and Jamie. But I know better. Anyway," she stroked his shoulder and upper arm a second, "you could do a lot worse than being your father's kid."

They hugged then. Carrie reappeared with both Brian and Taylor, and the whole group climbed into the Volvo and drove away.

"I can't believe they didn't want that armoire," Rita said.

"You want it in your room?" Della asked.

"You bet."

"I don't know why," Della said before they joined Kat on the porch. "It's too small to have sex in."

Pauline Freschatte was my friend, Barbara had written. *And like all good friends everywhere, she had an immense capacity for acceptance. Everyone who read her column in this newsletter saw this acceptance. Remember how she always gave you several different ways to finish a project and how she encouraged you to find the way that worked best for you? Remember how she delighted in readers' suggestions, never claiming any credit for being their inspiration?*

We expect our friends to forgive us when we blunder, but we rarely understand that to be our friends, they first must accept us as whatever we are. Pauline was that friend, and we are all poorer for losing her.

Della sat with the pages in her lap, looking out the window of her office. Before Ora and Isaiah had added the second floor, this room had been their bedroom, and it jutted out from the main house to give views of both the river and the street.

Now she looked to the street side and watched one of the Castleburg pickups head toward their gate at the end of the road. She's right, thought Della. Pauline saw what each one of us was and loved us anyway. Or maybe because of that.

She frowned as a second pickup followed the first. The gate at the end of the road led to a rarely used field. The field and the surrounding hills were what protected the Ladies Farm and Sydonia from the delights of dairy smells. Maybe they're chopping out the mesquite, Della thought. Maybe they're going to start grazing cows there. She knew she was just trying to distract herself from the column, because Barbara had recognized something about Pauline that she had felt only vaguely.

I would have gotten to it eventually, Della thought, if I hadn't let Barbara write the column. Anybody who knew Pauline would recognize it eventually. Barbara's just had longer to think about it.

It's funny, though, Della continued to herself. I never thought Barbara read *Sil-*

ver Quest, but she knew all about Pauline's column. Maybe she read the back issues on the coffee table.

Quickly, Della pulled the story up on the computer and finished reading it there. It took only a few changes before she laid it out in the newsletter. All it needed was a picture.

Hugh Jr. and Melissa had taken most of Pauline's photographs with them, but there was a large album lying on top of the pile of clothing on the bed in Pauline's room. Della climbed the stairs and pushed open the wooden door. It had only been a few days since the kids' visit and, other than Rita's taking the armoire and moving the writing table to the big office, no one had done anything to the room. Della took the album with her rather than leaf through it there.

She sat on the glider on the front porch, occasionally pushing a toe against the concrete floor to make the thing sway a little. Pauline had been PTA historian for many years, and Della suspected this album was from that period.

The photos were held in place by corner holders, and she began pulling the pictures out and sorting them into stacks according

to children. There were lines of kids in vegetable costumes and lines of kids dressed
as pioneers. She found both Jamie and
Robbie posed in front of a cardboard
Alamo, Robbie resplendent in gold braid as
Santa Anna, Jamie faking a faint in his
ragged Jim Bowie buckskin.

Some pictures were missing, and Della
supposed Melissa and Hugh Jr. had
removed most of their own. But there were
several of Richard's son—Richard's and
Barbara's she amended—and a few left of
Pauline's kids. There was even an early
one of Kat with Grant, and a later one of
her alone.

Toward the back, there were more photos missing. The ones that remained were
almost all adults, and Della looked carefully for a good one of Pauline. She could
always call Hugh Jr. and borrow one back,
but it would mean another day, and she
had to get this thing to the printer. "Why
didn't you think of it while they were here?"
she asked herself, but there were so many
things she hadn't thought of, it didn't seem
worth pursuing.

Della knew the kids had taken the Sydon
House album, the one that documented all

the stages of the renovation, but there were a few pictures here of Hugh and Pauline hammering and plastering. She smiled as she pulled one of Rita and Dave, evidently paying a neighborly visit, and then another one of Richard and Barbara on a canoe in the river.

She placed that one on top of a picture of Dickie in a Cub Scout uniform and glanced at it for only a second. I miss you so, she thought, not seeing Barbara in the shot at all.

Surely there's one of Pauline alone, Della thought, leafing through to the back of the album. Just one that shows her hair in its glory.

She almost skipped the one of Pauline in her bathing suit, but it did show her hair, so Della stopped and picked it up. This must be at Richard and Barbara's, Della thought, studying the picture of Pauline by the pool. This was before she'd jumped in, and her hair was lifted around her head by the wind as she squinted a little at the camera.

Della held her hand across the bottom part of the picture. If I crop it there, she thought, it will be perfect.

She stared a second longer at the picture, trying to remember the party. Where was I? she wondered. Maybe we hadn't arrived yet. Tony had just opened the second shop and might have had work to do even on the Fourth of July.

She shrugged. Maybe I was in the kitchen. She remembered that period as an endless parade of afternoons in the kitchen with her friends, working for hours on food that disappeared in minutes. It had been a struggle, she knew, but remembering that time now, it seemed rich with promise and the security of a certain place in a certain world.

Della pulled one or two more photos from the book, including a great one of Rita and her two girls at the Sydonia Peach Festival, then closed the book and stood up. She glanced for a second at the car parked out front. It belonged to the appraiser, who was walking over the property under Kat's supervision.

Thank God Kat could take care of that. All you need to do, Della informed herself, is scan this photo and get your newsletter to the printer.

Della had the image on her computer screen when Barbara knocked on her open office door. "Do we have any facilities for . . . are we wheelchair accessible?"

"Babe Didrikson," Della replied. "It's on the first floor, and the door's wide enough. Someone on the phone?"

"Yes, but they're asking about trails, and activities, I don't know what else. Is that Pauline?"

"Yeah. I think it's at your house." Della pulled the photo itself from the scanner. "Are they holding?"

"Oh, yes."

"Tell them we're okay for the whole first floor of the Ladies Farm, plus paved paths down to the river and the crafts barn. And about a quarter of the trail. But we can't do assistance, like lifting in and out of the tub or anything. We've got a bedside commode. And for a longer stay, we can arrange home health care."

Barbara watched her carefully, as if trying to memorize Della's words. Nodding, she backed out of the office and padded over to her new desk—the writing table from Pauline's room—in the big office. Della could hear her on the phone, explaining, clarifying. "And that will be two of you, for four days?"

She's good on the phone, Della thought.

But she wasn't Pauline, who had possessed personal knowledge of every ailment that struck anyone over forty-five.

"Mr. and Mrs. Sidney Turow," Barbara announced in triumph as she returned. "Mrs. Turow had hip surgery and she's still on crutches and in a chair for longer treks. Mr. Turow thinks facials, massage, and a makeover will aid her recovery. Isn't that sweet?"

Della's interest in their guests' lives had diminished to weak curiosity after the first few months at the Ladies Farm, but she understood the fascination. She remembered the first time a couple had had a vocal argument in the Sissy Spacek Suite and for weeks afterward she had agonized over whether they were able to repair the damage to their relationship.

So she smiled indulgently at Barbara's concern and reminded her to be sure to make up the Babe, since they rarely used it. Barbara reached out a hand to take the photo on Della's desk.

The clank of her bracelets, cloisonné bands in blue and silver, drew Della's attention from her expression. When she looked back up, Barbara was crying softly.

What now?

"That was the night," Barbara said, without Della having to ask the question. "That was the night!"

"The night?"

"That night. With Hugh."

Della considered telling Barbara that she was on deadline and couldn't play confessor this moment, but instead, she saved the image on her screen and closed out her scanning program. Why not wallow a little in Barbara's guilt over one night with someone else's husband? Besides, she had some questions.

"Barbara, did Pauline tell you she knew about this?"

Barbara shook her head and clutched the photo to her breast.

"Here," said Della, reaching for the photo. The kids might not want it, but she did. And she didn't want it soggy.

Barbara looked down in confusion, then released the picture.

"Even when she . . . when she had the heart attack," Della pressed. "Did she say something to you . . . you know, about that amethyst or something?"

Barbara shook her head even harder.

She backed away from Della until the back of her knees touched the loveseat, and she sat. "She knew."

"What makes you so sure?" Della asked. The doctor had told them that Pauline had had an undetected heart condition and that she could have died at any time. Yes, it could have been a sudden shock, he had answered Della. But it didn't have to be anything. Heart attacks are caused by heart conditions, not traumatic events, he had assured her as if she were the one with a guilty conscience.

"I just knew," Barbara said. "That's why they moved down here. It was right after that." She had stopped crying, but her face was stained with runny mascara.

"When she looked at me," Barbara continued. "I knew when she looked at me." The button eyes pleaded for understanding. "That she knew."

"You knew that she knew? Even though she never said anything?"

Barbara nodded.

"Do you think Hugh told her?"

"Maybe. That's what I like to think." Barbara shook her head. "No!" Her conviction grew. "I just think she knew. I think women, wives . . . they know when there's someone else."

"How?" Della could barely whisper the question.

Barbara looked out the windows that faced the river. "I knew even before Richard told me."

"Richard told you?" That damn doctor was wrong, thought Della, feeling her own heart pound. I'm keeling over any second.

"It wasn't a week after Hugh. And he had a meeting, just like all the meetings he had. Except there was just something about him."

"Perfume?" Della suggested. "Lipstick on his collar?"

"No, no," Barbara said. "Nothing like that. Just the way he was so affectionate. He started to bring me presents: silk negligees, perfume."

Della thought she should ask the obvious question. "Who was the other woman?" She closed her eyes a second as Barbara continued to stare out the window.

"She was just some real estate agent with an office in his building. Commercial leasing or something. She had a house over on the west side. He used to park right in her driveway!"

The tears had started to roll again, and Della took advantage of the moment to let out a long, slow breath and draw in fresh oxygen. Another one! She looked out the front windows and saw Kat bidding the appraiser good-bye. Well, thank God it wasn't Kat! she thought with the next breath. Thank God it wasn't either one of us! But she did wonder how many more even as she glanced back to Barbara.

Barbara pressed her lips together and raised her chin as if collecting her scattered composure. "Finally, though, he confessed to me. And he promised he would never do it again."

Again, Della forced herself to ask the obvious. "And did he?"

Barbara turned her head and looked at Della. "Oh, of course he did! He never got over what I . . . what happened with Hugh." She smiled apologetically. "He didn't ever know how to forgive."

"Richard?" This came out before Della could stop it. "He always seemed so indulgent," she suggested feebly.

Barbara shook her head. "Not about the big things."

Della remembered her job as consoler. "Barbara, you spent one night with someone and your husband couldn't forgive you. And you're supposed to forgive a lifetime of infidelity?"

"It wasn't a lifetime!" Barbara defended her husband. "Until that real estate agent, he was as faithful as any man, as faithful as Tony even!"

"Tony?"

"Oh, you know how the boys always teased Tony, he was such a straight arrow."

"Tony—my husband?"

"Of course. Richard and Grant and the others . . . they were always teasing him, the way he would call you during halftime, the way he never even would look at another woman."

"Tony looked at other women," Della said, but then she tried to remember. At least, she always assumed he did, and that good manners made him keep his adulterous desires to himself.

Barbara was shaking her head. "Not that any of us ever heard about. And he had his chances, too!" Now she was smiling with the memory. "Marjorie Schulkey, remember her?"

"Short blonde, kind of dumpy?"

"She was all over him." Barbara nodded at the photo Della had placed on top of the scanner. "At that party? Don't you remember her asking him to dance? And he said he had to go help you in the kitchen?"

How does she remember all this, Della wondered. "Marjorie Schulkey? Well," she said briskly, "she wouldn't have been his type, she was way too heavy. Tony liked tall, slender women."

Barbara eyed her quietly, and Della felt sorry she had mentioned Marjorie's weight. She rushed to fill the silence. "He sure didn't waste any time finding someone once I was gone."

Now Barbara tilted her head and furrowed her brow. "Why did you leave him, anyway? None of us could ever figure it out. Even Pauline."

Della sighed. "I don't know," she said, shaking her head. "We just wore each other out," she said. "We were exhausted from crying over Jamie, and we couldn't—I don't know—neither one of us could get enough energy to even care if things fell apart."

"Do you think you'll get back together?"

Della stared at Barbara. "We don't want to get back together."

"You might change your mind. Tony might," Barbara said, ignoring Della shaking her head no. "He sure seemed happy to see you at the cemetery."

"Well, we still have Robbie; we have to be civil."

"He was a lot more than civil. Maybe you should give it a try."

Who is this woman? Della wondered. Where does she live? Certainly not in the same world as the rest of us. She shrugged and turned toward the computer.

"Are you keeping that picture of Pauline?" Barbara asked.

"Yes. And here," Della reached over to her desk, "I found these, too," handing over the photos of the Morrison family from Pauline's album.

"Thanks," Barbara said, and wandered off.

Della did not let herself recall the conversation with Barbara until she had finished the newsletter, saved it to disk, and headed into Fort Worth to the printer.

So even Kat wasn't first, thought Della. And maybe the real estate agent wasn't the first. There could be hundreds! And Barbara knows about others. So maybe she knows about me.

Della shook her head. She was leaving Sydonia and she gave the Accord a little more gas. With the sun roof open and the air conditioner turned to high, she reveled in the day's sunshine, amazed that it was only early afternoon.

On her left, there was heavy equipment up on the crest of the Castleburg hill, but Della shrugged it off. I'll ask Kat when I get back, she thought, but she knew there wasn't anything too drastic. That field was the one that backed onto the end of their street, but she hadn't heard anything about any construction, so it was probably just some kind of well or stock tank venture. No one's building high-rises or factories, Della told herself. You can go back to worrying whether Barbara's planning to poison your food or smother you with your pillow.

She drove straight to the printer, where they took her disk and promised to call if they saw any problems.

Della had her list of groceries, of course,

but she put off her visit to the Kroger and instead drove over to West Seventh, on the fringe of downtown. A bell tinkled when she walked into the shop, and a bright-eyed young man behind the counter asked if he could help her.

"Is Tony here?" Della asked.

Chapter 8

"I wanted to bring you these pictures," Della said after the clerk had led her back to Tony's office. If Tony was surprised to see her, he gave no indication, and he smiled his thanks as he took the pictures from her.

"Don't you want them?" he asked.

"Actually, I was hoping you'd volunteer to have copies made for me and for Robbie. I was going to do it, and I don't mind dropping them off, but, barring funerals, I might not get back to Fort Worth until next month's newsletter."

He nodded, waved a hand to demonstrate his acceptance of the task. "You really like it out there?"

Della nodded. "You would too. It's quiet, friendly. And I have a river in my backyard."

He waved a hand at his desk—a platform, really, supported by file cabinets at either end of a windowless wall. "You don't think this is quiet and friendly?" His eyes were green with dark flecks in them, and they crinkled at the corners but stayed quite round when he smiled.

She noticed he had put on glasses to look at the photographs, but quickly laid them back down on the desk when he finished.

She was about to answer him when the clerk stuck his head in the door. "Here's your sandwich," he said, handing over a white paper bag.

"It's two-thirty," said Della. "Haven't you had lunch?"

"I was at the downtown shop," he explained. "Want half?" He pulled a sub from the bag and set it next to his French fries.

"I'll just steal these," she said, taking one of the fries. "Any ketchup?"

They occupied themselves with eating and exchanging bits of news about people they knew. She told him about Hugh Jr. and Melissa's visit, and he told her about their former next-door neighbors, who were moving to a condominium outside of Austin.

"How're you and Barbara getting along?"

Della felt her face grow warm. "Barbara? Fine. Why do you ask that?"

He shrugged, put one of the French fries in his mouth. "She's a little hard to take, isn't she? She used to hover over Richard like a helicopter. Not that it did her much good."

"What does that mean?"

"Oh, come on, you know about Richard."

"I don't think I do," Della muttered.

Tony was silent for a second. "I guess that was mostly after we split up. He used to like to get together for drinks, tell us all about it."

"Us?" She couldn't keep the alarm out of her voice.

"Oh, you know: Grant, Hugh, those guys."

"How come you never told me all this before?"

He looked at her, considering. "You never asked, I guess. I mean, it was after we were divorced, and we haven't really talked much, except about the . . . about Robbie."

He was right. They never spent time together. She didn't know why she was doing it now. "Did Marjorie Schulkey ever make a pass at you?"

She expected a blank look, and his grin stunned her. "That Barbara's a talker."

"How do you know Barbara told me?"

"Because she rescued me," he said, still grinning. "That woman had me pinned against the wall in the kid's room." He held his right hand in the air. "I swear it, she just cornered me." He shook his head, laughed a little. "I guess she had a little too much to drink. I just hate it when women drink like that. Anyway, she wanted to dance, and I kind of fled, and then, I was coming out of the bathroom, she just grabbed me and tried to kiss me. That's when Barbara comes down the hall calling 'Tony! Tony!' " He mimicked her in falsetto. " 'Tony, I need your help to get these dishes down for me. No one else is tall enough!' And she just drags me out of that woman's clutches."

"Saved by Barbara Morrison," Della said. "That's scary."

Tony nodded, took another bite of his sandwich. Della looked around the office, remembering the times they had used the long table to collate copies, the nights she had puzzled over the mysteries of binding equipment and the terrors of accounts payable. I could've just dropped the pictures at the photo place, Della thought, then called Tony and asked if he'd pick them up. Or asked the photo place to hold on to them for a month. Or asked Kat or Rita to get them next time they were in town.

"You ever hear from Suzanne?" she asked finally.

He shook his head no while he finished chewing. "Nah. She wrote me once, asked if I'd mind sending a few things she'd left, that was about it. Adios." He studied her a second. "You seeing anyone?"

She chuckled. "I don't know anyone to see. I guess I'll live out my old age surrounded by women."

"That's kind of what I always dreamed about."

They both laughed and Della stood to go. "I've got to be getting back," she explained. "I've got this shopping list, and someone has to keep an eye on Barbara before she kills off someone else."

He walked her out to the front. "The shop looks good," she said.

"Thanks." They stood for a second, letting the clerk watch them. Customers milled around the card displays and the self-serve copiers, and along one side several people sat at the computer stations. Della wondered if Tony would have had the fury to expand this business if Jamie had lived, but it was far too treacherous to consider.

"You take it easy," she said, and she felt herself leaning toward him.

He moved a little, pulling her into a clumsy hug. "Take care, Della," Tony told her. Then they pulled away from each other and she walked out.

She went to the grocery, then proceeded home, stopping only at Dave's to fill the tank. "How you holding up?" Dave asked.

"Oh, we have our good days and our bad." Della signed for the gas and tried to think of something sarcastic to say about his cemetery romp, but her sarcasm failed her. The convenience store smelled like gas and oil and Dave, in his coveralls, looked odd behind a counter featuring fountain drinks and sandwiches. Still, his resourcefulness impressed her.

He changes with the times, she thought.

She tried to explain that to Rita when she got home, but Rita was preoccupied with the news that Melissa was coming back to get her hair cut.

"Her hair cut?"

"Here we go again," muttered Kat. "Melissa is getting a haircut. What is so earth-shattering?"

"Her hair's like Pauline's," Della made an attempt at explanation.

"It's an odd time to be preoccupied with your appearance," Kat acknowledged.

"It's downright unnatural," Rita declared. "Not that that girl couldn't use a fresh look. That long, straight, bouncy stuff with the Farrah Fawcett fluff on top went out with . . . well, Farrah Fawcett."

"It's a way for her to visit us," Barbara said.

Della started. What was it that made her forget Barbara's presence until she spoke?

"What do you mean?" Kat asked. "You think she's cutting off the hair she's been growing her whole life because she needs an excuse to come to the Ladies Farm?"

The color rose in Barbara's face, but she stayed calm. "I think when someone . . . when we lose someone, we just want to try to stay close to them in any way. Maybe she just wants to be where her mother was. Where she remembers her mother being."

Well, that sure chilled the conversation, Della thought as the room grew silent. They were in the big office, with Rita draped over the loveseat and Barbara perched on the typist's chair. Kat was at her own desk and Della remained in the doorway, leaning against the doorpost.

"It's just a haircut," Kat said finally. "If it's a mistake, she can let it grow back. Did you know they're mining gravel at Castleburg's?"

She directed the last at Della, who caught the doorpost to steady herself. "Gravel?" She recalled the equipment up on the hill.

"The appraiser mentioned it."

Della shrugged. "I guess we'll have a few more trucks through here."

"I hate those heavy old things," Rita grumbled. "We can close every window in the house and we'll still all be covered with dust. How long's it take to get all that gravel out?"

"Oh, I don't think it'll be over quickly," Kat said. Then to Della, "He was asking who owned the mineral rights here."

Della frowned. "I'm sure Pauline and Hugh did," but she wasn't sure at all. "Why wouldn't they? Nobody's ever worried about mineral rights around here."

"Well, now, that's not really true," Rita countered. "Mrs. Myerhoff is friends with Dave's great-aunt, Gladys Hutto, and she says old Gladys 'bout killed that husband of hers, Ray, when she found out Ray gave away . . . and I mean gave . . . the rights to this nephew of his, Earl, who wanted to get in the gravel business. And of course they've got that big old place, nearly as big as Castleburg's if you count where the warehouse is, and all those cows and sheep, and that nephew just starts digging up everything, holes every- where and never finds a thing. And it's a good thing, too, because Mrs. Myerhoff says old Gladys might just have shot Ray if that nephew had come up with something and Ray had signed it all away." Rita finished with an expansive wave of her arm in the air before her as if encompassing the vastness of the presumed Hutto mineral empire.

"We own the mineral rights," Barbara said evenly. They turned to look at her. "When Hugh and Pauline bought the place, Hugh asked Richard to go over the papers with him before settlement, and Richard made Hugh have the deed changed to convey the mineral rights specifically."

Kat looked thoughtful. "That's good to hear."

"Well, not that it matters," Della said. "We're not mining gravel at the Ladies Farm."

"I doubt there is any," Rita said. "If there wasn't any at Hutto's, just across the river, there isn't any here."

"There is," Barbara said. "Hugh knew there was when they bought the place, it's just that it's such small acreage it wasn't worth digging up."

"Then," Kat said thoughtfully. "It wasn't worth digging up then. What about now?"

They all turned to Barbara, who shook her head. "I don't know. All I know was what Richard said: That the only mineral worth worrying about on the place was gravel and there wasn't much of it."

Della looked to Kat, whose eyes warned her to stay quiet and restrain her urge to lunge for Barbara's throat. She said she wasn't interested in even bidding for the place, Della reminded herself. But the rumble of the backhoe belied Barbara's demur. Gravel, Della thought. It could all go for gravel.

"Well, if we're not going after gravel," Rita interrupted the nightmare, "I've got to go sharpen my scissors for Melissa."

Della blinked, forced herself to stay both calm and in the present.

"She'll be here bright and early tomorrow morning," Rita reminded them. Then she rose and stretched, her knit top riding up to reveal the waistband of her lavender jeans.

"I'm not gonna be here for dinner," Rita called back over her shoulder as she squeezed past Della in the doorway. "Darlene's going out and she asked me to come over and mind the kid again. I'll be back tonight, though. I told her she better be home by midnight or I'm taking Tiffany home with me."

Kat shook her head at Della, but Della

only laughed as she made her way over to the loveseat. "The appraiser say when he'd have his report to us?"

"It doesn't go to us, actually. It goes to the estate, meaning Hugh Junior and Melissa. But Hugh Junior told him to go ahead and bring us a copy."

"When?"

"Next week some time. Won't take long. Don't forget, they just appraised the thing for the loan to remodel the barn."

"Yeah." The loan was another item Della wanted to forget. It had been Kat's idea, as a way of freeing two rooms in the house for guests and letting Pauline expand her crafts. It had also given them a place to install a spa and a mirrored room for aerobics.

But even with the schedule of freelance instructors in place and the steady flow of participants down the newly paved walk, Della doubted they were breaking even on the loan. She supposed the big selling point had been expansion of their programs, but what programs would they expand without Pauline?

Barbara shifted on her chair and the thing rolled a tiny bit before she steadied it by bracing a toe against the desk. "Shouldn't we be starting dinner?" she asked. "We checked in two more today."

"You checked them in?" Kat asked.

"Yes. They're in Oveta Culp Hobby."

"Did you get them signed for programs?"

"Well, they're only staying two days, so—"

"You didn't sign them up for any programs?"

"They're only staying for two days, so I thought they'd like the short-term things, so they each took a day of beauty and then," she glanced at Della, "that journal program."

"Students!" Della laughed. "At last." They had restructured the "Journal Writing as a Spiritual Journey" program to a series of self-contained afternoons to fit both locals and those who were just passing through. The locals, however, seemed less impressed than when Pauline was actually helping them write entries every day and sharing them in class.

"The need for self-expression is endless," Kat cracked.

"Well, it's what people like," Barbara defended herself. After Kat's cross-examination, she reminded Della of a wounded puppy.

"*Circus of the Stars* and the *National Enquirer* are what people like," Kat snapped.

"I've got to change before I start cooking," Barbara said, looking only at Della. "I'll be back down in just a few minutes. Meet you in the kitchen?"

"Sure," said Della, though she too had to change before she started dinner. "What's with you?" she asked Kat as soon as Barbara was out of earshot.

"Nothing. Why?"

"Nothing?" Della stood and motioned with her hands. "What's with you and Barbara?"

"Believe me, there's nothing with that woman and me." Kat ruffled her own hair with a manicured hand.

"Don't you think you at least should be civil, considering she's co-owner of the Ladies Farm? And could still make a bid on the whole place if she wants."

"Please do not ask me to be kind to Richard's widow," Kat said, pronouncing every word precisely and separately.

"I'm not asking you to be kind," Della said. "Merely civil."

"I'll be civil," Kat said sullenly. She

frowned. "But I think it's real interesting that she never said anything about the gravel."

"Well," Della pointed out, trying to be fair, "no one ever asked about it before. I think the best thing's just to try to get this whole thing settled quickly, so try not to piss her off. I'll grant her this," Della said, thinking about *Silver Quest,* "she's smarter than she looks."

Kat's expression showed she had already considered the possibility. "She wouldn't really change her mind? Anyway, I think Melissa and Hugh Junior want us to have the place."

Her eyes looked enormous and Della, who had always been enchanted by the sharp angles of Kat's cheekbones, for the first time noticed hollows beneath her eyes. "I just want this to be over," Kat blurted. "I want the Ladies Farm to be ours and Barbara to be gone and enough teachers and trainers to run the place without Pauline."

Della had always assumed that the Ladies Farm was just a convenience to Kat. It gave her a base from which to conduct her consulting business, and it gave her a home without the domestic responsibilities of a home.

"She treats us like we're her wives," Rita always grumbled, but she, like Della and Pauline, had come to appreciate Kat's steadfast determination that they live within their means, that they follow their own business plan, and that the Ladies Farm be more than a subsidized hobby. So maybe Kat's fierce attention to the bottom line indicated a different kind of devotion.

Della worried the corner of her lower lip and resisted the urge to tell Kat that everything would be all right. "Well, the teachers and trainers seem to be under control. Except," she added, "for 'Journal Writing as a Spiritual Journey.' But I'm working on that one."

"I know," Kat said. She shook her head and rolled her shoulders. "I'm just tired."

Della stepped around to the back of Kat's chair and massaged the back of her neck and shoulders. "We just have to concentrate on the guests," Della said. "Get the meals on, schedule the trainers, keep the rooms clean. I know it's hard about Barbara, but let it go, at least until things are settled with Hugh Junior and we know how to run the place without Pauline."

"I miss Richard," Kat said.

"I know," Della replied.

"I missed him the whole time Grant and I were dating, and after we were married, and then when we were divorced. And I barely saw him alone after I got married. But I never stopped missing him."

Della rubbed harder, kneading Kat's shoulder with the heel of her hand. "I know," she said.

Melissa arrived early, while the guests were still lingering over coffee and muffins. "Did Hugh send anything for me?" Della asked her after the introductions, motioning her to take a mug from the sideboard and help herself to breakfast.

Melissa shook her head no. "Was he supposed to?"

"Oh, I thought if he found something in your mom's journals that would help me with the class of hers I'm teaching—'Journal Writing as a Spiritual Journey'—he might send it along."

Melissa nodded. "He mentioned something about working through her journals." She grinned. "But I think he was so overwhelmed by having my little Californians for the day that he couldn't focus on it. Carrie made him stay home to give her a hand."

Melissa was pouring herself a cup of coffee when Rita breezed in, resplendent in a rhinestone-studded denim jumpsuit. "Don't get too comfortable," she warned Melissa. "You're up first, soon as I finish this coffee." She smiled and nodded at each of the guests. "Now, honey," she told one named Clara, who was sitting at one end of the table, "see how nice and firm your skin looks after that facial? You do that once a week and people'll think you've had a facelift."

Clara's friend Marty piped up, "I think I might like one too, if you've got time."

"Well, I can work you in," Rita promised. "I think you should have the mud pack. We'll do a good herb steaming, get those pores open, and then the purifying mud and mineral mask. About eleven?"

Marty nodded.

Della smiled. It really might be okay, she thought. Rita will keep expanding the salon, get an assistant or two, peddle lots more Day-of-Beauty packages. The aerobics trainer and the crafts lady will keep the programs going. And we can do a big marketing campaign for *Silver Quest,* get it into every senior household in America. If I can just get through this first journal class.

An hour and a half later, past introductions, a brief exploration of writing paper and pens, and a trembling recollection of her friend Pauline's description of journalkeeping as mapmaking of the soul, Della sat at the head of the dining-room table while four heads bent over four formerly blank pages. It's working! she exulted silently. They're writing!

She sipped her coffee, glad she had reserved the dining room for this group. With the sliding wood panels to the great room closed and the kitchen deserted until lunch, it was as private as the classroom in the barn, but with a prettier view.

Clara, the one closest to her, paused for a moment and caught Della looking, but only smiled and returned to her work. Della checked her watch. Ten more minutes, she thought.

Holding her breath, she pushed herself up from her chair and, coffee cup in hand, tiptoed into the kitchen and out to the salon.

She expected Rita to be ankle-deep in

hair, but she didn't expect to hear the buzz of the razor. She expected to see Melissa, but she didn't expect to see her sitting in the chair at the second station, hair intact and her face covered with a mud mask.

Della had thought perhaps Barbara would be there, hovering over Pauline's daughter, urging her not to part with too much of her crowning glory. But Della had never expected to see Barbara seated in station one, her expression tranquil as Rita finished shaving her hair line around the base of her head and up over her ears.

Chapter 9

"What are you doing?" Della asked when she caught her breath.

"We switched," Barbara chirped. "I decided if anyone's hair should be hacked off, it should be mine. So . . . age before beauty!"

Della blinked, but nothing changed. Rita, light twinkling off the rhinestones in her jumpsuit, was still finishing up with the razor. Melissa still sported the mud mask. Flops still lay under Rita's counter. And Barbara, her mountainous bulk draped by the pastel cover, sported a crew cut. In red.

"Your hair—" Della started, but stopped in the face of Rita's glower.

"No sense messing with it," Barbara said as Rita dusted off her neck with a soft brush.

"And are you still cutting yours?" Della asked Melissa.

Melissa nodded, obviously afraid of cracking the mask with conversation.

"I think we're looking at some shaping, maybe some highlights," Rita said, sweeping the drape off of Barbara and turning her to see the finished product.

Barbara, steady and serene, raised a hand and touched the top of her hair, testing her palm against the short bristles. "Oh, if Richard could see me now," she said.

Rita was shepherding Melissa to the back, where she would peel the mask and wash Melissa's hair.

"Why did you do that?" Della whispered.

Barbara smiled and continued to stare at her reflection. "It's so much easier to keep," she recited. "And," she turned to face Della, "I thought Melissa should see what really short hair looks like before she starts cutting. Now I'm going to get a facial."

Della checked her watch and shook her

head. "I've got to get back. C'mon, Flops," she invited. "Want to come to class with me?" The dog raised her head a little, then, with a sigh, settled back down at Barbara's feet.

"Traitor!" Della muttered, heading out of the salon.

In the dining room, Clara was filling her fifth page, but the others were chatting softly. "Would you like a minute more?" Della asked.

Clara shook her head and smiled. "Oh, no! I can finish this before bed tonight."

They took a turn around the table, sharing their entries. The class ended with an assignment to put their journals next to their beds, to write down their last thoughts at night and their recollected dreams in the morning. Della joined the others in the kitchen to help put lunch together, then headed out back. She found Melissa near the doorway of the barn, looking through the glass at the pottery class.

"You can go in," Della said. "They're probably finishing up anyway."

Melissa shook her head of newly trimmed hair. "I'm not sure I'm ready. Maybe another time."

Without discussion, they moved away from the barn and the ladies covering their clay with damp cloths. "I'm glad you didn't cut your hair short," Della said. Without discussing it, they headed to the river.

"Oh," Melissa laughed, "it was just a momentary longing. Something different. But this," she gestured at the new bangs and sculpted crown, "is probably change enough. Though I don't know how I'll recreate this without Rita around."

They reached the water and followed a small path into the trees that hugged the bank. "Your hair has beautiful color," Della remarked.

"Like my mom's." Melissa had obviously heard, and long ago accepted, the compliment. "Well, at least Greg won't be too shocked."

"Did he make his plane all right?" Della asked. Greg had left right after the funeral, leaving Melissa and the boys to stay with Hugh Jr. and Carrie.

"Just fine," Melissa said. "But he said the house is so empty without us, he can't bear it."

Della had to fight the envy she felt for the joy in Melissa's voice.

The path along the Nolan wandered back to town, and they followed it easily. "Your mother spent a lot of city council meetings lobbying for this," Della advised Melissa. "She was the first one to offer land for it."

"I know," Melissa replied. "She wrote me about it."

It wasn't much of a hike, more a stroll. At Pauline's urging, the path had been paved with large stones so that Ladies Farm guests could walk into town to visit the quaint shops filled with antiques and local art. Della wasn't sure about the quaintness—Sydonia clung to a fifties kind of dustiness—but the path did end at a flight of steps that took them to the front of DrugRite, seat of the finest soda fountain in central Texas.

"Oh, let's have ice cream sodas!" Melissa's voice was full of mischief.

"Sounds like lunch to me," Della assented.

Randi Buckler, who was about the same age as Melissa, motioned them over to a booth. From her post behind the counter, she called out, "Y'all want the special?" She shrugged when they shook their heads. Randi was the daughter of one of the courthouse clerks; though, as usual, Della could not remember if it was Wanda, Lu, or Kathy.

"I don't think Randi remembers me," Melissa whispered to Della as Della nodded her helloes to the table of Randall & Whitley, attorneys.

"We just want ice cream sodas," Della called back up to Randi, who nodded. "Chocolate with vanilla ice cream." She turned back to Melissa. "That okay?"

"Perfect." Melissa smiled. Her hair gleamed with the highlights Rita must have added this morning.

"Your hair looks great," Della repeated. "I just noticed the highlights."

"Oh, thanks." Melissa looked pleased. "I know Aunt Barbara just cut hers to prevent me from cutting mine all off."

"Well, it worked." Della shook her head at the memory of Barbara's shorn locks. "You have to indulge us, Melissa. You're all—you and your brother—all we have now of your parents."

"You and mom were close." Melissa considered a moment. "I didn't think of her as that close to Aunt Barbara, except with Uncle Richard."

A single word could be a betrayal, Della warned herself.

"But you know what?" Melissa gave a little laugh. "Aunt Barbara's a riot. You should have heard her yakking it up with Rita. Telling her all about Uncle Richard. You know that car she drives, that red Thunderbird?"

In an instant, Della's tender concern for Barbara's secrets boiled over in anger. Randi selected that moment to plunk the ice cream sodas in front of them, which saved Della from making digs about the gold-trimmed monstrosity.

"Randi," she said in an even, if slightly squeaky, voice. "Do you know Melissa? She's Pauline's daughter."

"Real sorry about your mom," Randi allowed. She and Melissa traded a bit of information . . . enough for Randi to establish her standing as a former cheerleader for the Sydonia Sabers and Melissa to explain, gently, that she had finished high school in Fort Worth. And that Randi, like many people in Sydonia, always enjoyed meeting the Ladies Farm guests who wandered into town. And that they would all miss Pauline's ceramics booth at the peach festival.

Then Della and Melissa sipped their sodas, and dug at their ice cream, and then the light lit Melissa's eyes again and she giggled. "Anyway, you know that car Aunt Barbara drives?"

Della nodded.

"You know why she drives it?"

Della shook her head.

"Because she and Uncle Richard? When they were in college? He had a T-bird convertible, a red two-seater, and that's where they first, you know, did it!"

Della propped her elbow on the table and rested her forehead in her hand. She rubbed a little, then lifted her gaze to Melissa. "And I thought I knew them!"

"I know," Melissa laughed. "Isn't that cool? She says, even though it's not the same model or anything, it's like Uncle Richard's still there. I thought that was so sweet!"

Kat was leaning against a counter, staring at Barbara, who had changed into a jade

pantsuit that billowed ridiculously for someone working in a kitchen. The jade and
gold disks that dangled from her exposed
ears gave her shorn head an odd balance
and, despite its egglike proportion to the
rest of her body, a fluid dignity.

Barbara grinned at Della. "I think I'm getting used to it," Barbara said.

"That's because you can't see yourself,"
Kat threw at her.

"Kat!" Della said.

"Actually," Kat tilted her head and studied Barbara, who hadn't moved, "it's kind of
mesmerizing. Especially with your jewelry."

Della agreed. Despite her size, Barbara
had a sleek profile and, with so little hair,
her eyes had become her dominant facial
feature, bearing an expressiveness that
had been overshadowed before.

"Melissa looks great," Della commented.

"I just whacked about three inches of
split ends off the bottom, did the highlights,
styled and shaped the top, gave her a
great facial, let her dish a little dirt about
her brother—he's really got an attitude
toward his dad—and voilà! another happy
customer," Rita reported, sailing into the
kitchen right on cue. She stopped to study

Barbara for a moment. "God, I do good work!" she exclaimed.

"You did a good job changing her mind," Della told Rita.

"She was saved by Barbara's sacrifice," Kat said, starting off sarcastically but ending with a limp acknowledgment of the effort.

Barbara, holding a bowl of gingered green beans for the evening's dinner, froze in the center of the kitchen, then turned again to the counter on which she set the bowl. "Shouldn't we grind some pepper onto these?" she asked with her back still to them.

"And a little salt," Della instructed. "But just a little."

It was amazing how quickly they got used to Barbara's new look. Della would see her sorting through buttons for one of the jewelry-making classes and that smooth head and those lined eyes, visible in profile, would remind her of some brightly painted Egyptian relief adorning the tombs of the powerful. Barbara seemed less weepy, too, Della thought. Maybe it was because she stayed so busy those next few days, teaching a jewelry class and looking after the front desk.

At any rate, Della was only mildly surprised at herself when she agreed to accompany Barbara into Fort Worth to pick up jewelry-making supplies. "I can pick up my pictures from Tony," she explained to Barbara, who insisted on taking the Thunderbird.

"I've got a few other errands," Barbara replied, "but I'll drop you at the shop and pick you up later."

Della started to ask her just to wait, since it would take only a minute to get the prints from Tony, then thought better of it. I can hang out with Tony for a little while, she thought.

The specialist was one whose life had been changed by Richard. As she signed her name on the patient registration, Barbara noted that the counter separated her from an office staffed by five uniformed women, each of whom seemed to be preoccupied with one or two single functions regarding stacks of color-coded patient files which they moved from station to station.

Barbara sat on the pastel sofa, smiled slightly at the other patients, and picked up a magazine. In many cases, these doctors had regarded Richard as their only friend, the only one who understood their frustration at the growing mountain of paperwork and regulation that kept them from seeing more patients. "If you don't manage your practice," she could hear Richard lecture, "it will manage you."

Richard had shown them how to manage, and the ones who had listened had thrived. Barbara sighed and patted the back of her neck, where her hair had been. The bare skin felt odd and Barbara smoothed the area over her collar to no avail. Tears sprang to her eyes and panic welled inside her. Quickly she withdrew her hand and raised her magazine in front of her face. Think of something else, Barbara ordered herself. Think of when your hair was long and brown.

The workshops had been her idea, and Richard had insisted that she be the one to greet the doctors who attended. "They like you, babe," he would say. "You make them feel welcome, get them in the mood."

At state and local medical conventions,

the credits for continuing ed lured the ones who had a glimmer of understanding that they needed something more than technical expertise. And Richard...oh! How could anyone resist Richard? Barbara thought.

It was funny that thinking about Richard could leave her grinning like an idiot, but thinking about her short hair made her cry. She knew the tears were about Richard, and not the hair, but she still cried at the wrong times. And there was no point crying here. These people would misunderstand completely.

They called her name eventually, and she checked her watch as she walked back to meet with the doctor. She would take her time in this consultation, Barbara decided. She would ask every question she needed answered, glean every bit of information, every detail to aid in the decisions she still needed to make. She had time, Barbara thought. Every moment she spent here would be an extra moment that Della would spend with Tony. And then, during the ride home, she and Della could talk about the Ladies Farm.

*   *   *

The young clerk knew Della this time, and greeted her as Mrs. Brewer before he led her back. Tony rose and approached when she entered, then stood awkwardly as if he weren't sure whether to step forward and embrace her or shake her hand. Della touched his shoulder, and he put his arms around her. "Here," he said, keeping his arm around her. "Sit down. Want a Dr Pepper?"

"Diet," she said, and he nodded toward the clerk, who disappeared and reappeared with two sodas. Tony reached to a shelf over his desk and retrieved a packet of photos, and they spent a few minutes going through them again.

"I wish we'd made another one of these," she said when she got to the two boys in their Alamo costumes. "For Robbie."

"Oh, I did," Tony said. "I had a whole set made for him; we can give it to him when he visits."

It was like him, she thought, to duplicate the whole set when there were only one or two prints Robbie would want. But she said nothing about that. Instead, she asked how the house was.

"Fine," he replied. "You ready for your interest?"

"Is it that apparent?"

They had left her equity unsettled, agreeing to have the property appraised and do an even split in return for her not pressing him to buy her out at the time of the divorce. But she wanted cash for at least part of her purchase of the Ladies Farm. The idea of a loan for the whole amount overwhelmed her.

"I figured you weren't coming in for just the pictures. Not twice in one month."

"Kat and I need to buy Pauline's interest in the Ladies Farm," she said. "I don't want to pressure you, but it's been a few years, and you look like you can manage it now."

Tony smiled, studied the top of his desk. "I guess I can. I guess I ought to sell that barn anyway."

"It would make sense," Della agreed. "Unless you've found some young honey who wants to start a whole new family with you."

He shook his head, pushed at some imagined stone on the floor with his foot. Finally he looked at her. "I guess I always thought you'd come back home."

There were too many answers to respond at once: that they couldn't go back, that she certainly couldn't live in that house again, that she had a different life now, that she was needed at the Ladies Farm. Not to mention that she still loved Richard, that Tony had lived in that house with another wife, that she and Tony weren't in love anymore.

Besides, what right did he have putting her on the spot like this? We went through all this when we split up, Della thought. Why do we have to go through it all over again?

Still, she didn't speak. Tony was, after all, the person who had loved her most. It wasn't his fault she didn't love him the same way.

He was a good father, she thought. And a devoted husband. He just wasn't—

What? she wondered. Just wasn't what? Exciting? Who would be exciting after twenty-five years?

It's not excitement, she told herself, looking at him looking back at her. It's Jamie. He turned away from me when Jamie died.

Della fixed on Jamie's death and the

loneliness that followed. Where had Tony been then?

He never understood the way Richard did. No matter what else—or who else—Richard did, he did that.

"Oh, Tony," she said finally. "You're just lonely since Suzanne left."

"It's not Suzanne I'm missing," Tony said. He sat down, pulling up a chair next to hers. "It's our life together. That's why I married her, I think. That's why she left, too. She knew it way before I did."

"Tony, you only miss it because you don't have it. You didn't like it much when you were in it." She smiled to show him she was just stating facts, not blaming him. "You thought it interfered with your business. And you were right in some ways; you weren't nearly as successful before we split up."

"Yes I was," Tony insisted. "We had already turned the corner here. I just was too inexperienced to know it. Look," he shook his hands in the air, "I didn't mean to spring it on you. You want your interest in the house. Fair enough. I'll call the real estate agent. But tell me you'll keep an open mind; that you'll at least see me." He paused. "You know. That we can go out."

"Go out?" For Della, going out conjured up sweaty-palmed teenagers at the movies and nervous introductions to hovering parents. Going out was a prelude to sex or marriage. We've already done that, she thought. Why would we go out?

"I'd just like to have dinner with you," Tony said. "Just the two of us."

"Oh, I don't know," Della teased. "My parents don't like me going out on school nights."

"Then try Friday nights," Tony suggested. "This Friday. I'll pick you up at seven."

"In Sydonia?"

"In Sydonia. At the Ladies Farm."

Della had had only a few male visitors at the Ladies Farm, and they had not led to much. The most interesting had been Eli Castleburg, who had called on her after his wife ran off with one of the county commissioners. It had been strained, at best, with most of their time together spent in his description of how important a wife was on a dairy farm, particularly the wife of the oldest son.

At least Tony knows everybody, Della thought. There won't be any silly giggling, the way there was with Eli.

"So you and Kat are buying the Ladies Farm," Tony said.

Della nodded, relieved to resume their earlier conversation.

"And Barbara?"

"She'll own half," Della conceded.

If Tony was surprised, he didn't show it. "Hard to imagine you partners with Kat," he said.

"Why?"

He shrugged. "She's hard, isn't she? I mean, she and Richard, they'd talk about hitting up a client, you'd wonder what the guy had left by the time they were done with him."

They talked a little more about Kat, Della conceding that the Ladies Farm was mostly a convenience for Kat, who traded business management for homemaking, and Tony acknowledging that she was no more avaricious than most men in business.

Tony took three or four calls, then left her alone while he tended the front counter. Della opened another Diet Dr Pepper and leafed through the paper sample books.

Quick-print shops had no need for fine writing papers, but Tony had samples of everything. Della ran her fingers over the linen weaves and deckle edges, imagining journals of fine writing paper covered with one of Pauline's special fabrics. A nice spiral bind, she imagined, black metal, so it would lie flat on a table.

Maybe even lines, printed in a variation of the pastel papers themselves. Peach sheets with cinnamon lines, pink with rose, yellow with gold. We could do a whole course, Della thought. Make the journal, then write in it.

We could print the lines on the small hand press. Or maybe Tony could give them a break on the color printer. I could operate the thing myself, she thought, smiling. During off-peak hours. And then we could bind them.

Tony grinned when she asked about the printing. "I'm sure we could work something out." She scowled to let him know this was business. He switched gears to talk about the binding.

"You'd do better to use a plastic spiral," Tony advised. "Much cheaper, and you could do it yourselves. Then, you make a cover with sleeves, that covers the whole thing, including the binding."

"We'd have to buy the binder?" Della asked.

"Yeah, but they're cheap. In fact," he grinned, "I've got a small one you can borrow. If you're interested."

He was showing her the binder, explaining how to judge the size spiral she needed, when Barbara showed up. "Am I interrupting?" she cooed. "You two go right ahead, don't mind me at all."

Della and Tony exchanged glances. Della explained what they were doing, and Tony carried the binder and a carton of spirals in mixed sizes out to the Thunderbird. He laid them in the trunk, arranging packages around the binder to keep it from sliding around.

"That should hold you," he said with a small grunt as he closed the car trunk.

"You're a good man, Tony." Barbara flashed a smile at him and patted the back of her head where hair used to be.

"That's kind of a cute haircut," Tony replied. "Like a teenager these days."

"Oh, you're so sweet to say that," Barbara responded. "But I know men. You always like long hair. But this is easier and now . . . well, now's a time when easier makes more sense for me."

After more awkward pauses, Tony hugged them both and they got into the car. "See you Friday," he told Della, closing the car door after her.

"We have to stop at the crafts place," Barbara said as they drove away.

"I thought you already went. What were you doing all morning?"

"Didn't you see my packages? I shopped." She glanced at Della. "What'd Tony mean: He'd see you Friday?"

"We have a date."

"You're kidding! That's great!"

"I don't know if it is or not." Della stared out the window.

They bought a lot of jewelry supplies— clasps, earring backs, silk ribbons, neck- lace strings—but it didn't take very long.

Barbara sailed up to the check-out counter and deposited her red shopping basket in front of the clerk. The girl, a teenager who Della thought belonged in school, interrupted her conversation with the clerk at the next counter and began ringing up their purchases.

"That's what I mean," the other clerk said in a loud voice, nodding at Della and Barbara.

"Huh?" their clerk responded, concentrating on counting each kind of trinket and punching the right keys.

The other clerk sported a name tag that said *Kelly* and chewed her gum and handled all the display items at her counter in a jittery way. "That's when I want you to shoot me," she said now.

"Huh?" their clerk, Kim, repeated. She pushed the total key with a flourish. "That's thirty-four seventy-three," she told Barbara. "Shoot you?" she repeated loudly, looking over at her co-worker.

Barbara rummaged deep in her leather bag for her checkbook, then searched again for a pen. "I thought we just had an account," said Della, her eyes on Kim. "The Ladies Farm."

"Oh, you do!" Kim said. "I didn't know. What happened to that other lady?"

"Pauline." Della said. "Pauline died two weeks ago."

"Oh, God, I'm sorry. Here, just sign this." She pushed the receipt in front of Barbara. "I need to see a driver's license."

Barbara sighed, then dug a little more in her purse.

"Shoot you?" Kim repeated again at her friend Kelly.

Kelly shot her a warning look, but grinned as she nodded at Barbara's back. "You know," nodding again.

Kim frowned. "What?" Meaning surfaced. "Oh, yeah. Here," she said to Barbara, "this is your copy of the receipt."

"And you'll just bill us?" Barbara asked.

"Yeah," said Kim, but by now she was breaking into laughter. She handed Barbara and Della the bags of supplies as she shook her head at the other clerk.

Barbara and Della exited to the laughter and spent a few minutes behind the car, rearranging the contents of the trunk. "I'll be right back," Della said, ignoring Barbara's startled expression.

She marched back into the store, where both Kim and Kelly were free of customers. "Come here," she said to Kelly. "You too," motioning to Kim.

They both looked at her but didn't move. "Right now, or I'm calling the manager."

Kelly looked about nervously. "Ma'am, we can't leave these registers."

"Just for a second," Kim contradicted. "What is it?"

They both approached. "Outside," Della said. "Right now." She herded them through the doors of the empty store, a third clerk staring as they left. Motioning to Barbara to roll down the window, she placed her hands over the two girls' shoulders and helped them lean down toward Barbara.

"These girls just wanted to apologize, didn't you, girls?"

"Yes, ma'am," Kim said.

"Kelly?" Della prompted.

"Yes, ma'am, we didn't mean..."

"Didn't mean . . . well..." Barbara shook her head to clear the confusion.

"What we mean," Kim took the lead, "is we shouldn't have been carrying on a private conversation while I waited on you. You didn't get our full attention, and I'm sorry."

"So am I," Kelly said quickly, ducking out from under Della's hand. "Bye now."

"Bye," said Barbara, studying Della. She waited until Della was back in the car before asking what that was all about.

"Kids with no manners piss me off," Della

said, adjusting the air vent to blow directly at her face. "They were making fun of us, and I don't think we should put up with it."

Barbara shrugged. "I'm so used to it, I never noticed."

"Well I noticed," Della said fiercely.

They rode without speaking. Barbara was a good driver, and the Thunderbird had a quiet, cushiony feel to it that made Della sleepy. Outside, the green had faded a little as summer rolled in and at places where there were no trees, the grass and the sky met in a white band.

Della felt shaky from her encounter with the two girls. She hadn't been afraid when she confronted them, but now she wondered what she would have done if they hadn't come with her. What if she had called the manager and the manager had asked her to leave? What if they had called the police?

She imagined Barbara bailing her out of jail, or, worse, calling Tony or Kat to bail her out. Worst of all, she could remember thinking the same thing as those girls—that she'd prefer death to being a middle-aged fat woman—and laughing aloud about it because surely a middle-aged fat woman would never get the joke.

And, of course, she and Kat had been just as tacky about Barbara in conversation just a few days ago. It's not the same, though, Della thought. I know better now.

Those girls know nothing, she fumed. Barbara has more wisdom in one fat pinky than they have in their entire cellulite-free bodies. She stared at the landscape, only slightly hillier now, but broken by stands of cottonwoods along the Nolan and groups of live oaks near small, neat houses.

"So where are you and Tony going for dinner?"

Barbara's voice jolted her back to the soft leather interior. Della shrugged. "Who knows? He's got something planned, I'm sure. I didn't ask."

"What are you wearing?"

"I don't know." Della shifted in the seat so that she was facing forward instead of out the side window. "I've got a silk pantsuit that I can wear. It's dressy, but okay if we end up getting barbecue or something."

"You should wear a dress," Barbara advised. "Men always prefer dresses."

The woman who had seemed so wise a second ago suddenly appeared dense. "I might do that if I were interested in encouraging Tony," Della said.

"You don't have to encourage him," Barbara said. "Just see if you like him."

"Like him? I was married to him! I already know everything there is to know about him."

"You didn't know he didn't run after other women," Barbara countered.

"I did know that," Della argued. "I just didn't think it was ... important. No, not important, exceptional, I guess. Look," she offered, "let's not argue about this. I'm going out with him and I'm more comfortable in a pantsuit. Okay? Let's change the subject. Where were you all morning?"

"Oh, here and there."

Della felt her annoyance growing. "I know it's none of my business, but could you be a little more specific?"

"I had to see the doctor."

"For what?" Della knew it was rude to ask but it was rude of Barbara not to volunteer answers to the obvious questions. "Are you sick?"

"No." Barbara shook her head. Then, "Yes."

Must be menopause, Della thought, though she would have guessed Barbara would be through it. She herself had sailed through menopause; it had resembled a special project that she attacked with a fitness program and a new set of vitamins, and it had left her with an altered internal clock that roused her earlier in the morning and a dread of leaving things unfinished.

Barbara didn't say any more, and Della glanced at her companion, but Barbara was studying the road ahead. Maybe she thought Della wasn't interested. "What do you mean, *yes?*"

Della saw Barbara's expression change. It seemed both softer and harder at the same time, with her chin raised slightly and her mouth in a tight line, but her eyes totally round and accepting. "I have ovarian cancer. They removed my ovaries in Dallas, but it had already spread and I'm starting to have other symptoms."

Her voice was filled with kindness, as if her greatest fear were frightening Della.

"Cancer! Are you sure? Did you get a

second opinion?" Della realized how insulting it sounded, but she couldn't stop herself from asking.

"Dickie sent me to someone. He insisted." She sighed, but now her voice sounded light, almost gay. "But the diagnosis is the same. One recommended chemo, one didn't, but even the one who did admitted it would just keep me alive longer. There isn't enough chemo in the world to stop this."

"Are you saying you're dying?" How could they be riding down the road to the Ladies Farm, how could Barbara be shopping and driving and worrying about what Della would wear on her date with Tony?

"Well, yes," Barbara said. "That's why I came to the Ladies Farm."

"To die?"

"Yes."

"Stop the car," Della said.

"Why?"

Why! "Because I can't talk to you about this while you're driving."

"Why?"

"I want to know why you lied to us," Della said finally. "There's a rest stop just past Foley Road."

Barbara pulled over.

They rolled to a stop at the center of a semicircular asphalt drive, next to which sat a picnic table, a metal trash can, and a sign proclaiming maintenance of the rest stop a project of Explorer Post 1053. The Explorers were doing a good job, Della thought as she opened the car door and walked over to the picnic table. She didn't want Barbara to drive off before they were finished and, as she seated herself, she watched the realization cross Barbara's face that she, too, must get out of the car.

She doesn't look sick, Della thought, but that wasn't really true. What she looked was fat and overly made-up. Della had attributed her pallor, her slow gait, even the creakiness that indicated pain, to Barbara's obesity.

She watched Barbara's earrings swaying as she approached. They were beaten copper and brass, and they glinted in the sun. The Explorers hadn't planted much in trees, and except for the shade provided by a green ash that overhung part of the picnic table, most of the area was in full sun.

Barbara was sweating by the time she reached the bench, and she sat down without trying to hide her exhaustion. "How long did you think we'd go without noticing?" Della asked.

Barbara looked at the empty road. "I would have told you this week anyway. But first Pauline died, and I had to push back my doctor's appointment; and I had to wait for Dickie."

"Dickie?"

Barbara met Della's gaze. "Dickie had that offer in Houston, but he wouldn't take it because he didn't want to leave me here. So I concocted this story about what close friends we all were, and how nobody could care for me better than Pauline and you and Kat."

Della started to speak, but Barbara waved her off.

"What do kids know about their parents' friendships? I just didn't want him hanging around Dallas waiting for me to die, and I didn't want him insisting I be shipped to Houston."

"Anyway," she proceeded smoothly but without speed, "I had to make sure he had accepted this arrangement before I told you all. Otherwise, I'd get you upset for nothing."

"And we might back out." The words escaped before Della had time to consider them, but the concept obviously was not new to Barbara.

"And you might back out. Particularly after Pauline died. And you still could. I wouldn't blame you. But you could wait until Dickie moves." She smiled tentatively, catching her lower lip with her teeth but holding a look of mild triumph in her eyes. "He accepted the offer yesterday. He'll be moving in the next month, and I promise I won't be any trouble until then. You know, Richard always wanted to be a doctor, that's why he started the business. So he could at least work with doctors."

Della let out her breath. So this wasn't about me at all, she thought. It was about Dickie. And Richard, who had always joked about not getting into medical school. And Barbara, Della conceded, silently. It's mostly about Barbara doing what she could for the two of them. For Della had no doubt that she considered Dickie's medical career Richard's greatest legacy.

"And you're going to die at the Ladies Farm?"

Barbara nodded. "If you'll let me."

Now Della looked out at the road, looked at the heat shimmering off the asphalt, studied the gravelly shoulder and the stunted grass along its edge. This is an unforgiving spot, Della thought. It's hot and dry in summer, probably cold and windy in winter. You can't even sit out at a picnic table in any comfort. What a place for a rest stop.

In her secret thoughts, Della had wanted Richard to leave Barbara, had wondered why he didn't. I'm prettier, she would think. I've got a much better body; I'm smarter; I work instead of sitting home all day. Now, though, the unthinkable occurred to her: It wasn't just loyalty to the mother of his child; it wasn't just respect for her position as his wife.

"How much longer—" Della kept staring at the highway, but she shook her head and started over, "What do the doctors say lies ahead for—"

"Three months," Barbara said. "Maybe less. But I'm not taking any treatments, and it's already moving into my bones. And my stomach. The oncologist I saw this morning says he's seen cases like this where the patient didn't last two weeks." Her voice was level. "But he thought three months."

"Why, that's not even into next fall."

"No."

Della turned and saw Barbara shaking her head. Don't cry, she started to say, but stopped herself. Of course we should cry.

Chapter 10

Barbara didn't cry long. As if she had been waiting for just this moment, she filled Della in on her medications, on the pain management session she would be starting in the next week, and on her discussions with the home-health people who would be able to care for her at the Ladies Farm.

Della listened and thought about how to convince Kat, about how little choice they had anyway, considering Barbara's ownership, about how lucky they were that the first-floor room was already so accessible. She imagined pushing Barbara onto the back patio, a plaid blanket tucked around

Barbara's lap and a shawl over her shoulders as they blinked at the early autumn sun. She pictured Kat, Rita, and herself lifting spoons full of broth to Barbara's dry lips. She saw them hovering at the door as the doctor emerged, shaking his head.

Meanwhile, Barbara spoke calmly about catheters and oxygen, meditation and pain management.

Slowly, afghans and fortifying soups yielded to the chores of fulfilling Barbara's wishes as they dealt with erosion of her bowel and bladder. Fury at Barbara, for her duplicity, for her use of them to promote her son's career, vied with fury at Richard for visiting this woman upon them.

She's dying, Della reminded herself. You wouldn't wish this on anyone.

Finally she held up a hand to halt Barbara's monologue. "I want to hear all of this," she said. "But you'll just have to repeat it to the others."

This time Della drove. Inside the air-conditioned bubble, the sunlight conveyed cheer without heat, and she managed a smile at the Castleburg cows, who congregated at the roadside.

Kat was in the office when they arrived

home, and Della wasted no time. "We need to get Rita," she told Kat. "Barbara has something to tell us."

Rita was in the middle of perming Mrs. Hutto, which gave Barbara time to change her clothes and enabled Della to clear her desk and return calls to the printer and Hugh Jr.

Hugh Jr.'s secretary informed her that he would like to meet with Barbara, Della, and Kat. Della repeated the request to Kat, who shrugged and was checking her calendar when Rita walked in. "What's up?"

"Where's Barbara?" Della asked. "This is her show."

"I'm here." Barbara walked up behind Rita and looked at them sitting around what had been Kat and Pauline's office. At her appearance, Flops abandoned her post at Kat's feet and advanced, tail wagging. "Doesn't anyone ever use the living room?"

"Guests," Rita reminded her. "Liable to bounce in at any second."

Barbara motioned them out the office door with one hand and scratched Flops' head with the other. "They are all with the pottery lady. She assured me they'll be at least another hour, and this won't take that long."

So the three of them—Della, Kat, and Rita—sat together on the sofa and Barbara, from the upholstered chair opposite, told them she was dying of ovarian cancer.

"Oh, honey!" said Rita, rising and rushing immediately to her. "Honey, that's so sad." She leaned over the chair, stretching an arm behind Barbara to gather her in a hug. "Does the doctor say how long?"

Della and Kat still sat on the sofa as Barbara, dry-eyed and factual, recounted what she had told Della earlier. Rita settled onto the floor next to Flops, but continued holding on to Barbara's hand as she spoke.

Della didn't need to look at Kat to feel her rigidity, and she didn't have to ask to know what Kat was thinking.

"Have you told Dickie?" Kat asked.

Barbara nodded and her eyes moistened. "He's such a good kid. He has a hard time accepting, you know, that treatment isn't . . . that there really isn't anything . . . that all his training is no help at all."

"So Dickie understands," Kat continued,

as Della squirmed, "how much care you'll be needing, what it will take while you're," she paused, "while you're in the later stages of your illness."

"Oh, of course," Barbara said.

"So you're planning on living with Dickie and Marcy in Dallas?"

Barbara looked at Della a second, then returned to Kat. "No. That is, I thought, if it's all right with you, I want to stay here."

"Here? Not with your family?" Kat's voice was amazingly level.

"Well, we're family!" Rita objected.

"I only meant—"

"Dickie is moving to Houston. He has accepted a fellowship there for post-graduate training."

"But he's a doctor!" Kat said. "I would think he and Marcy would be perfect . . . would want you to be with them, so they could look after you."

Barbara shook her head and Della noticed how her eyes had grown clear again. "Doctors all over the country would kill for this opportunity; he'll be working with the best heart surgeons in the world."

"How can he go now?" Kat asked. "When you're . . . so sick?"

"Because I told him to," Barbara said. "I told him that his father had provided a place for me as perfectly as if he'd foreseen the future. That I would be cared for by people who love me and that I could die at home. It's the only reason he feels comfortable leaving."

"And he should!" Rita said, rising once more to hug Barbara. "We will take care of you. He won't have a thing to worry about."

Kat's expression had not changed. Cautiously Della reached a hand out to Kat's arm. "Barbara thought she might move down into the Babe Didrikson," said Della.

"I'll pay for any equipment, of course," Barbara said. "And there's plenty of insurance; you know how Richard was." Barbara closed her eyes for a second and leaned toward Rita, who still sat on the floor at her feet. When she looked at Della and Kat again, her gaze was resolute. "And you understand, of course," she said to them, "this . . . the Ladies Farm . . . my interest . . . that passes to you."

The Ladies Farm! Della felt the muscles in Kat's forearm tense, but her unblinking expression remained unchanged.

"Barbara," Della murmured. "Shouldn't Dickie be the one—"

Barbara shook her head. "He doesn't want it and he'll never miss it." She smiled. "What . . . how much can one person want . . . in a lifetime?"

A person could want more than this, Della thought. More than dying of cancer and having to depend on the women with whom your husband was unfaithful. "Well, maybe we'll just spruce up the Babe Didrikson before you take up residence," Della said with a heartiness she did not feel. "Paint it, change out the drapes."

Barbara demurred with a soft shake of her head while Rita merely stared at Della's sudden gusto for décor.

Kat, meanwhile, remained wooden.

"Zaharias," Kat said finally, and they all turned to look at her. "Babe Didrikson Zaharias."

"If she had planned this," Kat said, "if she had plotted this for years, she couldn't have devised a better revenge."

She and Della had returned to the office by themselves, with Barbara at the barn to start a jewelry class and Rita back in the salon. "I know this is hard," Della began, but Kat cut her off.

"Hard! Slitting your wrists is hard! This . . . this . . . you don't . . . can't possibly understand!" She ended with her hands before her in the air.

Oh yes, I understand it all. The fury that the one he cared for more than you was fat and selfish and aside from a few years in the business never worked a day in her life. I understand it all.

But Della thought Kat had enough shock to absorb. And she ached once more for Pauline's forgiving ear.

"In a way," she said slowly, "this is what we wanted. She'll die and we'll get the Ladies Farm."

"After we nurse her through to her death. She doesn't even look sick."

"She is, though," Della said. "She's been hiding a lot. Medication. Weakness. That's why she takes those naps. We thought she was just lazy."

"I'm not going to feel sorry for her." Kat vowed. "I'm not."

"No one's asking you to feel sorry for her. And no one's asking you to take care of her."

"No? That's exactly what she's asking. She'll need constant care and we, all of us, will be nursing her." Kat ran her fingers through her hair, tugging on it a little as she reached the ends. "Why can't she go to a hospice?"

"You heard her: She wants to die at home. Our home."

"You sound like you want her here."

Della sighed and shook her head. "I don't know. I thought I didn't, but then . . . I don't know."

"It's just because she's dying and you don't want to be callous."

"No." Della shook her head. "It was before that." She looked at Kat. "She's not the way . . . not who I thought she was. You know what I mean?"

The anger and doubt in Kat's expression said no, but she did not speak.

"You believe all these things about someone, and her appearance fits what you believe, but then, when you really get to know her . . . know her personally, not just as someone's wife or mother . . . I don't know, it just turns out she's not hysterical and she's not stupid or lazy. And all those years I thought Richard just stayed with her out of loyalty . . ." Watch yourself, Della warned herself, watch it, but she continued, "I don't know."

"Richard was the most loyal person I ever knew," Kat whispered.

"I know," Della said. "But did you ever think . . . did you ever think maybe he really loved her?"

"Of course he loved her. When they were young and she was thin and they were just starting out. Of course he loved her then." Kat looked at Della sadly.

"Oh, Kat!" Della stepped forward and put her arms around her friend. Kat remained stiff a second, then hugged Della, resting her head on Della's shoulder.

"I feel stupid," Kat whispered. "He loved her all along, didn't he? Until the day he died."

Della nodded as Kat pulled away and reached for the box of tissues on her desk. "I think so. Kat," she said gently, "all you have to do is agree to let Barbara stay. I'll look after the rest."

"We don't have much choice, do we?" Kat whispered.

"No," Della said. "Not really. And it's what Pauline wanted. And Richard, I guess."

"How could he do this?" Kat pleaded. "How could he do this to me?"

"I don't know," Della said. At least that was the truth. "I'm sure he didn't foresee all of us here." She would bet on that. "I think Richard just thought he'd live forever, that he'd always be there to care for his wife." And for me, she added silently. He would have been there for me.

"She's kinder than I thought," Kat conceded. "I kind of admired that business about the haircut."

"Yeah." Della looked out the window as another truck rumbled by. "You okay?"

"No. But I will be."

They edged into a discussion about how they would accommodate Barbara's illness: how they would adjust to each level of Barbara's diminishing function. Kat became more tractable as they moved into logistics; these, after all, were manageable problems.

Della looked at her sturdy friend and tried to picture Richard holding her hand or singing old ballads while they danced in hotel rooms. It didn't surprise her that Kat was as vulnerable as anyone else to Richard's sentimentality. And Della knew

that Richard would have loved cracking
Kat's brittle shell.

But Kat's fierce protection of the memory
confused Della. From what Della could tell,
Kat and Richard had had a sporadic affair
that lasted a little over a year and ended
when Kat met Grant. Richard's just an old
boyfriend to Kat, Della thought. But maybe
when she compares it to her marriage, her
time with Richard seems more significant.

"Hello?" Kat was saying.

Della blinked, stared at Kat. "Sorry. I was
just . . ."

"Zoning out," Kat accused. "You do that
whenever the talk turns to finances. Did
you see the appraisal?"

"No."

"You need to look at it. It's a typical
estate appraisal, but I don't know if Hugh
Junior will go for that."

"You think he'll want more?" Della didn't
know why people shook their heads to
clear their thoughts. It made her a little
dizzy.

Kat shrugged. "I was asking you. You
know the kid."

Della shrugged back. "Not enough to
know whether he just wants to free himself

and his sister from the Ladies Farm or if he wants to cash in big-time."

"Well, if that's what he wants," Kat leaned back in her chair, "he'll have to look somewhere other than these two little old ladies."

There was other business, and the two spent an hour catching up on bookings, receipts, and building repairs. Della hadn't made ad calls for *Silver Quest* since Barbara's arrival; she and Kat pulled a prospect list and split up the calls to help get caught up. "There's an outfit in Michigan that does a campsite guide for seniors," Kat said. "I saw the book in a client's office, but now I can't remember the name."

"Prime Time Press," Della supplied. "We called them, remember? Mom and Pop, word of mouth, no ad budget?"

Kat nodded.

"But I'll try again. If they're still in business, maybe they've got a budget now."

Kat continued on about food budgets and their own advertising, which was minimal now that they had established a lot of repeat visitors. If she closed her eyes, Della could imagine that Pauline was out in the barn and that she and Kat were just taking care of business while Pauline taught journal writing.

Della wondered what Kat would do if she knew about Richard and the real estate agent, or about Richard and Della.

Kat's tough, Della thought. You could probably tell her everything.

I need Pauline, Della thought for the thousandth time. Someone to confide in.

After she and Kat finished, Della wandered over to the salon. Rita had two women from town under facials as she combed out the third. Nodding at Della as she worked, Rita described for the women the benefits of cucumber extract on aging skin.

"It cleanses the pores," she said. "The cucumber juices have just the right combination of acid to really get into those pores and clean them out. Then you finish with a nice, tingly, non-drying pore closer, and you've got yourself a face that's soft as butter. How're you doing, Della?" she continued, shifting gears without stopping her combing and circling her customer. "You want me to do something special for your big date?"

"Where is the nail polish?" Della demanded. "I just came down here to touch up my nails."

"Where it always is," Rita said. "In the cart."

"I meant, where's the cart?"

Rita waved her toward a partition, behind which sat the rolling cart with the manicure supplies. Della plucked polish and top coat from the cart, then returned to a seat under one of the dryers.

"Why don't you at least let me style you before you go out? I've got a spot that afternoon," Rita called to her from the sinks in the back.

"I don't want to make a big fuss over this," Della yelled back.

"I'll make it look casual," Rita called back. "No big hair, I promise."

After she returned to the salon and scooted her customers out the door, Rita undid her smock and tossed it over a salon chair. "You want me to finish those for you?"

Della paused with the tiny brush raised over her right forefinger, then shook her head. "I'm almost done. Are you finished for the day?"

"Are you kidding? I've got three more heads plus a barber. But the next one's not till four. I thought maybe I'd run over to Dave's for a while."

"That's going pretty hot and heavy."

"Oh, no!" Rita said. "Don't you start that about my ex-husband when you won't talk about yours! I confess doing it in a cemetery, and you won't even tell me you have a dinner date. I have to hear it from Barbara!"

Della didn't have to look up to see the indignation. "Barbara told you?"

"When she came down to get me."

Della put the cap back on the top coat and carried both nail polish bottles over to the rolling cart. "I guess her cutting her hair makes more sense now," Della said.

"I suppose. I sure do feel sorry for her, though. And I'm glad she's staying here, where we can look after her. So where are you and Tony going?"

Della smiled back. "I don't know. Just to dinner. I wish you wouldn't make such a fuss."

"It's good for you to go out," Rita said.

"I know. That's why I told him I would. But it really is just dinner."

"Well, that's how Dave and I started back, you know."

"Dave is persistent," Della said.

"He says some men never love more than one woman no matter what Old Pete—that's what we call his pecker, Old Pete—tells 'em. Don't matter where Pete goes, guys like Dave still just are thinking about that one."

Della started to laugh. "Old Pete? And you believe that?"

Rita shrugged. "Well, it's easy when I'm the one he's in love with. Besides," she smoothed her spiky black cap and tossed her head to make her earrings jiggle, "Old Pete's a little in love with me too."

"I'll just bet."

Rita looked at her a moment. "Della, haven't you ever done anything a little foolish just because your heart told you to?"

"Those were my hormones, not my heart."

"Well, your hormones, then. Didn't you ever just do what they said?"

"Oh, of course! That's what I'm telling you though: My hormones are not telling me anything about Tony."

"But they might," Rita countered. "If you'd listen."

Chapter 11

"Where's Barbara?" Hugh Jr. asked as he ushered them into the conference room. The glass tabletop reflected his gesturing hands as he motioned to the carafe in the table's center. "Help yourselves."

They had talked about it and had decided there was no point in telling him that they would inherit Barbara's share of the Ladies Farm soon enough. "Barbara's really not feeling too well," Della said. She smiled at Hugh Jr. and reached for the coffee and a glass mug.

"Sorry to hear that," he said. "I thought we could settle everything right now."

Della concentrated on pouring the coffee without dribbling anything onto the table and let Kat answer Hugh Jr.

"We thought . . . that is, we discussed it with Barbara, and she said what she told you: She's not interested in increasing her share of the Ladies Farm." Kat smiled at Hugh Jr. as Della passed her the carafe. "So, we're your best prospects. Fire away."

Hugh Jr. smiled and took a breath. "My parents put a lot of themselves into Sydon House and then the Ladies Farm. And while I credit the two of you, plus that hair salon, for a great deal of the effort that finally made the thing a going concern, I think you'll agree that the guiding spirit was always my mother."

He's found out about the gravel, thought Della as he continued. Della eyed the stack of journals and files that Hugh Jr. had set on the table before him. She and Kat had agreed they could go as high as fifteen percent over the appraisal, though they had vowed to try to hold him to ten.

"It was certainly her vision," Kat concurred.

Good move, thought Della. We'll be in total agreement right up until the moment he names his price. She could pick out

Pauline's fabric-covered notebooks in the stack and she imagined Hugh Jr. sifting through them, noting addresses and sending dutiful notes to his parents' old friends.

"Yes," Hugh Jr. resumed the narrative. "Her vision. And her planning. And her hard work. Her classes. Her décor. Her ability to get along with anyone, no matter how cruel they were to her.

"One thing she always warned me about, her great overriding admonition, was that there's nothing certain but certain change. And," he placed his hands flat on the table and sat back as if pushed there by the weight of the truth he was about to deliver, "change has overtaken the Ladies Farm."

You can say that again, thought Della.

"Change," Hugh Jr. repeated. "Ladies, I'm sure you understand. As my mother's executor, I have a responsibility to my sister . . . and to her children . . . and I hope, someday, my own."

As Hugh Jr. finally explained that he had talked to the Castleburgs about their gravel mining, Della exchanged glances with Kat.

"As you can imagine," Hugh Jr. said, "I now believe the Ladies Farm to be worth considerably more than the appraisal. Particularly this appraisal."

Della rushed to defend the honor of Sydonia. "I'm sure Mr. Tice was trying to err on the side of lower estate taxes."

"I'm sure." He smiled, but his lips stretched thin against his teeth.

"Hugh, we understand completely," Kat said. "Your mother was . . . I can't tell you how much she meant to us. And because of that, we want to do whatever's right for you and Melissa. So why don't you just tell us what you think is a fair value for your mother's interest in the Ladies Farm."

"Two hundred eighty thousand dollars."

"Pardon me?" Della heard her own words, but she wasn't sure who said them.

"Two-eighty."

"How did you come to that?" Kat asked in a remarkably cool voice. "The appraisal valued the whole property at less than two, and there's a hundred and thirty thousand worth of notes."

"I looked at the fair market value," Hugh replied in equally cool tones. "I let Castleburg make me an offer."

"Castleburg? The old man?" Della squeaked.

Hugh Jr. nodded.

"Does he know about Barbara?"

Hugh Jr. nodded. "That's why I'm so sorry she's not here. But I know you'll speak with her. Convince her this is in her best interest, too."

Kat's eyes narrowed. "Five-sixty for the whole thing? What'd you tell Castleburg? That you owned the whole thing?" She didn't wait for his denial. "Or that you'd get it all for him."

"You knew my father. He was impractical. If it weren't for my mother, he would have been hammering and sawing before they ever sketched out what the Ladies Farm looked like. She was the one who had the plans drawn, hired electricians and plumbers."

For how many years, Della wondered, would Hugh Jr. be blaming his father for mistreating his mother?

"We knew these things," Kat snapped. "We knew all your father's shortcomings, that's why we moved in to bail out your mother."

"And your mother knew them, too," Della rushed to add. "They were just one more part of the husband she loved."

Hugh Jr. looked at her a second. "Just one more part," he repeated. "In any case, it turns out that the prospects for gravel on the property are quite good, and that Dad, in his wisdom, decided to ignore those prospects in his pursuit of the good life."

"Don't you think your mom joined in that decision?"

"I'm sure she acquiesced."

"Where does this leave us?" Kat asked.

Hugh Jr. regarded her sympathetically. "The arrangement you had with my mother . . . it amounted to a lease, with payment being the services you provided." His hands rested for a moment on the stack of files and books, and he drummed his fingers thoughtfully. "We can continue it, of course, but you know, now, you would be tenants, running the bed and breakfast and paying part of the proceeds to the estate . . . to Melissa and me."

"Tenants!" Della couldn't help herself. "Tenants on the Ladies Farm!"

But Kat had seen the whole picture. "The Ladies Farm in the middle of a gravel pit," she said calmly. "How soon do you anticipate digging?"

"Not so quickly that you won't have time

to close things out and find yourselves a new place." He held his hands palms up in front of himself. "It's not our intention to put you on the street. But we—Melissa and I—can't afford to pass up Castleburg's offer."

"Unless, of course, we meet it," Kat said. "And assuming, of course, you have Barbara's cooperation."

"I intend to talk with her as soon as I can."

But not before we talk with her, Della vowed. Because if Barbara won't sell, if Barbara's giving us her half—

"You also should know," Hugh Jr. was saying, "that Castleburg's talked to the Huttos."

"The Huttos? But there's no—"

"No point to us arguing about it, is there?" Kat cut her off.

"I'll call Barbara this afternoon," Hugh Jr. told them. "Maybe come out later this week." He sipped cautiously. Then he smiled. "I think Barbara will go along with what we want: I think she owes us that much."

"What do you mean?" asked Kat.

"Hugh—" Della started.

Hugh Jr. pulled one of the journals off

the top of the stack before him and slid it across the table. "Read all about it."

"Hugh," Della said, "the Morrisons were good friends of your parents. If they hadn't bailed them out, time after time, your parents could never have held onto Sydon House."

"They lent my parents money," Hugh stated. "My parents paid back every penny."

"Read all about what?" Kat said.

"Barbara and my dad."

"What?"

Della shot a look at Kat, then plunged in. "Hugh, your father had a one-night stand with Barbara years and years ago. Your parents got over it. The Morrisons got over it. It didn't mean anything then, and it doesn't mean anything now."

"Barbara cheated on Richard?" The journal lay untouched on the glass table.

"Barbara and Richard lent your parents money at a time when no bank ever would," Della recited. "They refused to accept any interest, and they never once requested repayment."

"If it weren't for Barbara," said Hugh Jr., "we would never have moved out to Sydonia. That's why my mother agreed to that hare-brained scheme, that's why she gave up her museum job: to get away from the Morrisons."

"Barbara Morrison and Hugh Freschatte had an affair?"

"One night hardly qualifies as an affair," Della snapped. "Obviously, Pauline found it in her heart to forgive Hugh. And Barbara."

"That's what she told you," Hugh Jr. said. "But it tore her heart out when Barbara came back and she saw that amethyst my father gave Barbara."

"Your father gave that amethyst to Richard. As a gesture of friendship, to enable Richard to create a spectacular gift for Richard to give to his wife."

"Yeah, sure. Just because that wife was someone my father fucked!"

"A reconciliation gift," Della emphasized, ignoring Kat and wondering if Hugh Jr. expected her to chastise him for his language. "A sign that Richard and Barbara still loved one another, no matter what had happened between them."

"Hugh, your mother kept these things from you because she didn't want to hurt you . . . or anyone else. She wanted the

past to stay the past. She wanted you—
and us—to live in the present. To do what
is right now. And Hugh, doing what's right
means letting us—all of us, including Barbara—stay at the Ladies Farm. Your
mother welcomed Barbara to the Ladies
Farm. I'm sure she would want us," Della
looked at Kat, "all of us, to do the same."

"You mean, I should accept a low bid
from you so you can turn around and sell it
to Castleburg yourself?"

This time, he met her gaze after she
glanced once again at the stack of journals
piled in front of him. "Want to see the one
about you?"

Hugh Jr. was pulling another journal
from the stack.

Kat was staring at Della. "You slept with
Hugh?"

"No."

"Della?"

Della looked across the table at Kat. "I
had an affair with Richard," she told her
friend. "After I divorced Tony." She felt
Hugh Jr.'s gaze, but she kept her eyes on
Kat. "I was with him the morning before he
died. I'm sorry. I couldn't tell you when . . . I
couldn't tell you."

Kat was out the door before Della could say she was sorry one more time.

Della caught up with Kat in the ladies' room off the lobby.

"Get out," ordered Kat, disappearing into the handicap stall.

"No."

Della rapped on the closed door of the stall. "I don't hear any peeing in there."

"Go to hell."

"Come on, Kat. I know you're pissed, no pun intended, but you're going to have to come out sometime, and I'll be here when you do. So come out now, so we can talk."

"Go to hell."

"Kat!" Della banged on the door.

There was silence. "Okay." Della sniffed. "I can wait."

She returned to the mirror and combed her hair. She powdered her face and rubbed on blusher. "You got any under-eye cover-up?" she called out, but she wasn't surprised when she received no answer.

Della stepped back from the mirror and eyed the closed stall door. "Kat?" she called out once more. "You don't come out, I'm coming in."

She hooked her purse over her jacket on the corner of the door of the vacant stall. Then she knelt down, rolled onto her back and slid into the locked stall. "Why hi!" she greeted her pal, who sat, fully clothed, on the only place there was to sit. "Imagine finding you here."

Della flipped over onto her stomach and crawled fully into the stall. "Get out," hissed Kat.

Della shook her head, drew herself up until she was seated on the floor with her back against the tile wall. "Kat, I'm sorry. I just couldn't tell you without hurting you; I never thought anyone would know."

Outside the stall, the door to the ladies' room opened and someone entered.

"Excuse me?" Kat called out. "Excuse me, could you call the security guard? I'm being invaded here. Assaulted."

Della scrambled up. "Kat!"

"Help! Help me, please!" Kat called, but they both heard the woman step into the third stall and lock the door.

Della seized Kat and pulled her up.

"C'mon!" she said, throwing the latch. "We gotta run!"

Kat resisted for a second, then, maybe considering her position, grasped Della's hand and followed; and the two of them, hand in hand, stopped only to retrieve Della's jacket and purse, and then they fled.

Barbara supposed Hugh Jr. had called her because he wanted her to agree to meet with him before Kat and Della could get to her. She wondered why he was in such a hurry, and she suspected that he was worried about something, but none of that mattered. She would still get a chance to talk to Della and Kat before he met her for breakfast in Sydonia the next day.

But when Della returned, Kat was not with her. "She's spending the night at the Worthington," Della told her. Barbara saw that thin-lipped scowl and she didn't question further, but it was obvious enough things hadn't gone well. "Castleburg's offered him two-eighty for Pauline's share. Even if we meet it," Della clipped each word out, "we'll still be surrounded by gravel pits between Castleburg and the Huttos." Her eyes teared up even though Barbara could tell she was fighting it. "Kat decided to stay in Fort Worth for the night. We've all got a lot to think about."

Chapter 12

"Where have you been?" Rita scolded Della. "Tony called to say he'd be here at seven."

"Tony!" Della barely remembered that this was Friday and soon to be Friday night.

"Never mind that, what took you so long?"

Della didn't feel like recounting the fight with Kat, which no one had won, but which had merely wound down to silence punctuated by Kat's order to leave her at the Worthington because she wasn't returning to the Ladies Farm. "I told you, Kat and I got into a fight and she wanted to stay at the Worthington. I just went through all this with Barbara."

Rita's eyes narrowed. "You told us you fought; you didn't say what about."

"The Ladies Farm," Della said. "The Ladies Farm, the Ladies Farm, the Ladies Farm!" She yanked a glass from the cupboard and jammed it against the lever in the refrigerator door that dispensed ice. "We fought because we're scared. We can meet Castleburg's offer, but that doesn't do us any good unless we can buy out the Huttos and stop all this digging."

Rita still regarded her suspiciously, but Della didn't offer any more explanation. She didn't want to discuss how rotten it felt to tell your friend that you had had a much longer and much more recent affair than she had with the love of her life. Nor did she want to explain how greedy she felt not sharing the details, for which Kat seemed insatiable.

"Well, you've got just enough time to shower and dress, that's why I got Nancy to stay. We'll get dinner on."

"Shower." Della repeated. The drive home had not worked its usual magic, and she could not even sort out what she could reveal to Rita and Barbara. And she certainly could not manage a conversation with Tony.

"Are you okay?"

Della shook her head and collapsed onto a kitchen chair. Nancy had been washing vegetables, but now she turned from the sink to stare. "You want me to call an ambulance?"

"Oh, for God's sakes," Rita snapped, "no one is dying! Not now, anyway!" She turned to Della. "What's wrong?"

"Would you mind calling Tony for me?"

"Why?"

"To tell him I can't make it. Don't look at me like that, I can't! I've got to figure out what we're going to do."

"Well, if you're going to stand him up, you tell him. I'm damned if I'll do that to someone as nice as Tony."

Della shook her head. "He's just trying to get back in my pants because he hasn't got the energy to go after someone new."

"Well that's all Dave's doing, and you don't hear me complaining!" Rita shot back. "None of us has that much energy."

"Come on," she coaxed. "Be a sport."

"A . . . ? You break your own hearts! After all he's planned for you. You should be in that shower right now. You should be letting me do your hair."

Della didn't know which was tougher: going out with Tony and pretending nothing was wrong or explaining to him why she couldn't go out with him. She looked at Rita one more time, but Rita was not moved. "I'm going upstairs," said Della.

Della washed her hair and toweled it dry, trying to fluff it out enough that the roots didn't show. Then she stood in her towel for a long time studying the contents of her closet since her silk pantsuit was locked at the cleaner's, which had closed an hour ago. There weren't too many other choices; most of her clothes were tunic tops and washable slacks. Her red silk was far too dressy, jeans not dressy enough. Sighing, she pulled a white cotton dress from the back and hunted up a pair of white flats. At least it'll be cool, she thought.

At the mirror, she barely studied her face before she launched the routine. Moisturizer followed by concealer to hide the shadows under her eyes, followed by a moisturizing foundation, followed by a matted finish on her eyelids. She lined her eyes with an olive pencil; the least she could do was show she had tried. Then she rubbed on a little blush, powdered the whole thing, lined and filled her lips, and brushed on her mascara.

It doesn't work, she thought, pulling in her stomach as she studied her reflection in the full-length mirror. I'm too old to look innocent and too worn to look sophisticated. This thing's so white it makes my teeth yellow.

Tears welled up even as she ordered herself not to cry. You'll just have to do the whole thing over again, and this isn't worth one paint job, let alone two. Della marched herself back into the closet and yanked a denim jumpsuit from a hanger. It had an elastic waist and fake jewels on the yoke and always reminded her of something Rita would wear, but maybe Rita was right. Maybe a little gaudiness up around the neckline lured the eyes down from your crow's-feet and up from your belly. Maybe that was the best you could hope for.

She fished around in her closet for sandals with heels, then wobbled out to check the mirror again. It would do, she thought.

Tony arrived early, a sure sign of nerves. Rita talked and joked and fluttered around them until Nancy finally called her into the kitchen. "Now don't you bring her back too early!" Rita sang back over her shoulder. Della shrugged, but Tony laughed.

It didn't surprise her that they went to Wendells, but it disappointed her. Maybe there are no surprises left for us, she mourned. On a hill by the highway about thirty minutes out of Sydonia, it was the only restaurant in the county that sported both tablecloths and a wine list. She could remember driving out here from Fort Worth on Mother's Days past, the boys whispering in the back seat about the present hidden in the trunk.

They chatted politely, and Della surprised herself by remembering to focus the conversation on him. Men were easy to talk to, really. They could probably go the whole night without a single question about the Ladies Farm, or Barbara or Kat or Pauline.

Tony ordered wine, and she tried to be impressed; it was a new skill. They both had opted for the herbed chicken, and Della had to stop herself from offering to split one dinner. Men, she reminded herself, don't like it when you imply they can't afford a good meal. She wondered how he'd feel about doggie bags.

"Looked like you had a full house in the dining room," Tony said.

"We're doing all right," Della conceded. "Are your shops busy?"

"Pretty much. It always lags a little in midsummer, but I've come to expect it."

"Remember how terrified we were?" she recalled. "That first summer, when the schools closed and we didn't know how we'd make the rent?"

"You think much about back then?"

Della nodded. "More than I thought I would. It does make me happy sometimes, to think about the four of us back then."

He nodded, but didn't say anything.

The waitress had brought their salads, but neither of them had touched the food. "Tony," she said. He looked at her. "Tony, back then, did I ever, did you ever think I just joked my way through?"

"What do you mean?"

"You know: all that sarcasm. Did you think I refused to face things? That all I did was make fun of things?"

Tony considered a moment. "What's this about?" he asked cautiously. "Someone say something to you?"

It made her wince just to remember Kat's words: *Professional smart-ass. Can't face the truth in anything. Certainly can't tell it.* "Oh, Kat and I had a spat."

Tony studied her, then grinned. "Well, I always said you were a smart-ass."

"And nobody likes a smart-ass," she concluded. Tears filled her eyes, and she saw herself alone, isolated by the edge of her own attitude.

"God, Della, I just said you were a smart-ass."

"Oh." She shook her head. "It's not that. I'm sorry." She dabbed her eyes on the cloth napkin, then stared at it. "I've been buying mascara since I was fifteen and now I'm fifty-five. Forty years of mascara, all of it waterproof, and I never found one that didn't smear."

"You look fine," he said so automatically that it stimulated a torrent of fresh tears.

"I mean it," he insisted, but she just shook her head from side to side as he glanced nervously around the dining room

to see if anyone noticed he was with a sobbing woman.

"I'll wear a sign: *Not his fault,*" she said.
"Okay?"

"You know, you are a smart-ass," Tony
said.

"I had a fight with Kat," Della said. "Hugh
Junior got an offer from Castleburg—the
dairy next door—and we have to meet it or
lose the Ladies Farm." Not the whole truth,
but all true. "And he's buying out the Huttos
too, and the only way we'll keep ourselves
from being the center of the gravel pit is to
buy them out too."

"So why is Kat mad at you?"

"Oh, I think we're just both upset. All
we've learned since Pauline died. Since
Barbara showed up!"

Tony doesn't know, Della thought. And
Tony won't know. But she was seduced by
the idea of telling him, by the dream that
there would be one person to whom she
could tell everything.

"Is everything all right here?" It was the
waitress, bearing their dinners.

"Not much of a date," Della said as the
waitress moved away.

"It's fine," he said. "Why didn't you just tell me all this in the car?"

"I thought I could wisecrack my way through."

"Seeing the humor in things isn't a vice." He smiled a little. "I always thought your wit was one of your charms. At least when it wasn't directed at me."

"But it always is, sooner or later, isn't it?"

"Taste the wine," he advised. "Tell me how sophisticated and urbane I am."

She sipped, glad that there was no edge to the full, mellow taste. "Ultra-urbane, I'd say." She held the glass up to him in tribute, then sipped again.

Tony started to eat his dinner, and Della set the wine glass down and picked up her own knife and fork. The chicken was standard, bland middle-America chicken, the vegetables overcooked, and the potato wrapped in foil. Poor Tony, Della thought. This is as glamorous as it gets for him.

She remembered dinner on a patio between Taos and Santa Fe, with the stars blazing in the sky and the crunch and flavor of each grilled vegetable a delightful surprise. Fresh trout perfectly sauced, bread baked in a wood oven, the sights and sounds vying with the aroma of piñon and the flicker of a real candle on a simple, woven tablecloth. Of course, thought Della, the man who took you there was cheating on his wife. Whereas this man's fidelity became a joke to his friends.

Tony caught her looking at him and he smiled. "It's good, isn't it?"

"Yes," she replied.

They didn't talk much during dinner, but Della didn't mind. He accepted her suggestion that they split dessert, and she let him eat most of the pecan pie.

"You want to take a walk?" he asked her, taking her arm.

"Sure," she said. The stone walkway led to an overlook above the Nolan. It was already dark, but small lights illuminated the path, and the overlook, when they reached it, was deserted.

They sat on the bench and looked out into the darkness. With the lights from the restaurant obscured by trees, the stars that hung over the small valley sparkled in the moonless sky. "I always liked it here," said Tony, putting his arm on the bench and then, with no resistance, around her shoulders.

"Me too," agreed Della, though she couldn't remember ever coming here without the boys, who occupied themselves hurling rocks into the trees on the hill below the retaining wall. They would fight over who took the longest turn at the giant binoculars that cost a quarter for three minutes, and then they would howl when she and Tony insisted it was time to leave.

Tony always made Robbie give Jamie a head start in their race up the hill, and she had gladly yielded the front seat to the race winner for the ride home.

"What?" Tony squeezed her shoulder a little.

"You're a good father," Della said. "Did I tell you that?"

"I believe you did," Tony said. "Though I don't mind hearing it again."

"You're a good father."

"We were okay together," Tony granted her. "We had two nice boys. And our one son now . . . he's fine, isn't he?"

She nodded. "He got an education, he has a good job, he married someone nice, they have a nice kid."

"You think they'll have more?"

"Who knows?"

"You think he's afraid? Like maybe two would be bad luck?"

"Robbie?" Della asked. Maybe Robbie was afraid to subject Katie to the possibility of losing a sibling. She recalled Robbie standing in the middle of the living room, home from his first year of college in the middle of a school week to attend his brother's funeral. "Where is he?" Robbie had asked, his shirt hanging out of his pants, his car keys still in his hand. "I want to see him."

"Maybe he is afraid, and maybe he'll get over it. Maybe Laura will insist on another baby. Who knows?" She turned slightly toward him. "Are you going to make a move on me, or what?"

"Well, I was," said Tony, drawing her close. "But then we'll have to walk back up to the car and that might break the mood. So how about if we walk back up to the car and I drive to a secluded spot and kiss you and then we can see if we want to go to a motel?"

"Do I get the right to say no?" Della asked.

Even in the dark she could see a grin. "I'll take my chances."

In some ways, thought Della as she followed him up the path, he takes more risks than Richard ever did.

The spot he chose was the Boy Scouts' roadside park where Barbara had told Della she was dying. Della didn't even try to conceal it. He listened patiently, his arm around her as they sat side by side atop the picnic table next to the highway.

"Poor Tony," she said as she wound down the tale. "You can't get away from the difficulties of the Ladies Farm."

"Because you can't."

"Well, the Ladies Farm is pretty much my life."

"Why is that?" he asked. "I always thought you'd find someone else and get married. I can't believe you're still single."

Because when you were courting Suzanne, I was entertaining Richard with cozy, late-night dinners. While you were adjusting to stepchildren, I was flying off to meet Richard in Phoenix and Portland and New Orleans. You were filing for divorce and I was still looking over my shoulder while I drove to our tryst at some Hill Country retreat. I was hiding and lying and totally consumed by my secret passion. There was no time for making a suitable match.

Della took a deep breath, then shrugged. "Maybe there's just no such thing as Mr. Right," her voice as offhanded as she could make it. "I don't know, really. At our age, all the good men are married."

"Gee, thanks."

"Well, you were married."

"I was the only one in the relationship who seemed to notice."

"You think you'll get married again?" she asked.

"I don't know. What about you?"

"I doubt it. I've just been on my own too long, Tony. You know, you get used to it after a while, and someone sharing your life seems like an intrusion."

He pulled her close to him. "Don't you miss . . . you know . . . having someone to be with?"

"I miss screwing," she said. "I miss sleeping with someone."

"Me too," he whispered, nuzzling her ear.

It wasn't subtle, but it was effective. She squirmed a little and leaned into him. When he finally did kiss her, there was such sweet comfort in the taste of him that Della simply clung.

The motel, an inn at Lake Whitney, was predictable and the things he whispered to her were all the things she remembered from before. Della closed her eyes to hear him better. There was a thrill in knowing what came next and then having it happen exactly the way it should.

"Are you okay?" he asked her as she lay quiet in his arms.

"Yes," she said automatically. She didn't know if he meant okay with what they had done, or okay about the Ladies Farm or okay about Barbara dying or okay with the arrangement of pillows and blankets. But I'm okay for going to sleep in bed with Tony, Della thought.

Barbara dressed carefully. The diaper gave her a little more confidence, but she had to choose baggier clothes to conceal the bulk. She selected two pills from the bottle atop her dressing table and set them next to the glass of water. She wanted to wait until just before she left; it would give her a few extra minutes of eased breathing.

Resting in the upholstered chair next to

the window, Barbara looked over the slope down to the narrow river and then up again at the opposite bank. The early morning sun illuminated the tops of the cottonwoods that dotted the hill, turning their feathery silhouette from black to gray to a silvery green. She thought about Richard, about the way he was always up before she was. She would awaken to hear him humming to himself as he shaved, or, on weekends, to the coffee and toast he would bring on a tray.

Morning was always their time. No matter how late he came in the night before, no matter how angry her accusations, how ludicrously vehement his denials, Richard had always managed to make her early mornings a time when she felt treasured and protected, loved and desired.

Now, though, the step outside her door was Rita, who knocked softly and called her name. "You up?" Rita whispered as she cracked the door and peeked in.

Barbara motioned her in, and Rita almost wriggled with excitement. "Guess who didn't come home last night from her date with Tony?"

"No kidding?"

"No kidding!" Rita seated herself with a bounce on the edge of the bed. "That Tony! I could tell by the sound of his voice on the phone, he was going for it!" She pulled her lavender wrapper closer to herself and surveyed Barbara's outfit. "You all ready to go?"

Barbara nodded. "I'm glad for Della," she said, pushing herself up from the chair. "She's been alone too long."

She felt Rita watching her as she made her way back to the glass of water and took the two pills. "I've been thinking," Barbara said as she lifted her purse to her shoulder. "I think I'll go ahead and drive myself. I don't want Hugh Junior wondering if I'm okay."

Rita frowned. "You sure?"

Barbara smiled. "It's just a few blocks. Nothing to it!"

The walk to the car was the hardest part, but Barbara managed it, just as she managed to park in the front of the pharmacy and walk without hesitation to the booth at the fountain. The girl behind the counter, Randi, came out and poured her a cup of coffee and asked how things were at the Ladies Farm.

"Oh, I think we're getting back to normal." Barbara smiled and looked toward the door. "Here's my date."

Randi remembered Hugh Jr., and they exchanged polite greetings. Barbara ordered eggs and sausage with buttered toast.

"I believe in living dangerously," she joked.

"Look," he told her when their greetings were over, "I guess Della and Rita told you I've had this offer from Castleburg. Truth is, I'm uncomfortable about letting them explain the offer to you. Because it's up to you what you do, but you should know the whole story, and what's possible for you. Castleburg and his gravel could really set you up."

Castleburg was offering them two hundred and eighty thousand dollars each in exchange for the property. "Or you could do what I'm doing," Hugh Jr. said, sitting up and throwing his shoulders back. "He wanted to buy the property outright, but I pitched him a counter offer: I hold on to the land, he pays me forty percent of his gross. His gross!" Hugh Jr. smiled.

Barbara guessed it was the smile that

did it. Those large, even, white teeth, the flush, the hint of a dimple in the chin: It was Hugh all over, right down to the totally naïve pride in negotiating a really bad deal.

"They can see him coming," Richard would say, time after time.

"Hugh," Barbara said softly, "why don't you let me give you and Melissa two-ninety and be done with it?"

"Then you'd get forty percent of everything."

"Actually, Hugh, what I'd get would be the pleasure of letting Della and Kat and Rita continue the Ladies Farm. And the joy of providing you and Melissa with a sure thing, instead of forty percent of Castleburg's version of the gross."

His eyes had narrowed and his lips tightened. "It's what I should have expected," he said. "Isn't it enough that you ruined my mother's life? Why do you want to cheat Melissa and me?"

"Cheat you?" Barbara blinked.

"My mother wrote all about it," he told her. "She wrote about it when it happened, and she wrote about it for years after they had to leave Fort Worth and drag us all the way out here to get away from you. She

wrote about it every time you and your husband lent them money, and she wrote
about it when she saw that amethyst on
your fat little finger. And that's what killed
her. You and that amethyst!"

Hugh Jr. looked far more astonished at
his fury than Barbara felt. "Hugh, considering how angry you are, I'm especially
impressed with how hard you're trying to
be fair."

"You know," he picked up the theme, "I
could have really taken you, told you
Castleburg was offering one-eighty and
picked up the difference. You wouldn't
have had a clue."

"That's right," Barbara concurred. "You
could have." She regarded him quizzically.
"I appreciate your patience ... and your
generosity," Barbara said. "I just wish..."
Barbara looked down at her eggs, which
she had been moving around her plate, "I
do wish, Hugh, that there was a way for
Della and Kat to hang on to the Ladies
Farm. You know," she paused again, "the
way your mother wanted."

"They could stay," Hugh Jr. said, his
voice level and firm. "If they meet Castleburg's offer."

Barbara pressed her lips together and gazed down at her uneaten breakfast, amazed one more time that food no longer meant anything to her. You can eat anything you want, she told herself, and you want nothing.

"Della and Kat could meet Castleburg's offer," he repeated. "But they'd better decide fast. Because I'm giving up my forty percent if I do that. And Castleburg's waiting on me."

The morning was not nearly as awkward as Della had feared. Tony gallantly made a run to the convenience store for toothbrushes and orange juice, after which they managed a shower together and a pleasant breakfast at the nearby Waffle House.

She squeezed Tony's hand, and they sat across from each other, smiling dumbly and talking about going to a movie in the evening. "Of course, now I have to face Rita and her *I told you so,*" Della said.

"Hey, I told you so too, and you don't mind facing me."

"True. But facing you isn't real life right now."

He shook his head. "Della, what do I

have to say? I want to be part of your real life."

"Tony, I was just making a joke! This," she waved a hand around the Waffle House, "is not my life. Not yours either."

"Well, I don't think what we did was a joke."

"Did I laugh last night?"

Now he grinned. "Well, I thought I heard you giggling about halfway through."

"Gasps of pleasure, I'm sure," she said. "Anyway, I do need to get back."

"What are you going to do about Castleburg and Hugh Junior?"

"I don't know," Della replied. "And I won't ever know if I stay here."

"Does this mean our date's officially over?" He picked up the check and studied it.

"I don't know. If I say yes, does that mean I have to split the cost of the meal with you?"

Tony shot her a dark look and motioned her up. They were both quiet on their way back to Sydonia, and Della began to review her options with Kat. I could buy the Ladies Farm without her, or she could buy it without me. But it would be a financial stretch for either one without the other. And Della was sure that Kat, once she calmed down, would still want to be Della's partner.

And, assuming Kat and I can keep our own secrets, Della's plan continued, maybe Barbara would underwrite a note or something to help buy out Hugh Jr. or counter Castleburg.

Maybe I should just remarry Tony, Della thought, stealing a glance at him. I'm not that attached to the Ladies Farm. Or Sydonia.

It was pleasant to picture Tony and herself redecorating their old house, hosting dinners there, playing with Katie in the family room, even working together at the copy shop. It seemed very simple compared to the mess she was in.

"What are you thinking?" he asked.

"Nothing much," she replied. "This was nice."

"Nice?"

"What I'm saying is I'm glad you asked me, Tony."

"Oh, good. Then you'll see me again?"

"Tony, I'll see you again, but I'm not sure how serious . . . I mean, I don't want to rush into things."

"I don't know." He turned the car off the

highway and toward the square. "You seemed to be in a rush last night."

Della laughed, shrugged. "You know what I mean."

Tony sighed as they completed their pass by the square and turned onto Travis. "Well, I would like to see you tonight. We could go to the movies. Maybe in Fort Worth, this time. You could spend the night at the house."

Della swallowed. "I don't know if I'm ready for that. How about if we pick a movie and I meet you there?"

"Sure."

Rita was pacing the porch when they pulled up. "I feel like a misbehaving teenager," Della muttered. "Am I grounded?" she called to Rita as she got out of the car.

"Grounded?" Comprehension brightened Rita's face. "Oh, you're okay, I wasn't worried about you, you were with Tony. I'm just waiting on Dave. He's got to drive into Fort Worth with me to pick up Kat. The damn Worthington's throwing her out for making a scene in the bar. She called me in tears, drunk as a skunk, and we've got to go get her."

Chapter 13

"I'll go," Della volunteered. She must have climbed the porch steps too fast for her heart to be racing the way it was.

"No, Dave's on his way." Rita looked from Della to Tony. "Besides, you should ask Tony to stay for lunch. We've got a nice bunch of guests, and Barbara's making cranberry torte."

"I'll take Della to get Kat," Tony offered. "There's no sense dragging Dave away from the station."

Della didn't want to imagine a conversation between Tony and the drunken Kat. "I'm going to get Kat by myself," Della announced. "I'm the one who fought with her, I'm the one who has to make it up."

"Honey, she's real drunk," Rita warned. "She may just be spoiling for another fight now. If I were you, I'd take Tony."

"No!" This wasn't coming out right, Tony's expression was hardening as she watched. "Look, this is something I have to do by myself. It's not that I don't want your help. Honest."

"I'm going to call Dave off," Rita said. "You two can duke this one out. But hurry. They're about to put her butt out on the street!"

"Look," Della said to Tony, barely listening to Rita's exit, "this is between Kat and me."

"I get it," Tony said. "You don't have to keep repeating it. I'm just worried about your wrestling a drunk into your car, Della."

And I'm just worried about your hearing a drunk reveal that I slept with Richard. That we sneaked around for years while I built a new career and impressed the world with my independence.

Della reached a hand out to stroke the side of his stubbly face. "I'll take the car phone," she promised. "If I need extra muscle, I'll call for backup."

"Well, use leverage," Tony advised. "Plant your feet, grab her around the middle, and twist her into the car. She's a lot younger than you, don't let her strength surprise you."

"Oh, thanks," Della chirped, heading inside. No time to change clothes, but at least she could trade the sandals for some ground-gripping sneakers.

Tony was still issuing advice as she walked out to the driveway and fired up the Honda. He motioned to roll down the window, then leaned inside to kiss her. "Call me," he ordered.

"Yes, dear," she laughed, backing out onto the street with the window still open.

Once on the highway, Della called the Worthington and asked to be put through to Kat's room. When no one answered, she asked for the manager. That brought a cheerful young woman to the phone who knew who Kat was and confirmed that she still occupied the room she had checked into the previous afternoon.

"Well, I'm on my way to get her. I understand she's been asked to leave."

"I believe she's checking out shortly."

"You want to tell me what happened?"

"That would violate our responsibilities to our guests. I can say—"

"We're discussing a guest you're throwing out. I'm coming to relieve you of her presence. I suggest you tell me what happened. Maybe we can avoid a screaming fit in your highly refined lobby."

"Evidently, when Ms. Naylor realized we didn't open our bar at nine in the morning, she demonstrated her unhappiness by hurling chairs over the mezzanine balcony into the lobby. Thank God no one was injured."

"Did she say anything?" Della wedged the phone between her ear and shoulder to downshift as she merged onto the freeway.

"Oh, quite a bit." The voice warmed a little. "Most of it was directed at our maître d' and then at our security guards. She evidently started drinking quite early."

"I guess so," Della said, "if she ran out by nine." Della had never seen Kat drunk, but she had seen her angry and considered the wrath of Kat a force of nature worth avoiding.

The manager confirmed that Kat was up in her room and conceded that it was possible the present quiet might indicate that

Kat had either passed out or convinced one of the staff to run over to the liquor store for her. Della believed the latter, which might work to her advantage. Kat in a stupor might be far easier than Kat in a fury.

The manager met her in the lobby and escorted her to Kat's room.

They knocked first, the manager rapping with authority and calling, "Ms. Naylor?"

They heard fumbling, heavy steps.

Kat was a mess. Bunches of hair stood at right angles to her head. Her eyes were swollen, her clothes—the ones from yesterday's meeting with Hugh Jr.—bunched and wrinkled. Della caught just a whiff of the alcohol before the door started closing.

Della caught it before it slammed shut and pushed her way into the room. "Thank you," she said to the manager as she walked toward Kat. "We'll be out of here in just a little while."

"Get out," Kat said. "You get out now."

"Can't. The cops downstairs won't let me leave without you." Della grinned, trying to ignore the smell of alcohol-based sweat. "I hear you did a little redecorating."

"Bastards!"

Kat weaved her way over to the bed and swung at the tangled covers, then sat. Her words, when she spoke again, were precise. "I am not going back to the farm." She smiled and her red eyes glittered. "You just can't keep 'em down on the farm."

"Not after we've seen Richard," Della agreed.

"Shut up!"

"Can't, Kat. You're the only one I can talk to about it. You're the only one who knows. Well, you and Hugh Junior."

Kat considered this a moment, and Della took the time to survey the room. No puddles of vomit, she inventoried. One empty bottle of pre-mixed Margaritas. That was it.

"You're . . . only one too," Kat was mumbling. "One, two." She stared up at Della.

"We can't tell Barbara," Della said.

"No." Tears welled up in Kat's eyes. "Barbara's dying. Soon they'll both be dead and it'll be just us. Us two."

"Kat . . . Richard and I . . . that was a long time after you broke up with him."

"I know."

"I thought I'd go the rest of my life without telling anyone else."

"You told Pauline."

"Wouldn't you, if you could have?"

"Tried," Kat said. "Married Grant, called her. Lunch. But she canceled. Something . . . kids. Canceled."

"I wish now I hadn't told her," Della said. "Because of the journals. But it would have driven me crazy not to tell someone."

"Yeah," Kat said dully.

"You going to fight with me if I say we should go home?" Della asked.

"No fighting." She didn't look as if she could fight anyone.

"We need to settle your bill."

"Plastic." Kat was listing as she whispered and ended curled on her side amid the covers.

Della stepped over a mass of pillows and towels to help herself to the remote control. She checked Kat, who was awake but lying peacefully, then flicked on the television and walked herself through the on-screen directions for automated checkout.

The screen displayed an impressive bar bill from the previous evening, but no charge for damage. That'll come in a letter from the lawyer, Della thought. She selected the option to add any remaining charges to Kat's credit card and ordered the bill sent to the guest's address of record, then she looked at Kat again. The problem now, Della posed, is how to move this inert mass from bed to car without rousing her to resistance.

Stepping over the pillows once more, Della seated herself at the desk and reached for the telephone. In less time than it took to formulate and say "I'll rid you quietly of this guest if you'll cooperate," the young manager was at the door with a wheelchair.

"Kat, honey," Della whispered, kneeling close to the spot where Kat's head was sliding off the bed. "Kat, honey, I'm going to take you for a ride now."

The manager, whose name was Jennifer and who must have been working out regularly, helped hoist Kat to a sitting position and then slide and drag her into the chair. As Della propped Kat up, Jennifer, in a grand gesture, swept a blanket from the bed, folded it deftly, draped it over Kat's shoulder, and tucked it securely across her body. In one motion, Della realized, this child had concealed Kat's clothing and impeded escape.

Grabbing Kat's purse as she passed,

Della backed the chair out of the room, and Jennifer motioned her toward the service hall.

"We'll just take a nice ride in this elevator." Della pushed the chair in and smiled at Jennifer, who pushed LOBBY. Della fished for her keys. "My car's right in front. The blue Accord. Can you get it to where we'll be?"

Jennifer smiled and took the keys. There was a loading dock with a ramp on which Della had only to hold the chair to brake its descent. Then they waited until the Honda appeared. You just never know, Della thought, picturing Kat at her most familiar, suited and coifed and ready to take on the world. The car stopped in front of them.

Again, Jennifer's strength made it possible to load Kat into the car. "It's almost like a big sack of flour," grunted the young manager. "Except maybe riper."

Della smiled. Looks like Kat, talks like Rita, she thought.

"I cannot thank you enough," she told the young woman. She tried to press a twenty on her, but Jennifer resisted. "There'll be too many times when no one gives you a nickel," Della insisted, tucking the bill into

Jennifer's pocket. "Indulge an old broad. Besides," she said, "I took it out of Kat's purse."

She eased the Honda through traffic, glancing now and then at her seat-belted charge. Kat's head hung to one side, her eyes were closed, and she snored a little.

Once she hit the farm-to-market to Sydonia, she started to plan her explanation to Rita and Barbara. We'll get Kat upstairs and into bed, she planned, then I'll tell them about Hugh Jr. and Castleburg and the Huttos. But not about Pauline's journals. Or why Kat's so mad.

Then I'll take a nap, Della thought. On the recliner in Kat's room. So I'll be there when she wakes up.

But Kat woke up in the car.

"Who else besides you and the real estate agent?" she asked. "Who else?"

Della shook her head. "I have no idea."

"Would you tell me if you knew?" she asked.

"Probably. But I don't know anymore. I'll tell you something: I've lived with this for a while and the truth is, I've lost my curiosity about it. What difference does it make? Don't you think," Della asked, "it's funny he could do the same thing with you and me and some real estate agent?" She paused. "And Barbara."

"Who could?" Kat complained. "I used to think he just put up with her, but since she's been there . . . I don't know, she's not just some fat slob he ended up married to."

"No."

"But she's not like either one of us. And we're pretty different from each other."

Della grinned. "And he loved sticking his dick into all of us!"

She expected a strenuous protest, but Kat only gazed out the window and returned a muttered, "Yeah, he did."

"It was a lot more important to us, that's all. We thought it was meaningful. Maybe he did too, but not nearly the same way."

"It seemed pretty meaningful when it was happening," Kat said.

"I think that's what growing older means," Della advised. "You learn how time puts everything in its place. That body we thought was so glorious, that brought us so much pleasure? First it rotted, then it crumbled to dust. You could probably crush a fistful of his bones into powder now, that man who mattered so much to us."

Barbara was sitting on the porch when they pulled up to the Ladies Farm. Several guests were seated with her, and Della guessed she was reading them their horoscopes. *Be cautious with family member,* Della recited silently. *Romantic relationship heats up. What seemed a problem will furnish its own solution.* She pulled the car around to the back and they went in through the kitchen.

"I'm taking a shower and then a nap," Kat announced, heading for the stairs.

There was a note from Rita to call Tony and a note from Barbara that she couldn't wait to hear about Della's date. And then there was the voice mail from Hugh Jr. instructing Della to call him immediately. "Let me know when you're done with the shower," Della called after Kat. She started for the stairs. You must have been crazy to start up with Tony again, she told herself. Absolutely crazy.

She waited until she had showered to call Hugh Jr. back. Wrapped in her terry-cloth robe, her wet hair still dripping, Della took the phone from its base in the hall and carried it into her room before she dialed his number. Hugh Jr. answered on the first ring. He got right to the point. "I guess your friend Barbara told you she's offered me two-ninety."

"I . . . we haven't talked," Della replied, seating herself on the bed.

"She's really determined to hand that property over to you," Hugh Jr. said. "It's touching."

"Hugh," Della said, "Honey, I know how tough all this has been on you."

He laughed. "You're all the same, all that sympathy crap. Look, you don't know a thing about me or my life. All you know is that I have half of something you want and Barbara's got the other half. And you're playing us both for all it's worth."

Della closed her eyes a moment and took a deep breath. "Hugh," she started again, "what I'm trying to say is that I know, and I'm sure she told you, that Barbara is very sorry for what happened with your dad. But Hugh, that was a long time ago and you can't—"

"I don't care who's sorry," Hugh Jr. cut her off. "I'm just interested in getting done with this . . . getting done and maximizing

Mom and Dad's investment for Melissa and me."

"Hugh, what is it you want?"

"Barbara's offered me two-ninety. Why don't you offer three-fifty? That way, you can have the Ladies Farm and I won't tell Barbara you screwed her husband."

"Hugh," she started again, then stopped. Della had run out of responses.

"Think about it," he urged her. "It's your shot to get what you want: giving me what I want."

She held the phone away from her for a second, stared at it, then spoke into it. "Good-bye, Hugh," Della said.

Chapter 14

It was Saturday evening before Barbara, Della, and Rita gathered in the office. The guests had followed a dinner of beef Burgundy and crusty bread with a walk to the movie theater on the square.

"Kat's sleeping like a baby," Barbara reported as she sailed in.

"If your baby snorts in like a hog and whistles out like someone's grandfather," Rita amended.

"Hugh Junior's not going to be easy," Della announced to Rita and Barbara to get things started. "He's got a great offer from

Castleburg—two-eighty for his half, five-sixty for the whole property."

Rita looked shocked, but Della could tell that Barbara was not surprised. "I met with him for breakfast," said Barbara. "He thinks his ship's come in; not only does he want me to sell to Castleburg, he wants to forego the cash for a percentage of the gross."

"Unless, of course, we offer him even more cash. His latest call to me ups the ante to three-fifty."

"Three-fifty! For half?" Rita slapped Barbara's arm. "Honey, you're sitting on a gold mine!" She turned to Della. "Count me out. I'm not buying the Ladies Farm for seven hundred thousand dollars!"

"No one is," Della rejoined.

"Why don't you just move the Ladies Farm to another big house on the Nolan?" Barbara asked. "Or a big house in some other town?"

"Move the Ladies Farm?" Della reacted in mock horror, then slipped into an Irish brogue. "Why Scarlett O'Hara, land's the only thing in the world that amounts to anything, and we'll not be partin' with any piece o' it!"

"Well, Barbara's got a point," Rita said. "You might . . . we might do better with a less expensive piece of land."

"This is the Ladies Farm," Della said. "This house is perfect for the Ladies Farm, our barn is perfect for Ladies Farm classes, our riverfront is perfect for Ladies Farm canoeing, and our kitchen and dining room are perfect for Ladies Farm meals. If we have to, we'll go somewhere else. But for right now, we're staying here."

"Until I die, you mean?" Barbara's expression showed how well she understood Della's intent.

"Oh, honey," Rita started, "I'm sure that's not what she meant."

"It's exactly what I meant," said Della. "It's what we want, and I don't want you worrying about it."

"Besides, you shouldn't worry about anything," Rita chimed. "That's the worst thing you should be doing, it'll just, you'll just—"

"Die faster," Barbara said. "I don't want to die any faster than I have to. But I will worry if I think you're bankrupting yourselves because of some silliness about keeping a roof over my head. I can afford my own roof. And I can afford to do the right thing about the Ladies Farm." She took a breath. "I've already called my lawyer."

"What do you mean?" Della asked.

"I told you," Barbara said simply. "I'm transferring my interest to you and Kat. And you, Rita, if you all are agreed to that."

"We're agreed," Della said quickly. "But Barbara, the more I think about it, the—"

"There's nothing for you to think about." Barbara's expression, so self-contained and clear-eyed, unsettled Della. "My lawyer's working on some way of minimizing taxes, which is hard because it will precede my death so closely." She smiled apologetically and shook her head. "We— Richard and I—we should have done this long ago."

"If you had done this while Pauline was alive," Della observed, "Hugh Junior would control the whole thing now."

"Barbara, honey, how could you have known how it'd turn out," Rita jumped in. She stroked Barbara's shoulder, then turned back to Della. "And who'd have guessed Pauline's son would turn out to be such a little shit!"

"He just sees his chance to prove he's all

grown up," Barbara observed. "He's a good boy. He's just—"

"He's just a greedy bastard," Della broke in. "Don't make excuses for him. He sees a place to make a killing and he's making it."

"Well, he's killing us with it," Rita grumbled, then turned back to Barbara. "Oh, I'm sorry, honey, I shouldn't be saying 'killing' in front of you."

Barbara smiled. "Oh, stop worrying about that." She sighed. "But I do wish Hugh Junior were less bitter."

Della couldn't stand it. "Would you stop worrying about Hugh Junior! This isn't about anything you or I or anyone else did to traumatize him. And," she took a breath, anxious to steer the subject away from Barbara, "it's clearly not what his mother envisioned for the Ladies Farm. So let's get back to the question: Can we meet Castleburg's offer?"

"Even if I had the money, which I don't," Rita answered, "I'd never pay that much for this property. I wonder what he's offering old Gladys Hutto, if he's offering us this much."

Della waved a hand to dismiss the issue.

"I'm sure he's settled on some price per acre, plus an appraisal of the house."

"Maybe she would sell to you," Barbara suggested.

"Gladys Hutto?" Della asked. She looked to Rita, and Rita shrugged.

"I can ask Dave to talk with her. It's worth a shot."

"Even if they'll talk to us," Della said, "we haven't got the money."

"Of course," Barbara posited, "if the Huttos sell to you, young Hugh's deal with Castleburg won't go through."

Della frowned, looked at Barbara. "I'd forgotten that," Della acknowledged. "I guess it hinges on his delivering the whole thing, doesn't it? Our share, his share, and the Huttos."

"So all we need's a fortune to buy out the Huttos," Rita summed up.

"What we need," said Della, "is enough delay that Castleburg decides the only place he can dig is his."

"And a fortune," said Rita.

"And a fortune," Della concurred. "And . . . and . . ." she tilted her head to one side, "a visit to Melissa."

They sat looking at each other for a moment, piecing it together. Finally, Barbara spoke. "I think that's a wonderful idea!" Her eyes glowed. "Take a few days and go visit Melissa in California."

"You sure you want to go through with this?" Rita asked. "You sure you're not moving back into Fort Worth with Tony?"

"How'd that go?" Barbara chimed in. She looked incredibly cheerful. "Tell us what happened."

"Shoot! We know what happened. She and Tony staggered up the steps this morning, and she could barely walk!" Rita glowed with her own wit.

"So you're going out again?" Barbara asked.

"I don't know," Della said. "I don't know anything. I'm certainly not moving into Fort Worth," she told Rita. Della grinned. "After all, Eli Castleburg may regret his hasty marriage and try me again." She held up a hand to forestall more of Rita's opinion on how she should live her life and added, for Barbara's benefit, "Tony and I will probably go out again. But I don't think it's that serious."

"Spending the night together's pretty serious," Barbara said.

"She means serious with her heart, not her crotch," Rita answered on Della's behalf.

After wishing Rita and Della goodnight, Barbara climbed the stairs to her room, grateful that, after this weekend, she could move into the room downstairs. She knew Rita had gone over to Dave's, which meant that it was Della whom she heard knocking around in the kitchen. Barbara pushed Kat's door open, peeked in, and smiled at the racket. Still snoring, Barbara thought, closing the door again and continuing to her room.

On her vanity sat a box made of Popsicle sticks glued together and decorated with crayoned hearts. Barbara lifted the lid and removed the velvet bag that sat inside. Then she made her way back down the stairs.

Della was on the phone in the kitchen. "Tony, I don't know when. Okay? I'm sorry. I'll call you. I promise." She was walking around the kitchen as she spoke, pulling out muffin tins and uncovering the commercial mixer. Barbara stood at the kitchen entrance and watched, nodding to Della as

Della saw her and waved a hand to acknowledge her presence.

"Of course I want to, Tony. But I've got to take care of this. I'll call you." She shook her head and smiled sadly at Barbara. "Me, too. Bye."

"I hate that!" Della exclaimed, slamming a stainless steel mixing bowl onto the counter and fumbling the receiver back into its cradle. Della opened the recipe notebook out on the counter.

"Baking?" Barbara asked.

"Baking therapy now," Della replied. "Muffins. Starting with zucchini." She yanked a knife from the magnetic bar over the counter. "The way I feel, I might just bake them all, starting with zucchini all the way back to apple!"

As Della walked over to the refrigerator and pulled a sack of zucchini from a lower shelf, Barbara sighed and pocketed the velvet bag. "I'll help if you want," she offered.

"Oh! Barbara, you don't have to. I'm just working off steam! Why don't you have some tea and keep me company?"

Barbara plugged in the kettle, then

pulled a stool up to the counter. "Thanks," she said. "Want a cup?"

"Maybe later," Della replied.

She watched Della hack up the zucchini and run it through the food processor. In her few weeks at the Ladies Farm, Barbara had taken on the project of reworking the recipes in the notebook, devising low-fat versions of favorites based on substitutions of yogurt, applesauce, and skim milk for butter, oil, and eggs. She saw the project as a fitting cap to her life, putting to good use at last the knowledge gleaned through a lifetime of failed diets.

The water boiled and Barbara made herself tea. She watched Della as she worked, but neither one of them said much. Occasionally, Della would shake her head and press her lips together as if she were holding her ground in some fierce debate, but for the most part the silence was comfortable, broken only by the bustling arrival and cheery goodnights of their guests returning from their movie.

By the time Della had mixed the ingredients, Barbara had finished her tea. Barbara had planned to spray the muffin tins, but she found herself still perched atop the stool as Della lined the tins up on the counter and uncapped the no-stick spray.

"I'm thinking we need a little more flavor in that batter," Barbara said finally. "Lemon. Maybe a little ginger."

Della turned toward her. "Want to try now?" Her eyes were round and green, except that they tilted upward slightly at the outside, giving every suggestion—even an invitation to alter the taste of muffin batter—a faintly seductive undertone. Della's gaze always offered mischief, Barbara thought now. A willingness to test the limits for the laughs the challenge might produce.

Della reached up into a hanging basket where they kept dried things and retrieved a ginger root. "Let's grate this," she suggested.

"And a little lemon, too." Barbara peered into the bowl to measure what was needed. Before she could climb down from the stool, Della had retrieved a lemon, sliced it in half and was squeezing it over a sieve.

Della grated and stirred. She held a spoon with the batter to Barbara's lips for an approving taste, and Barbara nodded as she picked up a slight tang that would intensify in the baking. Then Della poured the batter.

"We have to make a note in the file," Barbara said. "Two teaspoons of the ginger. Then if it works, I'll redo it on the computer."

Once the muffins were in the oven, they made more tea.

"Want to sit outside?" Della invited. "We can light the citronella."

They made their way over the damp lawn to the wooden chairs. Barbara set the candle down and Della lit it, then they seated themselves on either side of the tiny table. They listened to the steady burble of the river ahead of them, and Della leaned her head back to look at the sky, where the stars were undimmed by the quarter moon.

"I love this," she said.

"Me too," Barbara agreed. She snuggled deeper into the chair. "Richard and I used to go to a spa in California, and every night we sat in this hot tub—our very own private one, on the patio of our cottage—and it was on the side of a cliff overlooking the ocean. All you could see were stars and all you could hear was the surf."

Through the darkness, Barbara could

see Della bite her lip. Finally Della replied, "I was at a place like that once: Costa Verde, south of Santa Cruz."

"That's it!" Barbara said, warming with the memory. "Richie and I thought of it as our own special place. Even when I knew about . . . you know . . . the others . . . the women..." damn! Why was this so hard? "even then it seemed that everything was okay if we could just get back up to those hot tubs in those hills." She stopped and found that she was trembling, but she had to go on.

"Della," Barbara said, "Della, I have to ask you to do something. Something important." Barbara took another breath and reached into her pocket. "When you visit Melissa—"

"Oh, Barbara," Della interrupted, "you want me to go back to Costa Verde?"

"Oh! No, no—no!" Barbara hurried to ease Della's mind. "Nothing like that. Nothing at all like that. It's just that…" She fingered the velvet bag. "I need you to conduct a financial transaction for me. It won't be hard," she instructed, "and it won't take too long, though it'll add a day or two to your trip." She was reciting now, exactly as she had rehearsed it. "And I'll pay for your airfare!"

"What's this about, Barbara?" Della's voice was politely curious, maybe indulgent.

Barbara withdrew her hand from her pocket and held out the velvet bag. "Here," she whispered. "There's a jeweler in New York who will buy these from you."

There was enough light from the candle to see Della's outstretched hand, palm up beneath the proffered prize. "What is this?"

"They're from Richard," Barbara said, and suddenly she had to tell it all.

"What?"

"They're from Richard."

"They, what? What are they?"

"They're what he gave me . . . over the years . . . whenever he . . . whenever we . . . we would fight about it. I would hear or see something, there'd be a phone call or something in the car, something, and then I'd follow him, or find out, and we'd fight and he'd promise not to do it again, and he'd start bringing me flowers and perfume and then we'd go to California and he'd fish out a diamond."

"Diamonds? This bag is full of diamonds?" Della had pulled the velvet sack away, and Barbara guessed she was opening it in her lap. She could see Della's outline, the line of her forearm and wrist, the hand disappearing into the bulk of the little velvet bag.

"There are twenty-three of them," Barbara said. "Not that there were twenty-three women," she explained quickly, "just maybe twenty-three arguments."

"Richard gave you these?"

Barbara nodded. "Yes."

"Gifts from Richard? Twenty-three diamonds? No wonder you stayed with him."

"No! Good God! You think I stayed because of diamonds?"

"Oh, Barbara, I'm sorry, I didn't mean that. I just . . . I don't know what to say about this. I've heard of making up, but this—"

"We didn't make up." Barbara couldn't control the trembling. "We never made up, really, we just kept on and on." She could feel her tears rolling, but she had control of her voice, so she continued. "He'd wait till he was sure . . . you know, that I still loved him and that I wanted to stay together. So the diamond was . . . it, you know, symbolized our love."

"Symbolized your love?" Della's voice was made for this skepticism.

"Everlasting," Barbara told her. She made her own voice light, airy. "You know: Diamonds are forever."

Della gave a little snort, but said nothing. Barbara could hear little clicking sounds as Della wiggled her fingers in the diamonds.

"Is this one, this really big one, is this a diamond too?"

"Yeah."

"It's really big. I can't wait to see this in the light."

Barbara sat without responding.

"I don't think I've ever seen a diamond this big!"

Barbara sighed. "Neither had I."

"You must . . . what did you say when he gave you these? Especially this one?" Della's voice was filled with wonder and Barbara had to concede it was an improvement over the earlier sarcasm.

"What was there to say? I told you: They're diamonds Richard gave me. So he could keep seeing other women. And I took them."

"Oh, Barbara!"

Barbara guessed Della was beginning to

feel sorry for her again. Poor Barbara, Richard's fat wife. "It's true."

"But you loved him."

"Yeah."

"And who wouldn't?"

"Evidently no one," Barbara said. "Evidently I was one of a small crowd." She heard Della take in a sharp breath. It didn't matter. Barbara just wanted to get done what needed doing. "Everyone loved Richard," Barbara continued. "And now he's gone. And I've got these diamonds. And they can help us. They can help us with the Ladies Farm if you'll take them to this man who knew Richard."

Alone in her room, Della took a handkerchief from her dresser drawer and spread it atop her dresser, then poured the diamonds onto the square of fabric. She counted and recounted. Twenty-three. Twenty-three arguments between Barbara and Richard. Twenty-three attempts to make their marriage everlasting. Twenty-three times Richard had told his wife that their love was forever.

She lifted the big diamond and held it up to the light. It was a marquise and she turned it different ways to see its edges. This was probably the first time, Della theorized. The real estate agent. When he thought he was only making this apology once.

She shook her head, placing the diamond back on the dresser. Once he realized how many he'd need, he probably bought them wholesale, worked out some sort of volume discount, went for quantity instead of quality. Della breathed out hard, then carefully pulled up the edges of the handkerchief and guided the stones back into the little velvet bag.

You promised, Della reminded herself as she pulled the drawstrings and tucked the thing into her shoulder bag hanging on the door hook. You promised Barbara you'd do this and now you have to. You have to follow the instructions she gave you and see the man she told you to see.

She tiptoed down the hall to check on Kat, who still slept soundly. Della stared at the recliner. I'll have to tell Kat about the diamonds, she thought, and felt far too weary to spend the night anywhere but her own bed. Somewhere down the road, Della promised silently.

Della crept back to her own room, thinking for only a second before she climbed into bed how unimportant Kat's reaction had become in the scheme of things.

The next morning, the guests snapped up the lemon- and ginger-enhanced muffins and Barbara gave Della a thumbs-up. She looked livelier this morning, Della thought, but maybe it was just makeup. And all that jade, Della thought, watching the sunlight flicker off Barbara's dangling earrings.

The guests were following Barbara out to the barn. Della knew that Nancy had helped lay out all the jewelry supplies, and that everything stood ready for the morning's enameling workshop. "All I have to do is sit and talk," Barbara had reassured them before she trooped out with her charges.

Kat had made her appearance without drama and now cleared the table and cleaned the kitchen with Della in harmonious silence. When they retreated to the office, Della told Kat what she thought they ought to do.

"Buy out the Huttos, kill the Castleburg deal?" Kat repeated. "How much is that going to cost us?"

"A lot. I thought we'd split three ways—you, Rita, and me—and I think we should send Dave."

"Dave?" Kat only looked half-awake, so her eye-widening seemed extreme.

"Dave Eleston, Rita's ex-husband."

"I know which Dave," Kat said. "I just don't know why."

"Because he's Gladys Hutto's great-nephew and they know him. He and Earl's father played football together."

"Ah, yes," Kat recollected. "The Sydonia Sabers."

"Well, it's something," Della said.

"And are you planning to barter with buttons and zucchini bread?"

"No. I have some cash. Do you?"

"A little," Kat confessed. "I'd hate to have to cash any CDs, though; you know how the penalties are. Maybe we could pay it out."

"Maybe. Plus Barbara's going to help. But I'm not sure how much."

"There's a delightful prospect." Kat shielded her eyes with her hand as if she were blocking strong sun rather than conversing in a shaded room. "I love the idea of being indebted to Richard's widow."

"It's not like that."

"No?" Kat shook her head. "Is there anymore ibuprofen in that desk?"

"How much have you taken so far?"

"Never mind. Just see if there is."

Della fished around in the center desk drawer, then tried the small one on the right. "Here," she said, handing over the white bottle. She watched in silence as Kat downed two of the pain relievers without water.

Kat glared at her. "This hangover's on you, you know."

"I know."

"Can't you even say you're sorry?"

"Kat, I've said it. Over and over. I'm sorry this hurt you, I'm sorry Barbara's here, I'm sorry Barbara's dying, I'm sorry, sorry, sorry."

"Except about Richard. Are you sorry about Richard?"

Della shook her head.

Kat looked at her. "I'm not either."

Della shook her head again. "I didn't expect you to be," she told Kat. "But I am sorry that it hurt Barbara. I didn't know . . . I guess I never thought about that part."

"There's something else," Kat said.

"What's that?"

"I appreciate your coming to get me yesterday."

"Yeah?" Della smiled at her friend.

"Yeah."

"Listen," Della said, "we've got one other thing we can try."

"What's that?"

"I'm going to talk to Melissa. Maybe she can talk to Hugh Junior."

"What are you going to tell her?" All the hung-over raspiness had vanished from Kat's voice. The question was low and clear and even.

"Everything," said Della.

Chapter 15

Melissa and her husband lived in the hills south of San Jose. Melissa's husband left for work around seven-thirty; Melissa drove the boys to school at eight-fifteen. She returned, pulling the silver minivan up behind the trees that probably blocked a carport, at eight-forty. Della, sitting around a curve in a rental car, gave Melissa five minutes before she pulled her own car to the front of the house, climbed two flights of steps to the entrance, and rang the doorbell.

This is a child who did well, Della thought, studying the heavy wooden door and turning toward the well-landscaped hill on which the house sat. Or at least married well. She heard movement on the other side of the door: indistinct sounds, then steps, then a silence of studying Della through the peephole, then the tumbling of locks. "Aunt Dell," the girl said, stepping backward.

She has to know, thought Della as she entered, that I'm not delivering good news.

"I've come to ask for your help," she told Melissa. They stood in a wood-paneled entryway. To her right, Della could see a living room with a hearth and an expanse of textured wall.

Melissa led her in the opposite direction, to a large kitchen with an oversized circle of a table.

"Have you talked to Hugh?" Della asked once they were seated, with cups of herbal tea and a platter of oatmeal raisin cookies before them.

"He's told me about the gravel mining," Melissa said. She fiddled with the embroidered collar of her denim work shirt. "Is there more?"

Della nodded and set down her cup. "I need to start with the worst news," she said. "Barbara is dying. She has ovarian cancer."

"Oh, no!" Melissa leaned toward Della. "Poor Aunt Barbara. Is she very sick? When did she find out?"

"She's known for a while. But she didn't want to tell us until she felt sure Dickie had agreed to move to Houston. Evidently, moving to the Ladies Farm was her way to convince him she'd be taken care of and that he should go on with his life."

"She seemed fine at the funeral," Melissa recollected. "Getting her hair cut and all. Isn't there something they could do: chemo or something?"

Della shook her head. "She's explored her options. Dickie's helped. But there's really nothing for her," Della said.

Melissa shook her head slowly. "She was always so sweet to me," she recalled. "When I wanted to go to school out of state, she was the only one who told me to go for it. 'Just try,' she said. 'If you can get accepted, you'll find a way to raise the money.' And she was right."

Della grinned. "Well, you were sort of everyone's daughter. The rest of us just had sons."

"Oh, I'll never forget the screaming—I mean screaming—argument they had over her."

"They who?"

"My folks. *What right did Barbara have to be advising their child!*"

"Who said that?"

"Oh, my father, of course."

"Your father?"

"Oh yeah. You should have seen my mom trying to calm him down. 'She's interfering in our family!'" Melissa lowered her voice and pressed her chin toward her chest in imitation. "'Just because they have more money than God,' blah, blah, blah! And of course, I was in tears, I just wanted to apply to Stanford, see if I could get in, try for scholarship money. And Dad, who was always so . . . you know, go for it! There was Daddy saying *don't you dare!*" Melissa held her hands in the air and smiled. "But I dared anyway and Daddy loved it and I guess I'm really sorry to hear about Aunt Barbara. What a shame. Is there . . . did you come because you need my help?"

"Yes." Della sipped a little more tea, uncertain now about how to proceed.

"You need money?"

"Oh, no," Della said. "I mean, not that we don't need money. But this is about costing us less . . . and maybe about your making less."

"Then this must be about the Ladies Farm." Melissa waved a hand to stop Della's explanation. "I knew Hugh was wrong about that gravel business."

"Well, the gravel business is only part of it." Della, with her elbows propped on the table, opened her hands palms up and extended them toward Melissa. "Hugh . . . Hugh is very angry with us. And he sees a chance to make a lot of money . . . for you, too, Melissa. So he's changed his mind about letting us buy out your mother's interest in the Ladies Farm."

"He told me that he had an offer from Castlebury Dairy," Melissa recalled. "But he told me you all could meet the offer and he'd take it."

"Well, he did say that." Della studied Melissa, who exhibited confusion but no rancor. "But he actually wants a little more than Castleburg's offering. Did he mention that?"

"No," said Melissa. "Why would he do that?"

Della chuckled and leaned forward a little, holding Melissa's gaze. "Honey, Hugh sees a way to make y'all a lot of money, but it does involve throwing us off the Ladies Farm. And it's pretty risky."

"But we agreed we want you all to have the Ladies Farm!"

Della pressed her lips together. "I know. But your brother learned some things that might justify a change of heart, at least in his mind. I'm hoping you don't agree. But Melissa," Della said, "I think you should hear what those things are."

Melissa threw her hands up in surrender. "Go ahead, Aunt Dell. Shock me."

"Barbara had a one-night stand with your father. And I had a long, long affair with Richard. Morrison."

Melissa stared.

"Shocked yet?"

Melissa nodded but stayed silent.

"The business between Barbara and your dad was a one-time event that shook everyone up, and they all—your mom and dad and the Morrisons—settled back down and remained friends. Good friends," Della said emphatically.

"And you and Uncle Richard?" Melissa's voice was quiet and quavered only a little.

Della wished for the millionth time that Hugh and Pauline had not insisted on those stupid aunt and uncle titles. It made everything sound more incestuous. "That was a little more involved," Della said.

"Does Aunt Barbara know?"

Della shook her head. "Not about me. And, no matter what happens between us or with Hugh, I am asking you to promise that you'll never tell her. She thinks . . . we are her friends. No matter what happened. We're the ones she came to. It wouldn't do any good, it would be cruel, to ever tell her that the ones she trusted most—"

"Well, I certainly won't ever tell," Melissa said. "But I don't really see why Hugh would be mad at you."

"Oh," Della waved a hand in the air, "he's not mad, just disgusted, maybe. And he sees it as a way to make a little extra."

"What do you mean?"

Quickly, Della ran through the choices Hugh Jr. had given her: Either she, with or without the others, paid a ridiculous price for the Ladies Farm, or Hugh Jr. threw them out, sold to Castleburg, and exposed her secret to Barbara.

"Hugh wouldn't do that!"

Della said nothing and waited for Melissa to consider the situation.

"He said he would?" Melissa queried. Della nodded. Then Melissa changed gears and grinned. "What did he say about Dad and Aunt Barbara? And how did he find out, anyway?"

"You know, Melissa, your mother," Della drew in a sharp breath, "your mother was our confidante. We told her everything. It's just that none of us was *her* confidante." She shook her head. "She had her journals. She told her journals. That's where Hugh found out about that one night."

Melissa reached toward her, but Della shook her off. "That's where Hugh read about your mother's shock on seeing Barbara's ring . . . that first day that Barbara showed up. Richard had it made from a large amethyst your dad gave him. Your mother . . . when she saw it she said she didn't know Hugh—your father—had given it to Richard. It must have shocked her, Melissa."

"Well, of course. Thinking about Daddy and Barbara—" Melissa broke off in a giggle. "Aunt Barbara and Daddy! I can't believe it!"

"Believe it," Della advised, not sure what was so amusing but fearing it might be the sheer improbability to Melissa that her father or any of his contemporaries could have had sex, let alone illicit sex with friends' spouses or spouses' friends.

"Where did this happen? At our house? At the Morrisons'? Don't say Daddy took her to some motel!"

"Melissa, I don't know the details. I only know what Barbara told me, which is that it happened once; it caused Richard, in her opinion, to become wildly unfaithful; it helped your parents decide to move out of the city; and the shock of recalling it—or maybe the shock of seeing Barbara's amethyst—may have contributed to your mother's heart attack. At least, that's what your brother seems to think." Della shook her head. "To be honest, it was one night a long time ago and hardly a reason to deny a dying woman a little peace."

Melissa shook her head. "You're saying

Mother died of shock? From recalling Daddy's little fling with Aunt Barbara?"

"I'm saying that's what your brother believes. Maybe. Which may make it a whole lot easier in his mind to mine gravel at the Ladies Farm." She took a breath. "The reason I came here, Melissa . . . the reason I need your help . . . is that we want to keep the Ladies Farm. We have to keep the Ladies Farm. Because, Melissa, you understand: We need a place for Barbara to die."

"I didn't think of that." Melissa slumped back in her chair, and her gaze fixed on the wildflowers that adorned the tabletop. Bluebonnets. Wine cups. Indian paintbrush. Yellow coreopsis. Pressed flat, then laminated.

Della waited.

"I don't . . . why can't we just wait until . . . we don't have to do this gravel deal immediately."

Della spoke gently. "The Castleburg offer goes away if Hugh can't deliver in time to dig pretty much all together."

"Maybe we could sign the deal but not dig right away," Melissa offered.

"Maybe," Della acknowledged. "But I think it has to do with the economies of mining the whole thing at one time. In any case, this deal kills the Ladies Farm." Della felt her eyes starting to brim and turned slightly from Melissa's gaze. Who would have guessed she'd wax sentimental over a marginal bed and breakfast in a nothing town?

"Oh, I'll talk to Hugh." Melissa waved a hand in the air as she spoke. "Surely he can delay the gravel mining at least until ... you know, until Aunt Barbara dies."

Della choked back her alarm. "Of course. Talk to your brother. If there's any way to get him to relent, we should try that."

"You don't think he will?" Melissa stood up and took both tea mugs with her to the sink. "Do you want more tea?"

"Look, you know him lots better than I do." Della stood and stretched.

"Do you want to buy us out?" Melissa asked.

Della smiled at Melissa. "It's become home, you know. Of course, we could barely meet the Castleburg offer. I don't know how we . . . how I . . . can pay the price for his silence too."

Melissa turned from the stove where she had set the kettle. "I'll talk to Hugh," Melissa said again.

Della resumed her study of the kitchen. It was a white and gray no-nonsense workroom, with a sink and grill-equipped island and a large window overlooking a redwood deck. But the counters were topped with canisters shaped like cartoon characters, and children's drawings adorned the stainless steel refrigerator and the bulletin board over the built-in desk.

The tea kettle whistled the end of their break. In a few minutes they were back at the table. Neither one of them had touched the cookies.

Melissa sipped tentatively from her steaming mug and drew back from the heat. "What is it you want me to do?"

"Sell us your interest in the Ladies Farm."

"To you and Aunt Kat?"

"And Rita."

"And Rita," Melissa repeated.

"We'll pay the full appraisal," Della hastened to assure her. "You won't really lose a penny. It just won't be gravel money."

Melissa shook her head. "I don't know. I have to talk to Hugh."

"What do you think Hugh will do when you tell him you want him to sell to us at the appraisal price?" Della queried.

"I guess he won't be happy," Melissa conceded. "But I think if I talk to him . . . after all, it's half mine. If I don't sell with him, and Aunt Barbara doesn't sell, then . . ."

"Then it all falls apart," Della finished. "Unless, of course, Hugh can convince Barbara she has a reason to join—"

"Oh, my God! Aunt Dell! You think he'll tell . . . oh, he couldn't do that!"

Of course he could! Of course he would! she wanted to scream, but Della merely pressed her lips together and looked at Melissa.

"He'd tell her?" Melissa shook her head. When Della didn't reply, Melissa said, "I can't just sell to you. Without at least talking to my brother, hearing his side. And Greg," she said as if just remembering she had a husband. "I have to talk to Greg."

"I won't push you, Melissa." Della

reached out to stroke Melissa's hand as it rested on the table. "But I want you to understand, it's not for myself. I mean, I'll be embarrassed if Hugh tells secrets," she closed her eyes for a second, trying not to imagine it, trying not to see Barbara's face, "but for Barbara, it would be the worst thing we could do to her. The worst thing I could do. And that's so cruel, Melissa. No matter how anyone feels about Barbara."

"No one wants to hurt Aunt Barbara," Melissa said. "But I can't . . . it's . . . I have to think about it."

"I understand," Della told her. "I'll wait to hear from you."

"Oh, Aunt Dell, I'm so sorry!" Melissa was beside her now, her soft hair brushing Della's face, her arm strong around her shoulder. "Oh, God! Of course I won't tell anyone, ever!"

Della put a hand out and drew the girl's head to her chest. She stroked the soft mane saved by Barbara's buzz cut and tried to remember how hard it was to lose people you love. Jamie's image—Jamie the way he'd been when he played with Melissa Freschatte and Dickie Morrison—blurred her vision and the feel of Melissa's hair made all those children seem real to her. "Your mother loved you so much," she told Melissa, holding her and rocking her. "So very much."

Della had no idea how long they stayed locked like that, but eventually Melissa pulled away and sat back up. "This is just a lot to deal with," she said, shaking her head and rubbing at her eyes. Like Pauline, she wore no makeup and her eyes, even red from crying, were round and luminous.

Della smiled weakly. "Life is full of surprises."

"Surprises!" Melissa laughed. "These are like explosions! No wonder Hugh's so mad!" Her tone grew confidential. "You know, it's always a surprise to learn you're not the center of your parents' universe. Taylor got up in the middle of the night one night and came down to get a drink and saw us dancing—oh, I mean jumping around, singing disco tunes and laughing . . . we were hysterical—and just got furious. I think he felt we'd betrayed him, having fun together like that, without him!"

"At least you had your clothes on."

Melissa shot her a quick look. "Yes. We do manage to do that in front of the kids."

Della looked down at the table and ran her hand over the surface. If you paid attention, you could feel that it wasn't perfectly flat, as if the laminate had followed the contours of some landscape, forming subtle swells and valleys. "You know," she said slowly, "we burdened your mother with our secrets. I did and I know the others did, too. She was such a good friend, such a trustworthy confidante. It's funny: In all this, the hardest part has been not having your mother to talk to."

"Yeah." Melissa reached over and took her hand. Then she looked at her own table. "You like this?" she asked. She motioned at the wildflowers. "Mom pressed these for me for over a year, then brought them to me right after Taylor was born." She gathered the cups and the plate of cookies and took them over to the sink.

Della read the signal to leave, and rose.

"That surface is almost indestructible." Melissa chatted on as she rinsed the mugs and put the cookies back in a blown-glass cookie jar. She returned to the table with a damp rag and wiped nonexistent crumbs from the tabletop.

Della exited no less anxious than she

had arrived, telling Melissa, as she hugged her once more, what a wonderful child she was and how much joy she had brought her mother.

"I'll call you," Melissa promised her, walking her onto the landing for the long staircase down the hill. "I won't do anything that—well, I'll try not to—hurt anyone. You, Aunt Barb, my brother..."

Della gave Melissa a quick kiss and stroked her cheek. "You take care," Della said. "I'll wait to hear from you."

"You're going home now?" Melissa asked.

"No," Della said, starting down the redwood steps. "New York. More business. Then home."

Chapter 16

She had booked a plain, midtown hotel. It was hosting a convention of community theater directors and, when asked if she were attending, Della replied yes without hesitation, thereby qualifying for the convention rate.

Early conventioneers were invited to assemble in the lobby for a look at a new off-Broadway drama by a promising young playwright. That should fit the bill, Della thought, shouldering her bag and marching to the elevator. She had no intention of spending a night in New York alone in her room.

The room, which offered a view of a brick wall and, far below, some sort of paved utility area, was clean and, by New York standards, spacious. Della checked the lock and secured the chain and pulled the drapes against what little sunlight reached her room. Then, seated on the bed, she unzipped her duffel and rummaged inside until she retrieved the velvet bag.

Carefully, Della poured the diamonds onto the handkerchief she had left in the bag. She spread them against the cloth and tried to imagine Richard as he presented each one to Barbara. Were they at dinner? In the car? Did he slip it onto her dessert plate when she'd gone to the ladies' room?

Della picked up the marquise and balanced it on the back of her ring finger, imagining it in a gold setting. Something simple, she thought. Maybe just baguettes on either side.

There are politics to diamonds, she reminded herself. Their value is inflated by a tightly controlled market. Their sparkle is dimmed by the exploitation of the workers laboring in the mines. Their meaning has been shaped by ad campaigns.

Still balancing the diamond, Della turned her hand a little. Even in the dim light, the stone sparkled.

Something that lasts, she imagined him saying. Something of value. He would place it on Barbara's breakfast tray when he brought it in the morning, the way she had described to Della. And Barbara would clutch it close to her, and keep it where no one could see, bringing it out when she needed the reminder that he was her husband forever.

It's just a lump of coal squeezed tight, Della thought, tucking the marquise back in the velvet pouch. A man could give you a million of them and it wouldn't mean anything.

Carefully, she replaced the rest of the stones in the pouch and placed the pouch in her shoulder bag. You're just a hick from Texas, Della thought. No one expects you to carry an evening bag.

She showered and dressed, then joined a group in the lobby. They walked together to a small restaurant featuring Jamaican food.

"I wish we had one of these in Tulsa," the man next to her commented. They were eating jerked chicken and a vegetable medley, the contents of which Della could not identify. She smiled and nodded at the man, whose name was Tom. "So, which theater are you with?" he asked.

"Oh, none really. I'm just along for the ride. My, uh, friend, Pauline Freschatte, directs a theater in Fort—uh—Wayne— you know, Indiana—and she invited me to be her roommate here. It's a treat for me."

"Oh, I'll have to look for her in the work-shops," he said.

"Yes. I told her I'd give her a full report on this production since she couldn't be here."

The charade worked for the length of the evening. Not much of a deception for a woman of her experience, but, Della reflected, the perfect way to keep her mind occupied the night before she sold the diamonds.

As an exercise in thoroughness, she penned a note to Pauline on hotel sta-tionery when she returned to her room. *Thin plot, clever dialogue, minimal set investment, three-character cast. Con-sider it.*

In the morning, before she checked out, Della set fire to the note with a book of

hotel matches and watched the ashes settle into the bathroom sink. Then she shoul-
dered her bags and left.

Barbara had written the man's name and
address in the detailed instructions Della
carried with her. When she called, Della
learned that the man, Max Jacoby, had
died, but that his brother, David, remembered Richard and had been charged with
honoring Max's commitment to repurchase
the diamonds.

Merely stepping from the hotel lobby into
the cab exposed Della to a big dose of
exhaust fumes. Even the crisp morning
couldn't alleviate the moist, gritty feel of the
air. "A warm one today," the cab driver told
her after she gave him the address.

I should have walked, she thought,
watching pedestrians pass her as she sat
in traffic. But the image of herself travers-
ing Manhattan with a sack full of diamonds
slung over her shoulder reassured her that
she had made the correct decision.

"You shop for jewelry?" the driver asked.

"Jewelry? Perhaps. I have a business
meeting."

"Ah. Jewelry business. You like jewelry?"
Della couldn't place the lilting accent.

"My cousin has jewelry shop. Right here." He pointed to the passenger window, and Della saw a row of stores offering windows full of jumbled goods: radios, watches, handbags, shavers. "You want to meet him?"

"I'm afraid I have an appointment and must go on," Della demurred. She pictured the headlines. CABBIE HIJACKS DIAMOND QUEEN. TEXAS DIAMOND QUEEN. CABBIE & COUSIN HIJACK TEXAS DIAMOND QUEEN. FIGHTING TO SAVE FARM CLAIMS BEAUTY ON WAY TO CASH IN DIAMONDS. Well, maybe AGING BEAUTY.

"Good bargains," the driver urged, but the cab moved forward.

"Another time," Della promised. There were lots of Hasidic Jews on the street now, men in dark suits with beards and curls of hair coming out of their sideburns. And dark hats.

They walked among crowds of other New Yorkers, working women in suits and running shoes, working girls in miniskirts and blond wigs, messengers on skates looking like neon streaks in their body suits of miracle fibers.

The driver stopped the car in front of a

doorway wedged between large windows that belonged to two flanking stores. She paid the driver and overtipped a little.

There was no sign other than a metal plate bearing a street number and the words "Trade Only"; the glass door, through which she could see the empty entryway, was locked. When she rang the bell, a young man hurried in from a side hall and cracked the door. "Yes?"

"Mr. Jacoby? I'm Della Brewer."

"Yes," said the young man. "Yes, Mr. Jacoby is waiting for you."

She was ushered to an elevator, then down a carpeted hallway to a small showroom and seated in a high-backed chair before an ornately curved table. In a moment a man and a young woman entered. "Mrs. Brewer?" He looked at her outstretched hand and looked away. "I am David Jacoby."

He had no sidelocks and his head was covered only by a black skullcap, but he wore a beard, full and black. The girl with him wore a long-sleeved blouse and full skirt, and a beret over her dark hair. "Can I get you something, some tea or a glass of water?"

"Tea, please," Della replied.

"Alana will stay with you," he said, leaving them.

"It's hot out," Della found herself saying.

"Oh, yes. In the sun," the girl said. "I hope you're not offended by Uncle David. He just can't . . . we don't believe in men and women touching that way."

"You mean the handshake? He won't shake hands with a woman?"

Alana looked down, and Della regretted her incredulity. "We . . . the way we live, men and women do business and can trust each other. It's not . . . please don't think he has no regard for women in business. It's just the contact that's a problem for him."

"And that's why you're in the room?"

Alana nodded. Della breathed out hard. "I'm not insulted, just . . . you know, even in Texas, men and women shake hands. I thought . . . the Jewish people I know are always hugging and kissing."

"Yes, we do," Alana insisted. "But a woman alone, to come in and do business this way. Uncle David could never take her hand."

Della smiled as Mr. Jacoby returned with

a tray. Of course, he thought I meant hot tea, she thought, looking at the cup and saucer adorned by a lemon slice and two sugar cubes. She'd forgotten that quaint Yankee custom of making you specify iced tea when you wanted it cold.

So the three of them clustered around the table and sipped tea. Mr. Jacoby explained that he had known Richard, but that Richard had always worked with his brother.

"Mr. Morrison was a fine man," Mr. Jacoby said solemnly. Della smiled a little and set her cup back in the saucer. "So," he said finally, "Mrs. Morrison wants to sell the diamonds?"

Della nodded and from her shoulder bag retrieved the pouch. From the counter that ran along the wall, Alana took a cloth and what looked like a microscope. "We'll have to identify each one," Mr. Jacoby said. He smiled, pulling a folded sheet of yellow ruled paper from his coat pocket. "But as they match up, we'll have the appraisal for each."

"Do you want me to come back?" Della said. "I could shop or—" She wanted him to know she trusted him.

"I prefer that you stay here," he said. He poured the stones onto the cloth and lined them up in rows. "We could bring you the newspaper, if you'd like. Or we can turn on the radio."

"It would be great to see a paper," Della lied. She knew it would be the *Times,* with its tiny print and serious stories and, much as she wanted to impress Mr. Jacoby with her erudition, she didn't think she could concentrate on anything except headlines. She reached again into her shoulder bag and retrieved a paperback. "Plus, I have a book."

It was a long morning, which Della would have preferred to spend at Saks or Bloomingdale's. I am entirely dependent on Mr. Jacoby, she thought. On his honesty and on his trustworthiness. The diamonds are in his hands (which struck her as well-scrubbed but rather chubby) and under his fingers; he could replace them with cubic zirconiums and I would never know the difference. Not to mention the small matter of how the money will come to me.

Mr. Jacoby worked noisily. He breathed heavily, he exclaimed loudly—beautiful! The way I remembered this one! exactly!

Aaach!—he snorted, he muttered, he chuckled. Della didn't know with whom he conversed; she tried answering the first few times but he ignored her.

She moved to the corner of the room, seating herself in an upholstered chair and propping her feet on a matching ottoman. All the while, Alana sat next to her uncle, making notes, handing him loupes, and smiling reassuringly at Della.

Della fought the urge to conjure more headlines. These are the people Barbara trusts. And Richard before her. Let them take care of you the way she promised.

Della cleared her throat. "You know," she said when Alana raised her head, "I could use a telephone. I need to check things at home."

"Of course," Alana said. She motioned to the phone at the end of the counter, near the heavily draped windows. "Would you like us to leave you alone?"

"Oh, no!" Della said. "I don't want you to interrupt the work."

She punched in a long string of numbers. Rita answered.

"Well, if it isn't the happy wanderer. Where have you been?"

"I told you, I had to visit Melissa."

"But we called Melissa and she said you left yesterday for New York City. What are you doing in New York City?"

"Holding a fund-raiser. What's going on there?"

"Barbara fell."

"Fell?"

"Passed out. Threw up and passed out, actually. It was a real mess. The good news is it was in the barn, and we could just hose down the concrete. The bad news is she cracked her collarbone. They said you could hear it snap—she was teaching jewelry—and she's laid up. We canceled those Turow people and put her in the Babe."

"What'd the doctor say?"

"That this was bound to happen, that she should use a cane or a walker, but we have to expect this, blah blah blah."

"Did they set her arm?"

"Shoulder. She's got kind of a sling to immobilize it, but she's okay for now, except we don't think she should be climbing stairs. When are you coming home?"

"Day after tomorrow, I hope. Is Kat there?"

"She's with the county zoning guy. That's another thing: There's all these inspectors. The health department, Texas Employment, zoning. Then some gravel guy came out to try digging samples, and Kat about chased him off with a shotgun."

"A shotgun?"

Rita giggled. "Boy, you should have seen it. She was madder than I don't know what. Like someone lit a fire under her. She says all this is a gift from young Hugh. They cited us for the kitchen, though."

"They who?"

"The health department. The dishwasher temperature isn't hot enough. We have ten days to correct it or they're shutting us down. Dave rigged something up, though. He and Tony got this thermostat—"

"Tony? What was he doing there?"

"Oh, I think he just borrowed a page from Dave's book and decided he should camp on the porch a little. It's a little harder for him, though, being as how his shop's in Fort Worth and all. But he was out here and Dave sure needed his help, moving all those appliances."

"Is he still there?"

"God, Della, you ask a lot! He went back to Fort Worth after he helped us get Barbara settled in."

Della exhaled slowly. "Did we hear from Hugh Junior?"

"Twice. Wants to talk to you and no one else."

She took Hugh's number from Rita and promised to call him.

"Did Dave talk to his aunt?"

"Well, old Gladys is pretty interested in the idea of a little cash coming their way," Rita said. Her voice brightened. "I told Dave all she talks about is moving down to the valley and living in some trailer camp on the river so's she can creep across and buy cheap prescription drugs in Mexico. I told her, that's like Russian roulette, getting your—"

"Did Dave set a meeting with them?"

"You don't have to interrupt," Rita said. "Next week. That is, if you're coming home."

"I will be home day after tomorrow," Della said through gritted teeth. "And I'd like to meet with the Huttos that afternoon, if we can."

"We'll try," Rita said.

Della sighed. "Is Barbara really okay?"

"I think so. We got that pottery lady to come do the enamel jewelry, and Nancy's working a little extra to help in the kitchen."

"I'll be there day after tomorrow," Della repeated.

"Barbara's boy came out," Rita reported. "He's nice. Handsome, too. That husband of hers must've been something."

"Oh, he was," Della concurred. "He was really something." She heard her voice quaver, and she felt the tears in her eyes, and she felt too tired to stop them. "Look, I'll be there when I can, okay? Tell Kat and Barbara. Tell Barbara to take care of herself."

"Well, everything's under control here. Just one more thing."

"What's that?"

"I'm marrying Dave."

"Oh, Rita! Are you sure?"

"Yes. And soon, too."

"You're pregnant?"

"Hope not," Rita chuckled. Then her voice grew serious. "I don't want to wait, Della. Barbara's slipping so fast, now. If you'll be home day after tomorrow, I want to be married the day after that."

"My god, Rita! How're we going to pull that off?"

"We can do it. I've already called the JP, and Dave's got himself a new suit."

"Well, if you're sure, I'm for it!" Della said, surprising herself with her own enthusiasm. "And I agree: There's no reason to wait."

Alana and Mr. Jacoby both swiveled around to look at her, and she smiled and shook her head to indicate it was good, if unexplainable, news.

"You take care," Rita said. "We'll leave the light on."

"I hope everything is good at your home," Alana said.

"Oh, it's under control," Della replied.

She picked up the phone again and dialed Hugh Jr.

"I'm waiting on your answer," he told her.

"I'm in New York, rounding up cash," Della assured him. She felt Alana's sidelong glance, but reminded herself she had to concentrate on saving the Ladies Farm.

"Are you agreeing to my terms?"

"I can't say, yet, Hugh. I won't know for a few days. Why don't you give us a week?"

"I'll give you five days."

Della thought. She'd have the cash. She'd close the Huttos within two days. Marry Rita off the day after. Get Barbara's signature on the deal for her half. And maybe, Della prayed, hear something good from Melissa. "Five days," she said, assuming from his silence that he had heard nothing from his sister.

Again, she hung up the phone and walked back to her chair next to Alana. Her tea was lukewarm, which suited her better.

"Have a cookie," Mr. Jacoby offered.

Della helped herself, then walked over to the window and pushed aside the curtain to see the street below. She leaned her head against the glass and closed her eyes. If she saw Richard now, she thought, she'd have to explain why things were such a mess. He sent us Barbara to take care of her and now she's broken her collarbone!

Well, it's his mess, Della thought, opening her eyes and looking down. They were only a few stories up from the street, and she watched the figures hurrying along the sidewalk. They all carried things: purses, briefcases, sacks, backpacks. The sun was still behind the tall buildings, and most of the street lay in shade. It must be terrible, she thought. Maybe four, six hours of sunlight all day.

She struggled to remember Richard during the time when he was buying these diamonds. The look in his eye, the excitement of his secret . . . had it been a thrill to give Barbara these gifts, or a sense of dread?

"Dad?" It was the young man who had answered the door. "Sam Marx. You want it?"

"Mrs. Brewer," said Mr. Jacoby. "This is my son, Elliott."

"Hello," said Della, not offering a hand.

Elliott nodded. "Hello." Still holding the door, he turned to his father. "So should we put the call through?"

Mr. Jacoby shook his head. "He's just asking about lunch. Tell him I'll be about an hour, but I'll call him."

Elliott nodded and backed out of the room. Mr. Jacoby smiled at Della. "We're almost finished. I appreciate your patience."

"I appreciate your help. Is there any more tea?"

"Oh, I think we're out," Alana said. She looked at her uncle.

"Oh, just tell me where and I'll make it," Della offered.

Mr. Jacoby nodded. "I'll go with you," Alana said. "We just have to plug in the kettle."

This is when they make the switch, Della thought. When I come back, he informs me that none of the diamonds is real, that the total value of all that glass is a buck twenty-five.

Della and Alana were the only people in the kitchen, which was equipped with all the standard appliances plus a large, round table. "So is everyone at Jacoby Brothers a Jacoby?" Della asked.

"Pretty much," Alana replied. She took fresh cups and saucers from the cabinet and pulled a lemon from a basket on the counter. "My grandfather and his brother started it, and they took in two sons-in-law as well as my father and Uncle David. So some of my cousins—the Spicers and the Rudnicks—aren't Jacobys, but we're all related." She looked thoughtful. "You must think it's medieval, working with family like this."

"No," Della protested. The girl's earnest

demeanor masked a quick eye. "No, in a way, that's what I've done. Sort of made a family—my friends and I—to run our bed and breakfast. The Ladies Farm."

"The Ladies Farm!" Alana repeated. "Where is that?"

Suddenly, Della found herself brimming over with descriptions of the Nolan River and the rolling hills around it. She talked about the shops on the square in Sydonia and the classes in the barn.

"It sounds more like a spa," Alana said. "And there are no men?"

"Well, sometimes," Della said. "But it's mostly women, mostly my age."

Alana loaded the tea things onto the tray, and Della held the door for her as they left. The girl's dark hair shimmered beneath the beret. "But if a whole group of women booked the Ladies Farm, then there wouldn't be any men," Alana said.

"Well, no," Della said, not sure where this was leading. She guessed at Alana's age, you had to consciously exclude men if you wanted an all-female environment. Della wondered if she should warn the girl that that would happen eventually anyway.

"My friends and I . . . actually it's a study

group . . . we've been talking about a retreat. But there would have to be a lot of arrangements about food and so forth." Della opened the door to the showroom and Alana followed her in, setting the tray on the counter. "Perhaps, though, if we simply agreed to a vegetarian menu, it might work."

Della fished a business card out of her pocket and handed it to Alana. "Call me in a few days. We can probably accommodate you. My friend Barbara is a whiz at menu planning. We'll figure something out."

Mr. Jacoby looked up for a moment, then returned to his work. "We're almost finished," he promised Della, picking up one of the diamonds with some sort of tweezers and setting it down on a scale.

She had returned to her chair and ottoman, but even though she held her book in her hand, she didn't read. She just held the book in front of her face, lifted and lowered her teacup, and stared at the page. Don't think about this too much, she advised herself.

The tea was gone by the time Mr. Jacoby pushed himself back from the table and stood up. "Aaach!" he exclaimed, clasping his hands and stretching his arms over his head. "A man can freeze in a sitting position if he's not careful."

"You will excuse me for a few moments? Then we will sit down and talk business."

Della nodded. The large expanse of white shirt revealed when his jacket fell away from his belly left her speechless. This man had sensed Richard's integrity and, she suspected, his passion. But she could not imagine such mass in motion over passion of his own.

Well, someone loves him, Della thought. Different people look for different things.

When Mr. Jacoby returned, he bore with him ledgers and files. After the teacups had been refilled, Della faced him across the ornate table, and he began by outlining Richard's arrangement. "Our price is locked in, of course, but you are welcome to refuse. It is based on our last three invoices from Tel Aviv, Amsterdam, and Johannesburg. Averaging the last three from each, we are obligated to offer you the highest of them, which this week is Amsterdam."

He laid a sheaf of papers before her.

"These are the invoices. They have been certified by our accountant, but you are welcome to show them to an independent accountant to verify their accuracy."

"Oh, no!" Della said without hesitation. "Barbara—Mrs. Morrison—was very clear, to accept your word."

"She is very generous," Mr. Jacoby told her. "So was her husband. Did you know him?"

Della nodded, but didn't trust herself to speak.

Alana, who had remained silent, smiled from her seat next to her uncle, who continued by placing a long ledger sheet before her. "The inventory matches exactly. You see," he pointed with his pencil to the various columns, "the weight, the clarity. No change. So, the value comes from last week's market, you see here, per carat, each stone valued separately."

He continued on, but Della's focus jumped to the last column, then down to the bottom of the page. She read it again, trying not to move her lips. Then she looked at Mr. Jacoby, who had fallen silent. "It's..."

"Yes," he said.

She had expected a lot of money, certainly over a hundred thousand dollars, perhaps two or three hundred thousand. But the figure written at the bottom of the ledger page was eight hundred eighty-three thousand, two hundred sixteen dollars.

"I thought..." she looked at him "It's far greater ... Barbara..."

"Her husband insisted on investment quality," Mr. Jacoby said. "He was very particular, very careful. He bought a great many diamonds. He brought them to us. We would select out one, maybe two for him, sell off the rest."

"I didn't..."

"He became quite an expert. They knew him in Europe, in Israel, in South Africa. Even in Hong Kong."

"He had a business," Della mumbled. "He traveled to find suppliers, then he was in licensing software."

"So I understand."

Della wanted to ask how many stones he had selected out, if they knew whether there were more, somewhere, given to someone else. And she wanted to explain to these people, to this man who would not take the hand of an adult woman, that she

did not merit their respect, that her relationship with Richard's widow was based on
fraud, that her relationship with Richard
had been adulterous.

"You understand, of course," Mr. Jacoby
said, "it is mostly the large one." He shook
his head. "That's the only one he bought
from me personally."

"From you?"

"My brother, may he rest in peace, had
died by then. It took him—Mr. Morrison—
weeks to decide: first to pick the stone,
then back and forth, back and forth from
Texas, as if he didn't know, couldn't make
up his mind."

"That was the last one, then?" Della
asked, startled.

"From us, certainly." He smiled gently. "It
was worth more than all the others put
together."

She shook her head to clear it. That
doesn't mean anything, she told herself.
Only that he was that much sorrier. And
that it's that much more money for the
Ladies Farm.

"I . . . it's the Ladies Farm, our bed and
breakfast," she stumbled, explaining what
she could. "This means I can . . . my

friends and I will be able to continue there. Barbara" she stopped for a second, "Barbara, Richard's . . . Richard's widow is very sick. We need . . . oh! this means so much!"

Mr. Jacoby and Alana gazed at her with the same set of brown eyes.

"It is much more than I expected," Della said again, but this time she was considering the quantity of cash. She looked at the small duffel and the shoulder bag that sat next to the chair.

"Perhaps we can help you there," said Mr. Jacoby.

Which was how she came to be met at the Amtrak platform in Penn Station by Alana, pulling a red, wheeled cooler behind her. "Cousin Della!" she called. "Cousin Della!" Like a child pulling a wagon, Alana made her way through the crowd pressing forward to board the express to Chicago. "Mama and I couldn't let you go back to Texas without fixing something."

By this time, she had reached Della and they stood facing each other as passengers continued to board. "Who would have guessed?" continued Alana. "A Jacoby from Texas!" Della saw a few smiles, then glanced down at the cooler. The bottom, she knew, was filled with stationery boxes packed with hundred-dollar bills.

"Now, don't open this until you're home, otherwise it will spoil, and the lox will stink up your whole berth!" Alana took Della's hand and placed it on the cooler handle. "And next time, you won't wait twenty years to visit!" With that, the girl leaned forward and touched her cheek to Della's. "They're shrink-wrapped, under the dry ice. Don't unpack till you're home," she whispered. "And there really is lox and cream cheese on top. And frozen strudel."

"Strudel!" Della exclaimed. "Your mother is too good to me."

"Apple and cherry," Alana giggled.

Della kissed the girl once more. "Thank you so much."

"You must call us," Alana said. "The moment you get home, so we know you're safe. And then write us a nice, long letter about Texas."

Della turned to board. The conductor stood on the steps, ready to help her get the cooler onto the train. From the corner of her eye, she saw David Jacoby, an attaché case propped against a tiled column, the newspaper held up in front of his face.

"They packed this one nice and full," the conductor said, lifting it up to the passenger car. "Ain't nothing like family for feeding you right."

"You're not kidding," said Della.

Chapter 17

The conductor teased her about her cooler full of home cooking, but Della laughed him off, refusing to share anything but the small sack of raspberry–almond tarts Alana had given her before she left Jacoby Brothers. Her fellow passengers accepted the sweets and shared her amusement that her orthodox cousins had insisted on sending her back to Texas with real—that is, New York—lox and cream cheese, not to mention the strudel.

When she changed trains in Chicago, she found herself ignored, which suited her fine. It might have been better to rent a car, but that, too, had its perils. You avoided the airport X-rays, she reassured herself; it would have been stupid to drive alone for three days with a cooler full of cash. You might never have reached Texas.

When they rolled into Fort Worth the next afternoon, it was Tony, not Kat, who met her train.

"Kat had to take something to the lawyer for Barbara," Tony explained. "What's this?"

"Take what?" Della asked, but Tony just shrugged and looked curiously at the cooler. "Oh, I just picked up this little red wagon in New York. We need to stop and get fresh bagels. It's filled with lox—that's smoked salmon—and cream cheese."

"I know what lox is." He took the handle and, setting the duffel atop the cooler, walked her through the station and out to the car. He caught her up on Barbara's condition (the collarbone felt okay, but the cancer had entered a new stage), on the parade of inspectors (the zoning people had no problems, but OSHA was concerned about chemical storage in the barn and the salon so he and Dave would have to put up a storage shed), the gravel mining (Kat had prevented them from taking samples and Hugh Jr. had filed a motion to compel them to allow it), and the Ladies Farm itself, which was full of guests.

Nancy's sister, Hannah, had been drafted to help with the cleaning, and Barbara had called a friend, Dottie, to take over the jewelry classes. Even Rita had been forced to bring in another beautician to help with the facials and manicures. "But she won't let anyone else do hair," Tony explained as they headed out of town. "She says she's the only one who can fix that Texas big hair."

Della smiled. "She's right about that. Though I don't know how she's doing anyone's hair if she's getting married tomorrow." They picked up ten dozen bagels— that would feed the guests, plus leave some for freezing—then drove straight to see the Huttos. They hooked up with Dave and Rita where the gravel drive met the county road and, after transferring the cooler to the back of Dave's truck, Della thanked Tony with a peck on the cheek and dispatched him back to Fort Worth.

"I hope someday you share the details of

your mystery trip," he said before he got back into the car.

Della wondered for a second what it would be like to come clean with Tony, imagining that he would simply accept it all and go on doing her bidding; then, she squared her shoulders and touched a hand to the side of his face. "Someday," she promised.

The Hutto house sat high on a bluff on the south side of the Nolan. From the back porch, where Gladys held court on an old sofa, you could see down to the river and across to the Ladies Farm. When you looked up and focused far in the distance on a clear day, you could see the outline of southwest Fort Worth.

Gladys Hutto was a chain-smoking, sausage-curled mound of a woman who, with her husband, Ray, received the delegation from the Ladies Farm with a pitcher of tea on the metal table and a case of Dr Pepper on the floor in front of the sofa.

"It's good to see you," Della said to her, then looked around for a place to sit. Rita inclined her head to the low stone wall that formed the porch, and Della followed her lead and rested her butt on the warm stones.

"You want to keep a lookout for snakes 'fore you settle in over there," Gladys warned with no particular urgency. "Little Ray like to have a fit the other day, playing with his action men over there. He comes in screaming, some damn snake knocked his little figures off into the bushes. Trying to get away from Little Ray, probably, but that child was furious. Wanted to find the thing and kill it, but we never did find it. Found a skin though. Rattlesnake. They're all over. That child's got a real guardian angel. We had to open five more boxes of cereal to replace that little plastic doll, too."

Ray spent the duration of the monologue holding up Dr Peppers and making eye contact with each guest. Rita and Dave accepted, leaving Della not much choice about following suit. She guessed the tea was for show.

"They're all over, this time of year," Rita picked up the conversation. "We find them on the asphalt path up to the barn all the time. Did Little Ray's mama get that job in Dallas?"

Della saw the agenda: First we talk about Little Ray; then Little Ray's mama, whose moving to Dallas would relieve Gladys and Ray of babysitting duties; then Little Ray's mama's no-good ex-husband, their nephew Earl; then confirmation that they had gotten Earl to sign back the mineral rights; then the reason for their visit. Should take five, maybe six Dr Peppers apiece, Della thought.

She watched Dave, who had not removed his coveralls for this appointment. He leaned against the house, one leg bent, stork-like, with his foot braced against the masonry. Every now and then he exchanged a glance with Ray, but for the most part, he stared down at his foot, silent.

Rita chirped on about Little Ray's mama and her new job, then listened as Gladys enumerated the virtues of her former niece by marriage.

"Lord knows she works hard enough," Gladys said. "Two jobs, most of the time, and not a bit of help from Earl with the baby. Not that he doesn't pay child support. Even so, it's a shame to see. Young people like that." She looked up at Della. "You have kids?"

"One boy who's grown. He lives in Portland," Della said. "He and his wife have a little girl."

Gladys continued her head-shaking. "That's hard on kids too, being an only child. Ray and I always figured we'd have a house full." She shook her head enough to make the sausage curls jiggle. "Didn't happen. Here we are with this big, old place and no one to leave it to but that half-wit Earl."

"I don't suppose anyone sets out to raise an only child," Della observed. The silence that followed assured her that Rita and Dave had shared her tragedy with Gladys and Ray. Bad move, Della chastised silently. Nothing stops a conversation faster than a dead child.

Finally, Dave picked up the earlier thread. "Well, now," he said, "Earl's okay. He just needs to find what he wants to do."

"He's bright enough," Rita chirped. "He's just not ready to be a grown-up yet."

"Twenty-five with a baby, that's pretty grown up," Ray said. He had settled in next to Gladys and spent most of the conversation studying his Dr Pepper. Now he shook his head in agreement with his wife. "That boy's worthless, I'm afraid. It's good his mama and daddy's moved on down to Corpus. It doesn't make them glad to hear from him."

"Your sister's down in Corpus, Ray?" Dave slid his stork foot to the ground. "I thought she'd settled in the valley."

"Nah. You know, her husband's people are there on the coast." Ray, as if suddenly aware that he had become the center of attention, clamped his lips and tightened his grip on the Dr Pepper.

"Well, the beach is nice, but I don't think I'd want to live where it's all that humid," Rita opined. "Especially with all those hurricanes."

"I want a nice little double-wide down on the Rio Grande," Gladys said. "Nothing fancy, just a little prickly pear and sage out front, nothing to mow and no fencing." She turned to Della. "So if you're here to make that happen, let's get on with it."

Nothing is ever the way it seems, thought Della.

"Well, not so fast!" Rita said. "This isn't

just Della, you know. Dave and I are in this too. And Kat."

"And Castleburg, if you don't hurry up," Gladys said. "Daddy, reach me another one of those Dr Peppers."

"Well now, Gladys," Dave said, "what are you looking at for this place?"

"Well, you know, it's over twenty acres," Gladys said. "I hear Castleburg's offering five-sixty for yours, and you've got less than ten over there, don't you?"

She was looking at Della, but it was Dave who answered. "I guess young Hugh's been 'round."

"Well, he makes some sense," Gladys replied. "Though I don't much like dealing with Dallas lawyers."

Now Dave shifted a little and planted both feet wider on the concrete porch. "Whatever happened with Earl's gravel adventure?" he asked Ray.

Ray shook his head and shrugged. "That boy."

"I don't think Earl could find gravel if you poured it over him," Gladys expounded. "That boy just does everything on the cheap, didn't want to hire the geologists, you know?"

Dave worked them through it slowly: how the unlikelihood of gravel and the fact that the Hutto place lay outside city limits made it less valuable; how the buildings at the Ladies Farm increased its value; how Castleburg's offer through Hugh Jr., was not all cash and that theirs—Della's and Kat's and Rita's—would be.

"It's not that Mama and I want to be greedy," Ray assured them. "We just want what's fair. After all, we've got our future to consider."

"And Little Ray's, too. His own grandparents can't do much for him, someone'll have to educate that boy. That's what Daddy means."

Mama and Daddy. Little Ray's future. Della resisted the urge to choke. She resisted the urge to describe the red cooler full of cash. She resisted the urge to ask if the sofa came with the property.

"The thing about it is," Della tried to speak slowly, "we don't want to mine any gravel."

"Well, we know that," Gladys said. "That's why we want to sell to you. I just hate thinking that old man's going to send those bulldozers over here and dig the place up."

"You know," Ray said, "when we built this place, the farm-to-market road was just paved. We were the first house on this side of the river."

"It's pretty over here," Della said. "I always love seeing those peaches come into bloom on the hill that faces us."

"I imagine those lady guests would enjoy a picnic on that hill," Ray said.

"Plus, you'll be able to rent out this house," Gladys said, blocking Della's impulse to tell Ray that their lady guests had enjoyed many picnics on his hill. "It's got three bedrooms, plus a big, old family room."

Della looked at the couch but held her tongue. The house is solid stone, she reminded herself. Even if you have to gut the interior.

"How's the kitchen?" Rita asked.

"Why, we had that designer down from Fort Worth just two years ago," Gladys said. As she spoke, she pulled a fleck of tobacco from her outstretched tongue. "Redid the whole thing, put in one of those islands. I prefer a big, old country kitchen myself, but he said this would raise the resale value. It's the latest thing."

"Well, let's go look at it!" Rita motioned Della off the wall. "No, no," she assured Gladys as the woman stirred. "You sit still. We'll look on our own, and we won't touch anything. I promise."

"Touch all you want," Gladys invited, settling back into the couch. "Open the cupboards, flush the toilets."

Inside, the paneling was dark, but real, Della saw. We could strip it, she thought. We can yank these drapes and put up wooden blinds, or shutters. We can strip the floor, too.

"I guess she just likes a sofa on the porch," Della murmured as she and Rita inspected the kitchen.

"Oh," said Rita, "that's one of those habits she picked up in Cuba, she says. She and Ray were down there before Castro. Some kind of bridge building."

"Bridge building?"

"Oh, you know. Ray's an engineer. I think Gladys taught school or something down there, too."

"Gladys taught school?"

"Well, not school, exactly. Some kind of science academy. She taught chemistry."

Della opened the pantry door and inspected the adjustable shelving. "You're joking, right?"

"No ma'am. Here's her degree, right here on the wall." Rita pointed to the alcove above a built-in desk. "University of Texas. I guess this is a mixed marriage. Ray's an Aggie."

"Kitchen's better than I thought," Della murmured, heading for the door.

"Where're you going?" Rita hissed. "Come here!"

"What?"

Rita shot her a fierce look and motioned her closer.

"What?"

"Dave's talking to them," Rita said.

"I know. That's why I want to be out there."

"Here!" Rita exclaimed in a loud voice, "look at the view out the side, toward town." Then in a whisper, "They won't talk if you're there."

"What?"

"For such a smart person, you sure are dense," Rita grumbled, guiding Della out onto the kitchen steps. "Dave's talking price. Right now. We can't go back out till he's done."

"What?"

"He's negotiating price!"

"That's why we need to be there. Price being the amount you and I have to shell out."

"Now you just sit right down on this step and let Dave handle that. He knows what we'll pay."

Della looked with astonishment at the woman who had seated herself on the wooden step. "I don't believe this. You're saying I should let your boyfriend determine how many hundreds of thousands I should pay for a place I'm only half-interested in. As in: Don't you worry your pretty little head, honey, we've got a man to take care of us?"

"Well, no one said that at all," Rita countered. "After all, Gladys is out there, and she's female. But Dave's kin, and they're all from Sydonia. It's home cooking."

Della eased herself down onto the step and looked out the back of what would soon be the Ladies Farm. "I hate it when you make sense," she muttered. Dave would negotiate a good price, probably without having to lead Gladys and Ray over to his truck to display the contents of the red cooler. Della was disappointed. She had enjoyed imagining the Huttos' reaction.

"Nothing's ever as good as you imagine it," Della mourned. "I rehearsed for this. I practiced my steady gaze for my final offer."

"I know, baby, but you can trust Dave." Rita patted her arm. "Try to keep your mind off it. Think about something else. Tell me what's up with you and Tony. Tell me what's in that cooler. Talk about anything else."

Kat knows, thought Della. Melissa knows. Hugh Jr. knows. Della leaned back and tilted her head up to the gathering dusk. But not Rita, Dave, or Tony. And maybe not Barbara.

Barbara knew she looked much worse. It had been less than a week since Della had left, but Barbara couldn't cover the purple wells beneath her eyes. "I'm feeling a lot better," she assured Della, but Della looked unconvinced.

She had wheeled a cooler into the room and Barbara, from her seat next to the window, looked quizzically at the thing.

"It's cash," Della explained. She pushed it right up to Barbara's feet and knelt before her. "Here." Della opened the cooler top, reached in, and pulled out a stationery box, setting it atop the wheeled hospital table.

Barbara watched as Della lifted the top from the stationery box on the table between them. The bills were packed neatly and wrapped in rubber bands. "They were transferring one twenty-five to you yesterday. That's the official sale, for the record," Della said. "Did you get it?"

Barbara nodded. "The bank called."

"The rest is here in cash: seven hundred fifty-eight thousand, two hundred and sixteen dollars." Della said it slowly and methodically and she looked shaken by the sum.

"Thank you for this," Barbara said. She took a breath. "For doing it, and for letting me help." She stopped and gulped for air.

"Barbara?" Della leaned forward, grasped her good arm. "Should I get someone? Do you need . . . is there medicine?"

Barbara waved her off and shook her

head. She tried to smile her reassurance, but the cough prevented it. "I'm just short of breath. The morphine helps." Barbara noted the alarm in Della's eyes, but knew she would have to depend on the others to explain that the low-level morphine doses were not the pain-relieving doping she would require later. She had to shepherd her strength.

"Okay," said Della, "you listen and I'll talk. I'm taking this money because I have no choice, just as we're letting you sign over your interest to us. But these are loans. And we—Kat, Rita, and I—will pay you back."

Barbara shook her head vehemently.

"Well, we'll pay it back to Dickie."

Barbara nodded, both to show she understood and to reassure Della that it was proper to plan events beyond her death.

"This money is far more than I ever expected to need, and the Hutto deal is a luxury. I mean," Della rambled on, "it's something we want because it'll help stop Hugh Junior and Castleburg, but we'll sell off a good part of it, and get that money to you . . . or to Dickie."

"How much?" Barbara asked.

"Three-fifty. Don't ask me how. Mostly because we promised them cash, quickly, so they can retire to the Rio Grande."

Barbara nodded. "And Tony?" She didn't have time for transitions anymore, and Della misunderstood completely.

"Oh, Tony went back to Fort Worth. It was Dave who negotiated the thing, even though I—"

Barbara shook her head. "You and Tony!"

"Me? And Tony?" Della smiled slightly, then shook her head. "Who knows, Barbara? I can't even make it to a movie with him." She paused and Barbara let her think for a moment. She really didn't know why she cared so much, except that dying changed everything and Barbara did have the urge to make that apparent. She wanted Della to understand that death could keep you from setting right the things that needed to be righted.

Della sighed. "I just don't know, Barbara. It's not," she hesitated, "it's not like you and Richard." Della looked startled by her own words, but she continued. "It's not like one of us did something that the other has to forgive. You can at least understand that."

Barbara nodded her agreement, signaling to Della that she understood the difference and didn't take it as a dismissal of Barbara's sorrow.

"It's just . . . I don't know . . . I'm not sure . . . after everything . . . Jamie and all that . . . I'm not sure I have the energy for that kind of relationship." Della, sitting on the bed and looking at Barbara, looked baffled, as if this were a new puzzle. "Tony really wants a marriage," Della confessed. "And I'm not sure I could be married anymore."

Barbara smiled a little and started to reach over to pat Della's hand, then stopped. There was something else to tell Della. "They weren't really mine," she said. "The diamonds."

"The diamonds?" Della frowned as if she were trying to catch up with Barbara's thoughts. "You said Richard gave them to you."

Barbara nodded. "I mean, I never felt like—"

"Like they were yours?" Amazement had enlivened Della's expression, and her eyes sparkled with wonder. "Whose did you think they were?"

Barbara shook her head. She sat for a moment, gathering her breath. "It was my payoff. Taking them, it was like saying Richard, what he did, was okay. But it wasn't okay. I took the diamonds, but it was never okay."

"Is that why you never wore them? Put them into settings? Rings? Necklaces?"

Barbara nodded.

Della's eyes blazed. "Those diamonds were yours. Don't you ever think..."

"Not the big one," Barbara whispered.

"The big one? That last one Richard gave you?"

It annoyed Barbara that Della whispered; Della had breath to spare. Look at that bosom heaving up and down with indignation! What did she know? Fury drove Barbara forward.

"He didn't give it to me. I found it." Gulp. "After he died. In a safe-deposit box." Another breath. "I didn't know about the box. I found the key."

"You mean, he never gave it to you?"

Barbara shook her head. "I . . . I was so upset . . . I tore the house . . . up."

"Tore the house up? Because he died?"

"Because he wasn't there for breakfast." Barbara got the whole thing out in one breath. "Even out of town ... I would call him in the morning, he would be there." She felt the tears starting, but she pressed on. "I called and called. Then I got home. I didn't know he was dead, I thought he was ... out. With someone."

"And you," Della said, "you thought he wasn't at home for your call because he was with some woman?"

Barbara nodded, picturing the mess in her mind: the clothes she had ripped from their hangers, the desk with its papers scattered, even his jewelry box upended into the trash, the gold cuff buttons glittering up from a tangle of old watches and Rotary pins.

"And the key ... you found it going through his things?"

Again, Barbara nodded, not bothering to explain that it was actually a small, blue folder bearing an electronically coded plastic card.

"And you found the diamond in the box?"

Barbara pictured her own hand, the amethyst sparkling as she reached into the trash and retrieved the small booklet guaranteeing the box holder complete confidence in the bank's security and integrity.

"Was there a note?"

Barbara could barely hear the whisper. She shook her head and looked at Della, but she couldn't speak.

"Oh, Barbara! He didn't live long enough to give it to you," Della said, reaching over and holding her arm. "Oh," Della crooned, moving over to the arm of the chair and clasping Barbara in an awkward hug.

Pain shot through her collarbone, and Barbara stiffened but did not pull away. It felt good to be held by Della, to have shared this awful thing with her.

"But at least you know," Della was murmuring now. "At least you know that he loved you, that he wanted you to have diamonds . . . to have beautiful things. That if he had lived, he would have given that last diamond to you."

Barbara stayed in the circle of Della's arm. She inhaled to give herself enough breath to speak a full sentence. Then, in a very low, carefully paced voice, she said, "Or maybe it was for the woman he was with that morning."

Chapter 18

Della stumbled up the stairs, her steps like thunder and her breathing a rasp against her lungs. She threw herself onto her bed before the door had swung shut behind her. She had left Barbara dozing in the reclining chair, the cooler stowed in the closet. Della doubted she herself would ever enjoy such sleep again, with or without drugs.

She looked at her own hand, palm up on the bed. The diamond had lain in that hand for only a few moments, and she had failed to grasp its meaning. She blinked and stared some more, imagining it there, imagining Richard putting it there and just as quickly imagining him depositing it in Barbara's bejeweled hand.

Should she have told Barbara that Richard had never given her jewelry? Or did that only make this possibility more significant?

Della rolled onto her back and held her left hand in front of her, modeling her fingers as if that enormous jewel sparkled over them. Other than her wedding band and a modest garnet with which Tony and the boys had surprised her one Christmas, Della had never worn rings.

Della closed her eyes and thought back to Richard holding her hand across a table at a Chinese restaurant. It had followed a rare weekend together, and she savored every detail in their particularly well-appointed hotel suite: the upholstered chair where she straddled him in the dark, ignoring the lights twinkling up from the city way below their window; the oversized tub where they had sipped vodka and crunched on caviar-covered nacho chips; the joy of starting awake in the middle of the night and finding herself next to Richard, who reached out to her in his sleep.

It had been Sunday lunch when they finally had left the hotel for the Chinese restaurant. Separated by a table, the greatest distance between them in a day and a half, she rested against the back of the chair and wondered if she possessed a nerve that had not been stimulated, or a speck of skin that had not been caressed. She was teasing him about making her sore when she reached for her fortune cookie, but he stopped her. He had paused a second, she recalled, stroking her fingers. Had he been contemplating her lack of jewelry? Or luxuriating in the feel of her skin?

Then he had placed the other cookie, his cookie, in her hand, and they had ended laughing, Della remembered, still giggling as they drove off in different directions.

I collected memories, not jewelry, she thought. I collected moments that couldn't be redeemed for cash and will never leave me.

Della opened her eyes. There was another possibility. She sat up and looked at her bedroom furniture: a double dresser, a lingerie chest, a straight-backed chair. She stood up and walked over to the dresser.

Barbara wouldn't do that, she told herself, pulling open the bottom drawer. But it was possible, wasn't it? Maybe Barbara knew all along and made up the story to torture you. Taking the truth to her grave.

There was a knock at her door. "Della?" It was Kat.

Another knock, then the door opened. "What were you doing in there so long?" Kat demanded as she stepped inside.

"I wasn't in there long." Della turned back to her dresser drawer. She was trying to help you, Della thought. She wouldn't—

"Did you tell her?"

Della felt around under the sweaters until she touched velvet. "Tell her what?" She grunted a little as she retrieved the glove box from the back of the well-packed drawer.

"What?!"

"What!" Della repeated with exasperation, closing the drawer and wheeling to face Kat's scorn. "I told her the diamonds were worth almost nine hundred thousand dollars and that you and Rita and I would pay back every penny to Dickie. I told her we'd sell off some of the Hutto place to raise some cash immediately."

Denying Kat had become too enjoyable, Della realized, and she shook her head to rid herself of the exultation of controlling even this one tiny part of the melodrama that had become her life. "No, Kat, I didn't tell her. And I won't. And you won't either. No one's telling Barbara." She paused. "Even though—you know—that doesn't mean she doesn't know."

"I almost wish she did, I feel so dishonest," Kat confessed. "I thought I could go through with this, but the sicker she gets, the worse I feel. I don't even mind the smell of Gucci anymore."

"I think the time to feel dishonest was back when you and I were sneaking around with Richard. That was dishonest. Keeping our peace now is just..." she shrugged, then looked at Kat again, "maybe barely decent."

Kat nodded miserably. "I know. I just needed to hear that."

"Well, cheer up," Della advised. "We've got a wedding ahead of us."

"Yeah."

"And a lot of work on the Hutto place."

"And a real nasty lawsuit from Hugh Junior," Kat contributed.

"I'm sure," Della conceded. She had decided not to check with Melissa until after Rita's wedding.

"And we'll always have each other."

"I suppose." Kat smiled a little. "I'm glad for it." She frowned a little at the glove box. "What's that?"

"Oh, I finally remembered where I hid something."

"You had diamonds too?"

"Not exactly." Della opened the box and withdrew a pair of gloves—worn, white kid that had belonged to her mother. "My fortune." Holding the gloves by the tips of their fingers, she shook them a little and a slip of paper fluttered out.

It landed on the bed next to Kat, who picked it up. "It is a fortune!" she laughed.

Della reached for it, but Kat held on. "*He loves you as much as he can,*" she read, "*but he cannot love you much.*"

Tony kept his promise to help Dave with the shed. They were already at work the next morning when Della threw open her bedroom window to get a glimpse of the hill on the other side of the river. She leaned out over the sill and looked beyond the

Ladies Farm barn to the small orchard and the rocky path that led to the Hutto house.

About halfway up and to one side of the path stood an outcropping of sydonite, and Della knew the view from there beat the one from the Huttos' back porch. This one hung out over the hill a little, giving you a glimpse of Castleburg's beyond the bend in the river. And it's ours, Della thought with satisfaction. Dave did a good job.

Below her, Dave and Tony were unloading Dave's truck. They had purchased some sort of prefabricated metal lean-to, which they intended to place over a concrete floor they had poured a few days ago. Next to Dave, Tony looked almost beefy. He was wearing overalls, which she had never seen before, and had a red bandanna tied around his head. Fugitive from the sixties, Della thought, withdrawing from the window but leaving it open. Welcome to the commune.

She dressed and made her bed. Then she headed down the front stairs, retrieving the paper from the porch before she headed for the kitchen. She had slept a little, but not well, and she needed a cup of coffee and her horoscope before she had to start breakfast.

Tony clumped into the kitchen. "Y'all got any coffee?" he asked, zooming in on the coffeemaker as he spoke.

"In a minute," she replied. "Try not to make so much noise, you'll wake the guests. If you didn't already with all that unloading."

"Boy, you sure get demanding when you own the place!" He reached into the cupboard and pulled down two mugs. It didn't take him long to know where they were, Della noticed.

Della busied herself with emptying the dishwasher and putting away the remains of last night's dinner. "I don't own it yet."

"Dave's sure you will. And you sure own the Hutto place," Tony said, walking over to her and putting a hand on her neck.

Della turned to him and resisted the urge to bury her face in his neck. This close, he smelled sweaty, with a tiny bit of soap fragrance left, and she steadied herself by planting both hands on his forearms. "If everything goes right," she told him.

He had slipped hands around her waist and now he pulled her a little closer. "We were right," he insisted.

"Yes, we were," she agreed.

"We were right the other night."

For a second, Della couldn't even re-member which night he meant, but then she recalled their date only a few days ago and smiled faintly at the memory of lying next to him. "Tony," she said, "aren't you afraid we're just falling back into this rela-tionship because it's comfortable?"

"Della, I'm not afraid of that, I'm hoping for it." He released her. "What's wrong with comfort?"

What was wrong with it? Della wondered.

Della shrugged and shook her head. "I don't know, Tony." Why was her voice shaking? "Maybe I'm beyond comforting."

He stomped over to the coffeemaker and poured himself a cup. "You know, Della, you may be smart, but sometimes you act stupid. And if you think you're . . . if you think anyone's beyond comfort..." His voice trailed off. "Or is it my comfort? Is it that I didn't do it right when Jamie died, so now I have to inch my way back, dance attendance?"

"Don't pull that crap on me!" She slammed a metal measuring cup down onto the counter, and it rang throughout the kitchen. "I'm not asking you to dance attendance. I'm not asking you to dance at all."

It must have sounded as stupid to him as it did to her, because he fought back a grin as he shook his head and advanced. "Come on," he said. "We'll dance anyway."

He hummed something she didn't recognize at all, then realized as they stumbled around the island that it was "Red River Valley." "I'm not mad at you," Della said. She had forgotten his penchant for kitchen dances to smooth over fights. At one time, it had been one of his most endearing traits. "And I'd love to sleep with you again. I just have a lot going on here."

"Just remember the Red River Valley," he crooned. *"And the cowboy who loved you so true."*

They stopped.

"I've been thinking about it," Tony said slowly.

"Sleeping with me?"

"That too. I mean, this problem of all those things you have going on."

"Well you have to admit, between Barbara, and Hugh Junior and the gravel mining and the OSHA inspector—"

"I know. But there's always going to be

something. The problem isn't how much is going on, it's how much we're willing to do to be together. So, if I live here, we could be and you could still manage this whole mess."

"Live here like at the Ladies Farm?"

"Well, yes. We're selling the house anyway, right?"

"Right."

"And I've got to reinvest the money and find another place to live, right?"

She nodded.

"So, I put it into a share of the Ladies Farm, you get a little more cash, and you and I can play all those night games you're so fond of."

"You want to buy into the Ladies Farm?"

"Well, it would give us a chance to be together."

Della listened to the muffled sounds from outside, trying to connect the ripping noises with a picture of Dave erecting the shed. Finally, she realized the pieces must have been packed in cardboard, and he was unpacking them. Where had Tony gotten this idea?

"You think instead of the Ladies Farm we could have the Couples Farm: You and I, Rita and Dave, Kat and whoever?"

"All I'm trying to do is give us a way to live a normal life in the place you seem determined to live it."

"You want us to live together at the Ladies Farm?"

"I want us to live together. You want to live at the Ladies Farm. Why is it so complicated? I'll commute into Fort Worth, you stay home and run the farm. It'd be great!"

"Tony, I can't talk about this now. Everyone'll be down here in a minute, we've got to start breakfast. Here," she reached up on the shelf and pulled down another mug. "Take a cup of coffee out to Dave."

"That's okay, we picked some up on the way over."

"You've already had coffee?"

"Just one cup," he said, lifting his mug. "This is my second. I didn't need to make up a reason to talk to you, if that's what you're thinking."

"No. Of course not. Is Dave moving in too?"

"Well, he and Rita have to live somewhere," Tony said lightly. "And Rita is buying a share, isn't she? Though I don't think anybody wants to make any plans with Barbara . . . you know."

"You mean, while Barbara's dying? She says it all the time, it's okay for us to."

"Well, it doesn't seem right to be assigning her room out from under her," Tony said. "I guess I'd better get back out there. Dave's liable to put that thing together inside out. He's good with motors, but he doesn't much care for construction."

The discussion about Barbara drove him off, leaving Della alone for only a minute before Kat and then Rita popped in and they began breakfast.

She said nothing to the others, glancing up only to smile at Flops, who wandered in to sniff around, then retreated back to Barbara's room.

Where would Tony fit in this? she wondered, arranging muffins in a basket. But she said nothing until they decamped to the office after breakfast, while the home health worker was helping Barbara bathe.

"She has her good times," Rita explained. "Usually first thing in the morning, and then around two. She'll have some lunch and then she'll feel like talking for awhile. Yesterday, she showed me how we could print the recipes off the computer onto file cards and then use those colored stamps Pauline made to decorate the cards."

"I told her we'd finish them," Kat said in a shaky voice. "Just the way she intends, with those stupid little carrots and apples stamped all over them."

"Don't sell her short," Rita warned. "She may finish them herself."

"Will she be okay for the wedding?" Della asked.

"Well, I hope," Rita replied. "Two is her good time."

Della tried to focus on logistics. "Who's coming? Do we have enough folding chairs? Don't you want flowers?"

"Well, my kids of course. Carla and her gang are driving over from Dallas, and Darlene and Tiffany are right here. You know, Darlene's always thought of Dave as her daddy anyways, so she's pretty excited. And we told little Tiffany she could be our flower girl."

"You're having a flower girl?" Kat asked.

"Well, she's already five and if she can't be her mamaw's flower girl, she's going to miss her chance. I don't think Darlene's remarrying anytime soon. Anyway, we're not having a procession, or anything. Darlene'll just dress her up in her Easter dress and she can sprinkle a few petals up there over the JP's feet, then Dave and I'll say our vows."

"We'd better count the folding chairs," Della said to Kat. "And check the freezer. And get some beer and wine."

"Now, Dave's already taking care of the drinks," Rita said. "You keep forgetting who owns the convenience store. I just need y'all to be there. To help Barbara. And, you know, to be there for me."

Her eyes had started tearing up, and now she broke down completely. "Here," Della said, grabbing a tissue from Kat's desk and bringing it to Rita. "All this is just such a surprise."

"Well, it's not like Dave's a stranger, we've been sleeping together for fifteen years if you don't count the years I was married to Larry the second time, and maybe some of them anyway, I don't even remember anymore. It's just a relief to make the decision and be ready to go on. It's like he's already living here anyway, all the work he's doing."

Kat and Della exchanged glances but remained silent while Rita wiped her eyes and blew her nose. When Rita finally looked up, Della said, "So you're planning on Dave living here at the Ladies Farm?"

"Well, yes. Husband and wife do usually live together, you know. That's one of the benefits of marriage, especially in a place like Sydonia."

Della could see that Kat was thinking that Sydonia's moral code had always proved elastic enough for whatever behavior Rita imposed on it but, thankfully, Kat said nothing. Della wasn't sure what to say.

"With the lodge up there, and all, we need a man," Rita said, "and Dave's certainly handy."

"Well, of course," Della said automatically, not bothering to point out that the lodge conversion was only theoretical. "But we'll have to talk about it . . . Kat and I. I don't think we should until . . . you know, with Barbara." She took a quick breath. "I'd like to wait until after Barbara's death to start redistributing the Ladies Farm, if that's okay with both of you."

"Why that suits me fine. As long as you

don't object to my husband and me sleeping under your roof in the meantime."

"We never objected before," Kat said
mildly.

Chapter 19

The WaLuKa trio brought the wedding cake over first thing in the morning. While Wanda had baked and iced the three tiers, Lu had busied herself producing a profusion of candied blossoms, gas pumps, and hair clippers to adorn the creation.

"Isn't this the most colorful thing you've ever seen?" Rita bragged. Kathy's contribution was the Ken and Barbie couple that topped the cake. The Ken sported coveralls with the name Dave stitched over the left breast pocket; Barbie wore a jewel-studded denim jumpsuit and a head of spiky black hair.

"Old teddy bear," Kathy confided. "I ripped Barbie's hair off, cut up a plush toy, and pieced together a wig. Thank God for Super Glue!"

"It's amazing," Della assured her.

"Don't touch," Darlene warned Tiffany, who had run in from the kitchen, where Kat had been showing her the little heart-shaped sandwiches they had put together the previous night.

The child wore shorts and a T-shirt; her pink, flounced dress hung from a hanger hooked over the back of a chair. "Are you ready to get your hair done?" Rita asked her. "I told her I'd pile it high on her head," she explained to Wanda, who stood blinking critically at her handiwork as if she wished she had a few more sugared gas pumps with which to edge the cake.

"How're you doing yours?" Wanda asked.

The trio regarded her quizzically, but Rita breezed past with Tiffany in tow. "Oh, not much to do with a head full of bristles," she sang out. "Darlene found me a little wreath to sit on top: baby roses. I'm thinking that's all I'll need. Barbara's lending me her diamond pendants. I don't want to look too busy."

Wanda, Lu, and Kathy exited though the kitchen; Rita and Tiffany disappeared through the living room. Darlene lifted Tiffany's dress off the chair and paused to admire the cake once more. "That sure is my mother," she laughed, shaking her head.

Della nodded. "I think so, too."

"Can I help you all?" Darlene offered. "I'll bet you could use a hand."

Della showed Darlene to the kitchen, where Kat was slicing celery and carrot sticks. Kat looked up. "We're just stowing them in these Baggies with marinade," she told Darlene. "Knives are on that magnetic bar over the counter."

Darlene was an adept slicer, and she, Della, and Kat had worked their way through celery, cucumber, carrots, and red and gold bell pepper before Dave and Tony started unloading the drinks.

First came the keg. Then came the trash can lined with Hefty bags and filled with ice and cans of soda.

Then they stomped inside, where Dave spied the cake. "How'd she like it?" he asked.

"She's overwhelmed," Della replied.

"She around?"

"In the salon." Della waved her hand toward that side of the house.

He nodded and started off. "I don't think she'll be superstitious," he muttered. "She didn't see me before our first wedding and that one didn't work out at all."

Tony grinned at Della, then studied the cake. "It's something."

"You knew, didn't you?"

"Knew what?"

"About Rita and Dave. That he was planning on living here."

"Well, honey, that's what I told you yesterday. But I don't think it was ever a secret about where they were heading. Rita has an inclination to marry."

Della sighed. He was right, but irritating. "So you figure if Dave can, why shouldn't you?"

"I figure Dave and Rita hit upon a good idea. I'm not too proud to copy it." He stood with one foot resting on a rung in the dolly.

"You feel like this would work for us?" Della asked. "Even when we couldn't live together before?"

"Yes ma'am. I do."

Della tried to imagine it. Maybe Rita and

Dave would take the place up the hill and she and Tony could carve themselves a suite out of her own and Pauline's room. Tony'd go off to Fort Worth every morning and would stop at the store for them on his way home. There'd be picnics on the hill, canoe trips down the Nolan, and deep conversation by the river under the stars.

Of course, reflected Della, Tony had never enjoyed picnicking, canoeing, or conversing. But he seemed more indulgent now.

"Maybe we ought to talk about it," Della granted. Tony's eyes widened, and Della wondered if that were panic at possibly achieving what he'd pursued. "We could go out in a canoe, next week. I'll fix us some lunch and we can paddle down to the landing below Wendells."

He grinned. "Are you asking me for a date now?"

"I guess I am," Della conceded. "But just a date. An afternoon date."

"A little regression therapy might be good for us," Tony allowed.

Della started to snap about calling an intercourse-free social occasion a regression when Kat poked her head into the dining room. "It's Melissa. On the phone."

"I'll just see how our shed's doing," Tony excused himself.

"I think I might have caused a problem," Melissa said.

"What's up?"

"Well, Hugh called this morning, and we talked."

"Well, we knew he'd be mad."

"Oh, he's more than mad," Melissa said. "He'll be filing writs for the next twenty years."

"What happened?"

"I think he called Castleburg, and he told Hugh something about y'all buying the neighbors' place—the Huttos'—and Hugh just thinks the whole thing'll fall apart, so he's heading your way!"

"Well," Della chuckled, "I'll be happy to talk to Hugh."

"Oh, Aunt Dell, he doesn't want to talk with you. He's going right to Aunt Barbara! That's why I'm calling. I think you better tell her—you know, about everything with you and Uncle Richard and all, because he's thinking when she hears it she'll sign her half over to him."

Della shook her head at Kat to indicate there was nothing to worry about, but Kat looked unconvinced. "What time did you talk to him?"

"Just now!" Melissa said. "From the car. I'm telling you, he's on his way there."

"Well, honey, we'll deal with him when he gets here. First, we've got a wedding to do."

"Aunt Dell," Melissa warned, "he's really mad. He won't even give me some of mother's things I wanted. It's real petty," Melissa continued. "And I don't think he's ever letting go of those journals. He's going through those things with a fine-tooth comb."

"Well, we can't control Hugh." Della tried to sound calm.

"I know. But I can control what I do, and I want you to know I'll sell my half to you all."

"Oh! Melissa," Della felt her eyes welling up and she turned away from Kat. "Honey, that's so . . . you are so wonderful and we appreciate this so much."

"It's what my mom wanted," Melissa assured her.

"I think so, too." Della gave Kat a thumbs-up. "Even so, this is a big step for you. You and your brother . . . that's sure not what your mother wanted."

"He'll get over it," Melissa said. Della could hear the effort to sound breezy.

"Honey, you take care of yourself." As she hung up the phone, Della turned her back to Kat and held the receiver in place for a moment to calm herself. Think carefully, she counseled herself. Think it all through.

She murmured a few words to Kat to dismiss any fears, then walked down the hall to Barbara's room.

If Hugh gets to Barbara, Della thought, she might just blow him off. She might already know what he's going to tell her. She might not care anymore. She might recognize him for the bitter, obsessed loser he is and not pay any attention to him.

Della put one hand on the door knob and knocked with her other hand. "Barbara?" she called.

"Come in." It was the voice of the home health aide, a young Jamaican named Lydia.

The odor hit her as she opened the door. It was the smell of shit and it came in a wall of warm air that made the room shimmer in its own heat. "We are just getting cleaned up," said Lydia. Her Caribbean lilt made *getting* two words: *gett ting.*

The soiled linens made a huge, tightly wrapped ball on the floor next to another ball of red plastic bag, which no doubt was the receptacle for the articles with which Barbara had been cleaned.

"The bridesmaid wore a diaper," Barbara whispered. She sat in the wheelchair and wore a cotton robe over what looked like a hospital gown. Flops, oddly patient, settled next to the chair.

"Better than a maternity dress," Della rejoined. She stepped over the balled-up linens and sat on the edge of the freshly made bed. "How you doing?" She reached over to take Barbara's hand. Flops lifted her head a moment to look at Della, then laid it back down.

"Oh, smelly but okay," Barbara said. Her voice grew a little stronger. "Lydia's going to help me in the shower, then I'll get dressed." She managed a smile. "Can't keep the bride and groom waiting."

They sat awkwardly for a few moments, Della leaning forward and stroking Barbara's hand as Lydia busied herself carrying bundles out of the room. "Anything I can get you?"

"Makeup," Barbara said.

"Pardon?"

"Do my makeup, after the shower?"

"Oh, sure," Della agreed. She stood as Lydia approached the bed to lay out Barbara's clothes. "Just like a high school pajama party."

Barbara managed a smile.

"Are you in pain?" Della asked.

"No, no." Barbara lifted a hand, then dropped it. "Just weak."

"You are ready now for your shower?" Lydia asked. Barbara nodded, and Lydia wheeled her away, Flops following a step behind.

Della supposed she should shower and get dressed now, too. Most of the kitchen work was done; Nancy and her sister would take care of serving the food after the wedding. There was no point hanging around in her work clothes.

She wandered through the living room and peered out back. The folding chairs were lined up under the live oaks before two pedestals, which sported arrangements of white gladiolus, purple irises, and flaming birds of paradise.

In the salon, Rita had tortured Tiffany's tresses into an elaborate configuration of curls on top of her tiny head and was now lacquering the creation into place with a can of hair spray. Della nodded toward Darlene, who stood with Dave just out of range of the hair spray, but she didn't stop to talk. She knew better than to break Rita's concentration.

Her own outfit for the wedding was silk, a flowered, matronly thing that screamed for a wide-brimmed hat. As she combed her hair, Della recalled Tony's garnets and, smiling, went searching for the old jewel box she kept on a shelf in the closet. There, among the high school trinkets and dime-store pins selected by her children for birthdays past, she found the garnet pendant.

Della sifted through the cache a little more to find the matching ring. Thankfully, it was a small stone that didn't look outlandish on her pinky, since that was the only finger it would fit now. If we do remarry, she thought, we'll have to get new rings.

She stopped in the middle of fastening the necklace. My God! she thought, then shook her head. This Hugh business has you rattled, she told herself. Forget it.

And she did, at least while she applied

Barbara's makeup. "You sure you're up to this?" Della asked.

"The question is, are you?" Barbara retorted. "I want the full treatment."

Full treatment meant using almost every type of makeup in what Della judged to be a world-class collection. "Moisturizer first," Barbara directed. "Then the eye-toner. Make sure it soaks in before we do the foundation. And use the yellow concealer under my eyes, the green stuff around my nose . . . counteracts the red."

Barbara was a patient craftswoman, Della thought, preparing her palette step by step. It was fifteen minutes before she spread the foundation over Barbara's face and could begin coloring and contouring. Barbara kept her head still, her muscles relaxed, as Della layered two colors of blusher beneath Barbara's cheekbones.

Full treatment meant false eyelashes, with which Della was unfamiliar. Barbara instructed her, advising her on how to avoid lumps in the adhesive that held the lashes to her eyelids, counseling about using a toothpick to place the edge of the lashes exactly at the base of her real lashes.

"You must have had these made for you," Della marveled. "They fit exactly."

"My indulgence," Barbara murmured. "No two eyes the same, you know."

"Hold still another sec," Della said, pulling the top off a soft pencil liner. She outlined Barbara's eyes in a smoky plum, then shadowed them in a slightly lighter shade. Lydia had laid out the lavender silk pajama suit with a floral scarf. Della worked to match the color over Barbara's eyes, then picked up a rust from the scarf for the lips.

They didn't talk much. Barbara watched her in the dressing table mirror, but after the eyelashes, she said little. "Are these your earrings?" Della picked up the amethyst drops and, when Barbara nodded, gently put them on her ears.

Della stood back and assessed her work. It looked garish and overdone. The slashes of color beneath Barbara's cheekbones screamed bad taste and the false eyelashes stuck out way too far. It looked all the things Richard would have hated, and it looked all the things at which Della had always laughed. But it hid the dark circles and gaunt cheeks and yellow color and, despite the chair, once they wheeled Barbara out to the lawn, no one who didn't know would guess she was dying. And everyone who did know could forget for two hours.

Della checked the clock on the dressing table. "Here," she offered, reaching for the lavender silk. "Let's get you dressed."

Della managed to get the suit onto Barbara's body, lifting her to a standing position only once to pull on the pants and kneeling before her when they got to the shoes. She pushed Barbara's feet into her gold flats, then stood. "I think we're ready." Della walked behind the chair and turned it.

Barbara grunted a little, and Della paused to see that the chair hadn't caught on anything as she turned it. "You okay?" she asked.

Barbara waved her hand a little. "Ring," she said.

"What ring?" Della asked.

Barbara replied by waving her hand again, and the lavender sleeve conveyed the message.

"You want your amethyst ring?"

Barbara nodded.

It took a moment to search through the

jewel boxes—Barbara had always resisted using the safe—but she found the ring in a Popsicle-stick box probably made by Dickie in Scouts. "Here," said Della, leaning down and taking Barbara's right hand. "Let's put this on."

It wasn't until she was wheeling Barbara toward the ramp to the back that Della realized they had forgotten to dab any Gucci behind Barbara's ears.

Oh, well, she thought, watching Tony greet Barbara. We can do it later.

By the time Hugh Jr. called, Barbara had been parked on the aisle of the first row. Darlene sat down next to her, and Flops settled herself at their feet.

Della let Kat hurry her out to the kitchen. "I think he's calling from the car," Kat hissed. "He said if I didn't want him busting up this wedding I'd get your ass to the phone now!"

"I'm in my car," Hugh Jr. said without preliminaries. "I'm coming to see Barbara."

"I'm afraid that's impossible," Della said. "Barbara is attending a wedding, after which she needs to nap. She's very sick, Hugh."

"You're the sick one, Auntie Della. Pretending to be so kind to Barbara when you were fucking her husband." Della stayed silent. "You want to protect Barbara, you meet me in Sydonia this afternoon and sign over your interest in the Huttos' place. Or, you pay me four hundred thou for my interest." Della did not reply. "Did you hear me?"

Della stood holding the phone to her ear and watched Nancy and her sister follow Kat around the kitchen as she showed them what to serve. She saw Tony leaning against the cabinet drinking a Dr Pepper. And in her mind she saw Richard, saw the blue eyes and the steel hair and the barrel chest, heard his deep laugh, felt his hand on hers. That isn't much, she thought, over which to destroy someone else's peace. I could slip away during the reception, she calculated. No one would notice. Maybe he'd agree not to announce it until after Barbara dies. I don't have to have the Ladies Farm. I can go anywhere, do anything, start another bed and breakfast. Barbara could die in peace.

"Hello?" It was a demand, but she could not respond, could not rouse herself for one more deal, one more arrangement.

Somehow the snarling in the telephone

grew fainter until she noticed Tony staring at her and realized she held the receiver out in front of her as if it were some anthropologically significant specimen of late twentieth-century technology. Della slipped her thumb up over the reset button. The snarling stopped.

She smiled at Tony. "Hugh Junior's on his way," she said. "I think we should complete the wedding before he gets here."

Tony stepped forward and Della rested her arm on his and let him lead her outside and to her seat.

Chapter 20

Rita had toyed with the idea of having music during the ceremony, walking down the aisle to CDs of Rodney Crowell singing "Life Is Messy" or Juice Newton doing "The Sweetest Thing I've Ever Known Is Loving You." Then she remembered that her previous wedding, her second to the wretched Larry, had begun to the strains of Kenny Rogers and Dottie West belting out "I Feel Sorry for Anyone Who Isn't Me Tonight" and she decided a dignified entrance, preceded by the flower-strewing Tiffany, would suffice.

The disadvantage to having neither music nor rehearsal was that no one knew when to start. The JP looked toward the house and nodded, but Rita was fussing with the bow on Tiffany's dress and didn't catch the cue. When she finally did look up, the JP, who was Wanda's brother, Paul, had turned to speak to Dave. Rita returned her attention to Tiffany's bow.

Seated between Barbara and Tony, Della shook her head. "We need to transmit eye-contact messages to Rita and the JP," she muttered. Tony snorted, then, ever so casually, slipped his arm around her shoulder and stroked her hair. This brought a smile to Barbara, which prevented Della from snarling at him to stop petting her like a dog. Dave, meanwhile, continued to listen to the JP while casting anxious glances toward his bride.

Finally, Rita looked up and Dave motioned her forward. With a little push, Rita launched Tiffany, who marched resolutely down to the chairs filled with guests, then stopped for a moment to contemplate the aisle between the chairs. Somewhere behind Della, Darlene hissed at the child to toss the flower petals, which Tiffany did. Then, with further urging, she moved forward a little. Then she stopped to distribute more petals.

Tiffany had drawn almost even with Della when Rita, decked out in peach silk and crowned with a wreath of white rosebuds, sauntered down the hill. She frowned slightly as she closed the gap between herself and her granddaughter, who was tossing more petals; then, after Darlene gathered Tiffany to her and cleared the path, Rita joined her groom before the JP.

In deference to Dave's choir friends, who had driven down from Fort Worth, the JP read a little bit of the Methodist service, then asked who was giving Rita in matrimony. Della and Kat helped Barbara to stand and said, "We are."

They sat again and Della had only one more bad moment, envisioning Hugh Jr. crashing over the hill as they were asked if anyone knew of any reason why this couple should not be joined in matrimony. As it turned out, the JP didn't ask. He read a short recipe for successful marriage clipped from an advice column, then asked Dave to place the ring on Rita's finger.

Dave reached into his breast pocket and pulled out a gold band and placed it on Rita's ring finger and recited the vows he and Rita had written. Then Rita slipped

Dave's ring off her forefinger and placed it on his ring finger and recited the vows back to him: *I promise to be your wife, to love you and take care of you, to support you even when we disagree, to respect you and to share everything with you—money, children, jokes, music, happiness, and sorrow; to be honest and nonviolent, with or without weapons; to be your best friend and your strongest ally for ever and ever.*

Then Dave and Rita kissed, and everyone clapped and cheered as Carla and Darlene ran up and tossed the remaining rose petals all over their mother and stepfather.

"For ever and ever?" Kat whispered to Della, but Della just shrugged.

"What were they supposed to say: for as long as we're married?"

Cameras flashed and Kathy's husband, who had been videotaping since Tiffany's appearance, made the guests return to their seats so the bride and groom could make a proper recession.

The guests, gamely withstanding the heat that was oppressive even in the shade of the house, clustered around the long tables filled with food. "Mom," said Carla, "you've always been one to plunge right in and Dave, you've always been one just to wear down the opposition, so we don't have any doubts about how you two got together again. We just want to wish you well and tell you, Dave, welcome back. It's like you never left."

One of Carla's sons undid one of Tiffany's curls, beginning a chase, joined by Flops, through the round tables set under the trees; WaLuKa posed in front of the cake for Kathy's husband to tape; Rita and Dave kissed long and repeatedly for various friends with cameras; Kat shepherded people toward the brisket and then back past the keg; and Della leaned against the post on the back step and watched the side of the house, where the driveway curved down from the street.

A few of their Ladies Farm guests, bewildered at being included in the wedding, stopped to chat with her, primarily about the cake; but, for the most part, she stood alone and let the wedding teem around her. Lydia was holding a cup out to Barbara, who took it slowly and sipped tentatively, then handed it back.

Della watched Barbara look up and catch Lydia's eye and Lydia nodded. She saw Lydia wheel Barbara toward the house and, as they approached, she held the door open for their entrance. Then, resuming her post, she wondered where Flops and the children had gone. "Expecting company?" Tony asked, holding out a cup of beer.

Della shook him off. "Young Hugh's pretty mad."

"I had Dave call over to Simmons ... you know, where the highways intersect? ... and he just called back to say his youngest saw a blue Volvo driven by a man heading toward Sydonia."

"So I am expecting someone," Della said.

Della looked around at all the people, then she smiled, marveling at her own calm. "Well, at the least the wedding's over and Barbara's gone back to her room. He can't spoil that."

"Maybe we ought to meet him out front."

"That's a good idea," Della said, starting toward the side of the house. "But you don't have to come. This really isn't your fight."

"I have a vested interest in your future," Tony pointed out. "We have a date next week."

"Wait here," Della said, motioning toward the porch as they rounded the house.

"What're you doing?"

She didn't know why she expected him to follow directions, but she shrugged and let him follow her instead. She hurried over to the cars in the long drive by the house, and she couldn't help a smile at Barbara's Thunderbird, gleaming red in the sun.

"Get in if you're coming," she instructed. The key, in Ladies Farm fashion, was in the ignition, and she turned it before Tony had settled in. Quickly, she backed out into the street, which was lined on both sides by the cars of wedding guests. It took only a little maneuvering to get the T-bird perpendicular to the flow of traffic.

"She won't need this," Della explained, getting out of the car as quickly as she'd gotten in. Tony followed and they stood for a minute on the dusty road in front of the Ladies Farm, listening for the hum of an approaching car. Truck traffic from Castleburg's had been rerouted for the day, and they had returned to the solitude of a dead-end street.

"What's he coming out here for, anyway?" Tony asked. "Why doesn't he just file his writs and be done with it?"

Della peered down the road but saw

nothing but neighbors' houses, some old gingerbread cottages, some fifties-style ramblers. "Oh, he thinks he can bully us into doing what we wouldn't do otherwise."

"All this over a few dollars?"

Della sighed and turned toward him. "All this about Hugh Junior's chance to strike it rich." His silence begged further explanation.

"Look, we've messed up his deal with Castleburg. So his fall-back is to sell to us. But he wants more than the appraisal. So if he gets Barbara to sell him her interest, he's got it."

"I thought Barbara was giving you her interest."

"She is. Those are the papers Kat took to the attorney the other day." It was warm in the sun, particularly in a long-sleeved silk dress. Della felt the sweat on her face and in her armpits, but there was nothing to do but wait on Hugh Jr.

"So it's over, isn't it?"

Della nodded, then shaded her eyes with her hand and looked down the street again.

"Then why is Hugh Junior on his way here?" Tony's exasperation was clear, but

Della sensed something additional, perhaps suspicion that she had orchestrated
this confrontation.

"To fight." She took a breath. "To hurt
us—me—for keeping him from doing what
he wanted." Della hoisted herself atop the
Thunderbird's hood and patted the spot
next to her in resigned invitation to Tony. He
had taken off his jacket and tie, and his
open collar showed the strength of his neck
where it met his shoulders. She stared a
second, remembering that particular point
with pleasure.

Tony squared his shoulders and looked
down the street so intently that Della had to
stifle a giggle. "Tony, he's not coming to
beat us up."

"Then what—"

"He has Pauline's journals, Tony," she
said a little too sharply. "He knows all the
things that we—Rita, Kat, Dave, Barbara,
Richard . . . all of us—confided in her over
the past twenty years."

"This is stupid," Tony grumbled.

"Yes it is."

"He just wants to throw a tantrum. Upset
us all with each other's secrets. Punks like
that make me sick!"

Perception dawned at the same moment
the blue Volvo appeared. "Tony," she
asked, amazed, "what did Pauline know
about you?"

He shot her an annoyed look as he slid
off the T-bird and stood braced to meet
Hugh Jr.

It seemed like only a second before
Hugh Jr. slid to a stop at the T-bird, which
blocked his path. Della had envisioned a
confrontation in which Hugh Jr. stayed
seated in the car, but he was already slamming his door behind him. Della decided to
keep her perch.

His sandy hair had thinned to the point
that Della could see his scalp when he lowered his head to charge them. "How
sweet," he sneered. "Uncle Tony and Auntie Della. Together again." He faced Della.
"Calling out the troops?"

"Have a seat, Hugh," Della invited, patting the same perch she had offered Tony.
"Can I get you a drink? Some barbecue?"

"You know what I want: I want all of you
off the Ladies Farm!"

"Hugh." Tony stepped forward and
offered his hand. "Haven't seen you since
your mom's funeral. How're you doing?"

Hugh eyed him nervously, but extended his hand. "I'm sorry to meet you this way." He gulped, and Della realized Hugh Jr. was addressing his scoutmaster. "What's happening . . . this has nothing to do . . . this is between me and . . . her!"

"Hugh, honey, don't point," Della said. "It's not polite."

"I want you out!" he said, his voice rising. "Get out of my way!"

"Hugh, honey," she started again, "we want—"

"Move out!" Hugh demanded. "Now!"

Without awaiting her reply, Hugh Jr. jumped back into the Volvo and backed up.

"Della!" Tony reached for her but she was already jumping off the hood as Hugh Jr. backed down Travis to give himself a running start. They were well out of the way when Hugh Jr. made contact.

As a bulldozer, the Volvo was less than satisfactory. Hugh Jr. made contact in the exact center of the T-bird, pushing the whole thing a few inches as it crumpled the middle. The Volvo's vaunted safety features protected Hugh Jr. and the car from much damage, but it did deploy the airbag. Hugh Jr. didn't seem to mind.

As the airbag deflated, the Volvo backed, though not nearly as far, and struck again, dead center.

The noise of the first collision had attracted a few wedding guests who, by now, had called to their fellow revelers. As Hugh Jr. backed the Volvo yet again, people in party clothes scurried up the hill by the side of the house.

Wham, crunch! This time he caught the T-bird toward the front, turning it into a parked car on one side of the narrow street as the Volvo stopped mid-section of a pickup on the other side. Hugh Jr., a little dazed, alighted once more.

Della and Tony ran toward him. "My God, Hugh," she said, "look at your lip!"

That feat, of course, was physically impossible, but Hugh Jr. did touch a finger to his mouth and then stared at the blood on his fingers. Tony pulled out a handkerchief, which Della took impatiently. She reached to dab at Hugh Jr.'s lip.

At least he's got his teeth, she thought. You never knew with airbags.

"You know, Hugh," Della said as conversationally as possible, guiding him to a seat on the grass, "you could have just walked between the cars and gone into the house."

He slapped her hand away from him and tried to rise. That was when Rita attacked.

"You son of a bitch!" she screamed, leaping at his head and tumbling him flat. "You crushed Barbara's car!"

It took a second for Della, knocked aside in Rita's leap, to recognize the object with which Rita was flailing at Hugh Jr.'s head and shoulders. The bits of flying icing, however, confirmed the identity of the weapon as the buzz-topped Barbie.

"You bastard!" Rita yelled. "You ungrateful, spoiled turd!"

Dave by then was reaching over Della to grab hold of Rita. Tiffany, terrified and screaming, had latched onto Rita's knees, while Tony concentrated on Hugh Jr., who had roused himself to counter Rita's efforts.

Wham! Wham! Wham! The Barbie struck with such ferocity that her head flew off. Rita continued to beat Hugh Jr. about the head, but Dave finally managed to drag her and the clinging Tiffany backward on the lawn.

Della, who had pulled herself to her

knees, looked at Hugh Jr. with Tony's arms around him from behind.

"Take it easy," Dave was calming Rita. "He's too hurt to know what's going on."

"I'm not hurt," Hugh Jr. mumbled.

"Take it easy," Tony took up the mantra. "Maybe you should lie back down." Della watched him trying to ease Hugh Jr. back in his arms.

Suddenly, Hugh Jr. flexed his shoulders and squirmed hard. "Let me go!"

"Hugh!" Tony commanded, squeezing tighter. "You don't want to do this, son."

"I'm not your son!" Hugh exclaimed, breaking free and half-turning toward his recent captor. "Your son's dead and he didn't even like you when he was alive!"

It didn't take any effort at all for Tony to punch Hugh Jr. with his right hand. They were both still on their knees, and Tony didn't draw back much, but Hugh Jr. was too stupefied to duck, and it landed on the right side of his jaw with a convincing crunch.

"Tony," Della cried.

Hugh Jr., his body still twisted around so he could face Tony, couldn't manage to punch back. The only thing that kept him from falling, Della saw, was Tony's left hand, which had reached out to steady the boy by his shoulder.

She half-crawled, half-scooted over to the tableau.

"You asshole!" It was meant to be hissed or screamed, but Hugh Jr. could only mumble in Tony's direction. "Your son hated you and your wife cheated on you!"

"That's enough," Tony said. The hand on Hugh Jr.'s shoulder pulled downward once more, and Hugh Jr. did not resist.

"Tony—" Della started.

"Hush!"

Della retrieved the fallen handkerchief and tended the bleeding lip. Tony squatted near Hugh Jr.'s head, a precautionary hand on his shoulder.

"Don't you think we should take him over to the emergency room?" she asked Tony. "He might have banged his head, that second or third time."

Tony studied Hugh Jr., whose eyes still blazed. "Let's just sit still for a few minutes," he proposed. "Let them get those cars moved."

They sat for a few minutes, Hugh Jr. resting oddly against Tony's lap, Della dabbing at the lip occasionally and helping Hugh Jr. with the glass of water someone had brought to them.

Della supposed Dave had called the wrecker that appeared so felicitously. Once the Thunderbird was dragged away, the Volvo could probably be backed into the drive, leaving the street clear for dispersing guests. Now, they milled around the street and hung over the porch. Della wondered if anyone had even sliced the cake that Rita had robbed of its ornament.

Della didn't see Kat or Rita. Maybe they were comforting Tiffany or reassuring the guests that no one was seriously hurt.

The T-bird, except for its crunched-in middle, still gleamed in the sun. It's a good thing Barbara went back to bed, Della thought. Telling her won't be nearly as bad as her seeing it.

Hugh Jr. began to wriggle again as she smoothed his hair back and tried to feel for lumps on his head.

"Easy, now," Tony repeated automatically. "Let Della look after you."

"She slept with Uncle Richard," Hugh Jr. choked out, wrestling free of Tony's grip but still lying flat on the ground. "Your wife and Barbara's husband!"

Hugh Jr. was coughing and spitting, but he finally stopped sputtering.

"Tony," Della tried again. "Tony, it's not true, at least not the way—"

"It is true," Hugh Jr. spat out. "She's a bitch, and when I tell Aunt Barbara, when Aunt Barbara—"

"Hush!" Tony commanded again.

That's when she finally heard Flops howling. It took a second for Della to identify the sound, and another second to realize that it came from the house. They must have called the ambulance, she thought. He's heard the siren.

Tony held her gaze and they waited, Hugh Jr. silent between them. There was no siren.

Della stood, awkwardly, and ran toward the house. She tore through the living room and down the hall, rushing past the Huttos, past Darlene and Tiffany and the shaken members of Dave's Methodist choir.

Flops sat in the middle of the hall with her head lifted toward the ceiling, howling at a chilling pitch. "Oh, God!" said Della, not knowing if she whispered or screamed. "Oh, God."

Chapter 21

Lydia emerged, ignoring the dog as she walked straight to Della and took both her hands. "Mrs. Morrison passed," she said. "Her poor heart give out, I think. But she passed peaceful. Just lying quiet."

"We have to call Dickie," said Kat, who had appeared in the hall.

Della started and dropped Lydia's hands. She thought she should turn around and push these people out of the hallway, maybe stand triumphantly on the porch while Hugh Jr. lay vanquished on the ground. Instead, she stepped forward and opened the door to the Babe Didrikson Zaharias room, closing it again behind her.

The blinds were drawn and the curtains closed. Della approached the bed, with its smoothed and straightened covers tucked neatly up under Barbara's chin. She pulled the chair up to the bed and sat next to Barbara, looking at her bristly hair and her slack face. She didn't know why people described the dead as peaceful. Barbara didn't look peaceful. She just looked dead.

And of course Jamie.

Della reached a hand out to touch Barbara's brow.

She had identified Jamie's body herself. The police had come to the house while Tony was down in Sydonia helping Hugh with his failed copy shop. Della could have waited for Tony, but she didn't. She went straight to the hospital, where her son was still connected to pumps and monitors that would preserve his organs while she signed papers giving them to someone else.

Barbara still felt warm. Della reached under the blanket and touched her fingers. "They covered Jamie so I wouldn't see he was crushed," Della told Barbara. "But his face was okay, except for the tubes. And he wasn't cold yet." Della clutched the fingers a little tighter. "It's not the way Hugh Junior said, you know. Jamie never hated us. He was just a teenage boy and he was angry about the car. So he took it when he shouldn't have, that's all."

Della shook her head. "I don't know why Hugh Junior said that, except to hurt Tony. He wasn't even friends with Jamie. Not like Dickie."

She squeezed the hand a little, but that just gave her a sense of the weight of it. Even the hand of a friend grew heavy in a dead body.

"Tony was so angry, he thought—I don't know, maybe he still thinks it—Jamie really did hate us. But Richard knew. Richard was the only one who could talk to Tony. Or me."

There was banging at the door, then it opened. "Della?" It was Kat.

"Just give me a minute," Della said, calmly. "Then you can stay with her."

"Stay with her?"

Della sighed. "Just a few minutes," she

said again, but Kat was already backing out of the room.

"It may take Kat a lot longer to make her peace," she advised Barbara. Then she sat for a moment, holding Barbara's hand under the covers.

"I shouldn't have done it. But after Tony and I split, there wasn't anyone I could talk to about it. And then, Richard came to me to help Pauline, and I learned that you can make yourself feel better—feel whole and powerful—if you throw yourself into helping someone else. Richard showed me that. And he was the only one I could talk to."

Della shook her head, leaned forward. "And then, then it was . . . he was what I had, Barbara. Richard on a weekday night; Richard for a weekend out of town; Richard on the phone, Richard in a restaurant. But you were the one, Barbara. You were his wife. His one and only wife."

It's all out now, Della thought. Tony and everyone else know about Richard and me. They know about Barbara and Hugh. They know everything. And nothing.

It was all jumbled together in her mind: the Huttos and the Ladies Farm, Tony and

Hugh Jr. The only thing that seemed clear was the remembered comfort of Richard's embrace and the feel of Barbara's velvet pouch full of diamonds being handed over in the dark night beside the Nolan.

"He never gave me jewelry," she assured her friend. "He never gave me diamonds."

She gave a final squeeze to Barbara's hand.

Lydia must have undressed Barbara right after the wedding ceremony, for she wore a pastel gown that did not flatter her arms and neck. Della saw this because she drew back the covers. She looked at Barbara's white legs, stick-like as they extended from the bulk of her body. The skin on her arms and neck was slack and yellowish, and there was a great deal of it.

"Tony and I have a date next week, if he's still talking to me." She looked at the amethyst ring on Barbara's hand and started to smile, but she could not. "So maybe," Della leaned down close to Barbara and whispered, "maybe I got away with it."

She was on her knees now beside the bed, resting her head on the mattress next to Barbara's hand. "Maybe," she whispered, "that's why it feels so rotten."

She heard steps beyond the door and the drone of insects outside, but she stayed that way, with one ear pressed to the mattress and her eyes opened, staring at one small section of Barbara's body.

Finally, Della shook her head and pushed herself up. She stepped over to the dressing table and plucked a heavy bottle from the top. "Here," she told Barbara, unstopping the bottle. She tipped it over on her finger, then dabbed the perfume behind Barbara's ears, along her collarbone, and between her breasts. The scent of Gucci filled the room.

Della leaned forward to stroke Barbara's face. "That's better," she told her friend, touching the bristly red hair and watching it spring back as her hand passed over it. "Much better."